The Centaurs
and Other Stories

The Centaurs
and Other Stories

by
André Lichtenberger

translated, annotated and introduced by
Brian Stableford

A Black Coat Press Book

Visit our website at www.blackcoatpress.com

ISBN 978-1-61227-184-2. First Printing. June 2013. Published by Black Coat Press, an imprint of Hollywood Comics.com, LLC, P.O. Box 17270, Encino, CA 91416. All rights reserved.

TABLE OF CONTENTS

Introduction

Les Centaures, roman fantastique by André Lichtenberger, here translated as *The Centaurs*, was originally published by Calmann-Lévy in 1904. A second edition—from a copy of which this translation is taken—was published by J. Ferenczi in 1921, augmented by a new preface. The other three stories included in the present volume, "Gulliver chez les Vichebolks," "La Curieuse aventure de M. Cuffycoat" and "Mowgli revient du front," translated as "Gulliver in the Land of the Vichebolks," "Mr. Cuffycoat's Curious Adventure" and "Mowgli returns from the Front" respectively, were published in the collection *Pickles, ou récits à la mode anglaise* [Pickles; or, Stories in the English Style] (Crès, 1923).

The stories in the latter volume, although heavily ironic, are *hommages* rather than parodies. As noted in the author's afterword, the Wells pastiche had previously been published in the *Revue Mondiale*, and the other items might also have appeared in the same publication, in which the author's work was frequently featured, in the years immediately prior to the date of the book publication, following the end of the Great War. The fourth item contained in *Pickles*, which I have omitted from the present collection, is "M. Pickwick et les Boches" [Mr. Pickwick and the Boche].

André Lichtenberger was born on 29 November 1870 in Strasbourg. He was the son of the Protestant theologian Frédéric Auguste Lichtenberger, who was a professor at the University of Paris for many years, and whose books include *Étude sur les principes du protestantisme* [A Study of the Principles of Protestantism] (1857) and *Des éléments constitutifs de la science dogmatique* [On the Constitutive Elements of Dogmatic Knowledge] (1869). André's older brother Henri became a professor in German literature at the

University of Paris and wrote numerous books on that subject. André was educated at the Lycée de Bayonne, the Lycée Louis-le-Grand and the Sorbonne, where he completed a doctoral dissertation on nineteenth-century socialism. He married Jeanne Sauterau in 1895. He wrote several further books on socialism, including a study of *Le Socialisme Utopique* [Utopian Socialism] (1898), as well as numerous novels and short stories.

Lichtenberger was better known for his political activity than his literary work in the early years of the twentieth century; he was the *chef du cabinet* of the radical Republican Paul Doumer when the latter was the President of the Chambre des Députés in 1905-06 and he was the editor-in-chief of *L'Opinion*, a political periodical he co-founded with Doumer. He was also the deputy director of the Musée Social for many years, and was appointed an Officier de la Légion d'honneur for his work in that context. As a writer of fiction, he won praise for his attempts to capture the psychology of children in a number of narratives, beginning with *Mon Petit Trott* [My Little Trott] (1898), but his fiction was very varied in kind, including contemporary fiction, historical novels set in various eras and children's stories.

Les Centaures, one of three fantasy novels that Lichtenberger wrote—the others being the "missing link" fantasy *Raramémé* (1921) and the prehistoric fantasy *Houck et Sla* (1930)—must have seemed like something of an anomaly at the time of its first publication, but a memoir written by his daughter Marguerite, *Le Message d'André Lichtenberger* (1946), records that it was the author's favorite among his own works, and suggests, with some justification, that it ought to be regarded as an extended poem in prose rather than a fantastic novel.

The novel reflects the author's strong early interest in the Symbolist Movement, for whose members the ambiguous figure of the centaur became a significant motif. Maurice de Guérin's prototypical Symbolist prose-poem "Le Centaure" appeared in the *Revue des Deux Mondes* in 1840 and the short-lived Symbolist periodical founded in 1896 by Jean de Tinan and Henri de Régnier was entitled *Le Centaure*. Centaurs play significant emblematic roles in several of Régnier's early Symbolist fantasies in verse and in prose, including some of those translated in *A Surfeit of Mirrors: Symbolist Tales and Uncertain Stories* (2012).[1]

In 1896, Lichtenberger was the editor of the French edition of the international literary periodical *Cosmopolis*, for which he successfully solicited work from Stéphane Mallarmé and *Les Centaures* includes an obvious *hommage* to "L'Après-Midi d'une faune" [The Afternoon of a Faun] (1876), which presumably indicates one of the seeds of the imaginative process that produced the novel. Fauns also feature very widely in *fin-de-siècle* Symbolist poetry and prose-poetry, including notable works by Albert Samain, Catulle Mendès and Rémy de Gourmont. There are, however, three other obvious precursors of considerable specific significance to *Les Centaures*.

One of the three precursors in question is Rudyard Kipling's Mowgli stories (1893-95 in *Many Inventions, The Jungle Book* and *The Second Jungle Book*; all reprinted in the version of *The Jungle Book* contained in the 1909 *Complete Works*), from which the convention of nomenclature applied to the various species of animals is taken. As the last story in the present collection illustrates, Lichtenberger was perfectly familiar with the stories in question, and had an obvious affection for them. "Mowgli revient du front" reiterates the sentiments expressed in *Les Centaures* in a manner that adds a further order of magnitude to the already-pronounced disenchantment of the earlier work. It is worth noting that the naming convention appropriated by Lichtenberger was also borrowed, some years later, by Edgar Rice Burroughs in *Tarzan of the Apes* (1913), which makes an interesting contrast with Lichtenberger's novel is providing a speculative archetype of Rousseauesque "noble savagery."

---

[1] Available from Black Coat Press, ISBN 978-1-61227-076-0.

Further archetypes of noble savagery are featured in a sequence of stories by J.-H. Rosny Aîné featuring exotic hypothetical offshoots of the human family tree, including the prehistoric fantasies *Vamireh* (1892)[2] and *Eyrimah* (1893)[3] and—perhaps most significantly—the aborted lost race story "Nymphée" (1893)[4]. Like Tarzan, Rosny's archetypes of noble savagery are fully human—and even more so, in some ways, than the rival humans whose mastery of the elements of technology allow them to drive their supposedly nobler kin to extinction—but "Nymphée" introduces more exotic quasi-human species and might have been a more interesting novel than the other two had Rosny managed to complete it rather than issuing the fragment as a hastily-rounded-off novella. All three stories, however, envisage Romanticized relationships between their leading characters and their environments that supposedly encapsulate something precious lost by humans in the process of becoming civilized. Lichtenberger must have been familiar with them, and his own prehistoric fantasy is evidently influenced by Rosny's work in that vein.

The third work to which "Les Centaures" probably owes some debt of inspiration is one of the significant precursors of Symbolist prose fiction, which undoubtedly influenced Régnier in his use of similar figures: Anatole France's "Saint Satyre" (tr. in different versions as "San Satiro" and "Saint Satyr"), the first story in the collection *Le Puits de Sainte Claire* (1895; tr. as *The Well of St. Clare*). The story is a poignant comedy in which the tomb of an accidentally-canonized satyr becomes a refuge for the ghosts of all the mythical species of the Golden Age, banished from the world by the triumph of civilization and oppressive religion. That

---

[2] translated as "Vamireh" in *Vamireh and Other Prehistoric Fantasies*, Black Coat Press, ISBN 978-1-935558-38-5.

[3] translated as "Eyrimah" in the same collection.

[4] translated as "Nymphaeum" in *The World of the Variants and Other Strange Lands*, Black Coat Press, ISBN 978-1-935558-36-1.

erasure is seen by France as a tragedy deserving of a plaintive elegy rather than a victory over pagan superstition, and the attitude obviously struck a chord in Lichtenberger's mind. In "Saint Satyre," however, the Golden Age has faded away quietly, having run its course; Lichtenberger imagines a very different conclusion, whose narration has closer echoes of the vitriolic tone of the final story in *Le Puits de Sainte Claire*, the masterful novella "L'Humaine tragédie" (tr. as "The Human Tragedy").

Although Lichtenberger was a radical activist, his particular socialist ideals are more closely related to the eighteenth-century utopian writers he celebrated in his early books on that subject than to the political movements of his own day; his rapid disenchantment with the Russian experiment is clearly demonstrated in "Gulliver chez les Vichebolks," and "La Curieuse aventure de M. Cuffycoat" adopts a condescendingly cynical view of H. G. Wells' modern utopianism. By the time Lichtenberger wrote those stories, however, he had largely despaired of the possibility that political effort might achieve anything very much in the way of social amelioration; whatever optimism he had been able to muster before the Great War died therein, and the flagrant misanthropy of *Les Centaures*, tacitly stripped of its nostalgic element, must have seemed to readers in 1921 to give the narrative a relevance above and beyond its refraction of the world of 1904. From then on, Lichtenberger's literary work became a Voltairean exercise in cultivating his garden, taking refuge from a world that seemed closer to the worst possible than the best.

The Golden Age of *Les Centaures* is no Garden of Eden, even in the relatively blissful section set on the Fortunate Island; if feline predators refrain from molesting lambs there, it is only because of the threat of sanctions. Even so, the creeping tragedy inflicted upon its quasi-magical forest by climate change does remove an authentic golden gleam from it, and the illusion maintained within the novel by poor Kadilda, that there might conceivably be something worth having to be attained by way of intercourse with humans, remain the dream

11

of someone who has refused real experience, and is fundamentally confused as to her own nature and identity.

Lichtenberger's bleak resignation did not, however, lead him to abandon his principles; he remained a radical idealist, who would doubtless have been considered a dangerous enemy by the invading Germans when they took possession of Paris in June 1940, had he still been there. Most biographical sources allege that the reason he was not was that he was already dead, having died in Paris on 23 March 1940—an affirmation confirmed by, and probably originating from, the text of *Le Message d'André Lichtenberger*—but other sources give the date of his death as 23 March 1943. The latter contention appears to be derived from an obituary in a Moroccan newspaper; if it is correct, he must have managed to get out of Paris, and France, before the city was occupied. If the evidence of *Les Centaures* can be taken seriously, however, he was not the kind of man who would think it appropriate to run away; it is possible that whoever died in North Africa in 1943 was someone else, who had merely borrowed his name, perhaps considering, on the basis of *Pickles*, that such masquerading was fair play.

Brian Stableford

THE CENTAURS

Preface to the Second Edition

There is, unfathomably, the prodigy that something exists. Between the gulf of the past and the gulf of the future, over the gulf of terrestrial mud, human being emerges momentarily, bewildered and amazed, among the impenetrable mysteries of Time, Space, Matter, Causes and Ends.

An ephemeral atom of atoms, he grasps the universality of the aspirations of his heart and his brain. He is as incapable of deciphering a tiny part of the enigma in which he is comprised as a gnat is of raising itself by the beating of its wings above the atmosphere that contains it. Ill-served by his imperfect senses, he only receives partial and misleading impressions of things. They excite baroque images within him, which engender erroneous conceptions that he is incapable of transmitting without making a travesty of them.

For each of us is sequestered in the dungeon of his own self. Insurmountable barriers isolate us from our neighbors. Each of our thoughts only belongs to us so long as we imprison it within us. As soon as it is formulated and exteriorized, it is refracted and deformed, and becomes estranged from us. We are understood on the basis of what we have never conceived, loved or hated for what we are not. No one knows me. I do not know anyone. The lover who believes, for a second, that he is fusing with the one he loves, is as mad as the genius who claims that his paltry candle can light a path for humankind.

Something else is as implacable as the solitude of the individual; it is his need to escape it. There is a desperate ardor within him to emerge from himself, to cling on, in time and

13

space, to something les ephemeral, less impalpable. Rather become demented, or immediately enter into the unqualifiable, than trudge on alone over the indifferent planet, in the bleak and enclosed universe.

Now, by virtue of the unbreakable laws that rule him, a human being attaches himself to other beings. My individual life is contiguous with others. Other, more ample lives loom over it. Blood-ties create physiological affinities between those they unite. Corresponding intimacies are born therefrom. If I am impregnated by them, something is glimpsed through the loopholes of my cell. I cease to be completely cloistered. A ray of light from beyond reaches me.

Family, race, fatherland: if I fortify within myself the consciousness of these realities that nature imposes upon me, if I incorporate them within me sufficiently to participate in those less temporary existences, which condition, enclose and prolong mine, yes, truly, the wall of my prison part and split. Horizons are revealed, sufficient for my paltry lungs to dilate, for my myopic eyes to recreate a glimmer.

Family, race, fatherland: it is to affirm and simultaneously to glorify the validity and beneficence of those intuitions that I have written.

A number of my novels deal specifically with the family.[5]

The others are entitled *Les Centaures, La Morte de Corinthe, Monsieur de Migurac, Kaligouça le Coeur Fidèle, Tous héros* and *Juste Lobel, Alsacien.*[6]

The common thought is this: under the penalty of unintelligence, ugliness and impiety, let us clarify and define within us the consciousness of our race. Let us be able to live, act and die with it. Thus will I subsist on a less miserable and less

---

[5] Author's note: "See the Preface to *Biche* (Plon et Nourrit, publishers, 1920)."

[6] Author's note: "With a few similar tales in which the fantasy of fiction further disguises the idea: *La Folle Aventure, Gorri le Forban, Le Petit Roi.*"

doomed earth. Thus, death will be less atrocious and less complete for me, which will satisfy or deceive—what does it matter?—my need to love and my preoccupation with eternity.

Before the War, the grave wounds of which caused us to despair of the fatherland, intellectuals gladly took an anarchic pride in detachment therefrom and in acrobatic or abnormal mind games.

Those games have their advantages.

Such a manner of rising above the confusion gives egotism comfortable alibis that can appear elegant.

It is perfectly permissible for the mole to deny the Himalayas and for a sophist to deny the fatherland, and even universal gravitation itself.

To defy reason, to contradict a fact, is an attitude devoid of intellectual probity, but it is possible to find amusement in it, and even satisfaction.

If an appetite for logic and intellectual honesty rules us, we will set aside recompenses as vain and sterile as the rebellions of a child against the corner of a table into which he has bumped.

I can refuse to live.

If I live, I can only live in accordance with the spark of reason that is within me.

Let is illuminate out desert and our darkness with the only gleams that it allows us to glimpse.

All the mystery of existence remains impenetrable to us, but amid Space and Time, they indicate to me how to live and die with less mental poverty, physical horror and intellectual confusion.

Let us not refuse the blind man's staff...

A.L.,
January 1921.

Part One

It is the powerful joy of spring that is ripening. In the radiant sky, the sun is setting. The green dome of giant oaks and tall beeches is transpierced by oblique sunbeams. Life is exalted by their flame. The grey and brown trunks light up. The mosses and fern glisten, sprinkled with pink, yellow and blue, at the hazard of sparse florets. The violets emit perfume in gusts. In the fiery foliage, the birds chirp. The undergrowth rustles; parting the brambles and furze, the quadrupeds sniff the descending freshness. Life is swarming urgently in the underwood.

As broad as a river, a stream of sunlight cuts through the forest. Once a fire born of lightning, was propagated by the complicit fury of the wind. On the ground thick with ashes, fertilized by light and the infiltration of water, the splendor of nurturing plants has blossomed.

Axor and Pilta are grazing side by side. From time to time, the stag pauses, raises his head or readjusts his antlers and contemplates his hind with his moist eyes. Seductively, he rubs his damp muzzle against Pilta's neck. She resumes grazing, greedily.

Pilta shivers. Axor straightens up at the same time.

Ten paces away, in a thorny thicket, two yellow eyes are focused on them. Seeing that he is discovered, Raram, the jaguar, emerges entirely, yawns nonchalantly, blinks his eyelids, swings his spotted tail several times to the right and the left, yawns again and takes a step forward. Axor and Pilta, their gaze suspicious, brace themselves on their legs. It has been a long time since Raram was last seen. Some said that he had emigrated to hotter climes. Previously, he swore to accept the truce. He promised not to kill without Klevorak's permission—but his memory is short and his humor as sly as the claws he conceals in his silken feet. He loves blood. The charnel-pit is a long way away. Perhaps, forgetful of the law, he prefers fresh venison?

Suddenly, however, with the same gesture, Axor and Pilta lower their heads into the grass again, and raise them up placidly, their muzzles overflowing with succulent stems. Raram has laid his ears flat along the two sides of his flat face; he listens, purring dully, spits angrily, and coils up in a thicket. Axor cheerfully scratches the new velvet of his antlers against the trunk of a young ash tree.

Like Axor and Pilta, like Raram, the people of the forest have heard. With little hurried and comical bounds, the entire tribe of rabbits regains the edge of the trees. Lull, the hare, ever timid, has preceded them, calling his doe. Roebucks jostle one another, trying out their young horns. The white cattle in the large herd get to their feet heavily. At a slow pace, pausing to chase away a fly or collect a perfumed tuft of grass with a sudden bite, they too move off—and with distracted gazes, they follow the furious gallop of Konnionk, the wild sow, enraged by her undisciplined piglets, which she scolds. Thus, everything that lives steps aside, to make way for those who are coming.

Because the sun is lower, the shadows are beginning to elongate, and ruddy glimmers brighten the green carpet, which they light up in places. Grey and nimble, two weasels race away and disappear. The cattle stop chewing the cud; at a lithe trot, Herta and her wolf-cubs have crossed the clearing. Konnionk shakes her little ones, which are squealing loudly, by the ears.

At first, there was only the confused rumor of the forest. Then something like a distant rumble gave evidence of the approach of a herd. Soon, the rattle of hooves became distinguishable, with the murmur of voices and the breaking of branches. Now there is the cadenced rhythm of galloping, and cries are echoing in the air—the calls and laugher of the sovereign animals.

The forest-dwellers along the triumphal path have paused. There is no fear in their gazes. Even the goat-kids are not huddling close to their mother. Entirely brave, Tutul's young nibble the thyme, and wrinkle their mobile noses mockingly at Volp the fox, who pretends not to see them. And in spite of the frightful odor she emits, Pilta remains beside the she-wolf, careless of her drooling fangs. Who, at the approach of the Dominators, would dare to violate the law they have imposed?

The gallop is more sonorous. The ground shakes. Necks extend. A confident curiosity is in their gazes. It's them! At the edge of the luminous clearing, the triumphant herd of Centaurs—the six-limbed people; the sovereign people; the children of the sun—surges forth. As they pass by, noses sniff, muzzles extend, hackles rise. On both sides of the avenue into which they have raced, a murmur of welcome greets them.

A stride ahead of his people runs Klevorak, the king. He bears his illustrious head high, whitened by the years but unbowed. Scattered by the wind of his progress, the abundant tresses of his hair fly around his bushy head. Like wings of snow, his great beard floats on either side of his rigid neck. The wrinkled face with sparkling eyes has been tanned by countless suns. Beneath the flaring nostrils, a proud smile uncovers intact teeth. The torso stands up tall, as gnarled and hard as the trunk of a chestnut-tree. The bronzed skin of the arms is studded with the formidable roundness of their muscles, and the large hands with enormous fingers are twirling a young uprooted beech. In spite of his age, the brown coat of the lower body remains glossy; four limbs with robust hooves carry the chief along at a rhythmic gallop, and the tail that nervously swats his polished flanks is still thick. His piercing gaze strays alternately to the right and the left; his thick lips part slightly and with an amicable whistle he salutes the tribes of beasts who venerate the peaceful strength of the Centaurs.

Behind the chief, the herd races in a joyful tumult. In accordance with custom, Herkem has remained with half the herd at the Red Grotto; the rest are here. Above the others,

Hark the Rude raises his scarred face, his striking beard and his broad chest, like that of a three-year-old bull. The other day, Spirr, the panther, in violation of the truce, killed a goat-kid. Hark; caught him ripping his victim apart in a thicket of laurier-roses. Drunk on blood, Spirr, spat and leapt at the centaur's throat, scoring his face with his claws. Hark grabbed him by the tail with one hand, whirled him around at arm's length and smashed him against the trunk of an oak. Spirr's mewling would no longer frighten the kids in the forest. Thrown in the charnel-pit, his cadaver served as a reminder to the flesh-eaters of Klevorak's inflexible law.

Hark's rival is Kolpitru the Giant. Although Kolpitru's height falls slightly short of that of the red-haired centaur, he surpasses him in the unusual power of his lower body, the depth of his thorax, and the volume of his arms, as stout as thighs. Without bracing himself on his legs, Kolpitru can stop the humped black-maned aurochs Mumm in his tracks, seizing him by his horns. Between Hark and Kolpitru there is an authentic jealousy. More than once, in the mating season, they have come to grips. Hark is the superior in terms of agility, but Kolpitru is perhaps the stronger.

All around them, exchanging playful words, running, whinnying, rearing up to collect a leafy branch in passing, or half-turning, slipping their withers with the flat of the hand to challenge them to race, are Tregg the Gray, Horok of One-Eyed, Halkar, Yahor and all the rest.

With an irritated gaze, Sakarbatul the Beardless searches the bushes. The other day, Tregg assures him, a few fauns drunk on cherries mocked his polished chin, boating about their pointed beards. Sakarbatul has sworn to pluck the cheeks of the first capriped he meets. The whole herd knows about his plan, and in enjoying the comical combat in advance.

Among the males, Haidar is the most handsome. His torso stands up as straight and smooth as the bole of a young palm-tree; his evident flanks are like those of a greyhound; four white patches circle his gleaming legs, and the plume of his tail, the color of night, sweeps the fallen leaves on the ground.

Gladly, in their capricious course, the centauresses draw near to him, rubbing their moist flanks against his, and seeking the gaze of his brown eyes with theirs. Impudently, Mimitt tickles his shoulders with a juniper branch, and when he turns round, provokes him with bursts of loud laugher from behind the abruptly-drawn curtain of her hair. Disdainfully, though, Haidar shakes his black locks and the lustrous curls of his silky beard.

What do Mimitt, Bagalda and all the rest matter to him! Last year, perhaps, they pleased him; perhaps they will again next summer. In the present season, he does not care about them, any more than the old ones with flabby breasts, the toothless Hurico or the lame Sihadda, obstinate in disputing her weary bones with the charnel-pit. The ardor of the summer sun has not yet inflamed the males with the despotic madness of love. Already, however, one sole desire is warming Haidar's loins. With a kick he drives away the brazen Mimitt and Bagalda, and shoulders away the pushy Poltico in order to gallop side by side with the one who retains his gaze every day, all the way from the Red Grottos to the rheki field, and from the rheki field to the Red Grottos: Kadilda, the white centauress with the eyes of a gazelle.

She is so beautiful, Kadilda the blonde, Kadilda the white, Kadilda the virginal! Who could be insensible to her triumphant grace? Klevorak himself feels pride swelling his heart when his eyes fall upon the last-born of his blood. No matter how far the memories of the old ones go back, none of them can remember such a prodigy: a centauress white from the crown of her forehead to the tips of her fingers, her four feet and her tail. So fine is the skin of her face, her slender torso and her arms that the blood comes to the surface there, putting a pink tint into her cheeks, at the rigid tips of her young thrusting breasts and the palms of her excessively soft hands, which are lacerated by brambles and prickly holly. When Kadilda capers in the meadow, her blonde hair undulating around her, one might think it a fleece of foam flying from waves. In all the tribe there is no one who leaps more nimbly over the trunks of fallen trees or importunate bushes, bounding into the air as Titt the skylark soars into the sky in the summer dawn.

Thus, for two seasons already, at the approach of the fecund ardors of the solstice, the males have pressed around her, coveting her with their avid eyes, filling their dilated nostrils with the voluptuous odor of her young body; of all those who are old enough for love, there is probably none whose words and gestures have not testified to the centauress the violence of his desire. Even last year, some preferred the fawn coat and skittish humor of Mimitt. This year, in the opinion of all, Kadilda is the most beautiful, and well before the torrid season, careless of the rest of the females, the males seek to rub against her and pursue her with their profound gazes.

Will Kadilda refuse herself again, as she has done for two years? Neither Hark the Rude, nor Karak, nor Kolpitru has received the promise from her for which they hoped, and when she sees the handsome Haidar veer sideways and steer toward her, she increases her pace, parting slender hindquarters with her hands, she slips between the old ones, and to support Sihadda's unsteady gait she passes an arm round her waist, while obstinately veiling her face with the other in a sign of refusal.

With loud bursts of laughter, all those she has driven away mock Haidar's disappointment as anger creases his forehead, and they all congratulate the virgin. She keeps silent, annoyed to see gazes seeking her out, but as Papacal playfully tries to part her hair and stroke her with his stout fingers, she rears up; her face appears, all pink, and raising her hand, she slaps the insolent one in the face with a resounding blow. Then the centaurs' joy burst forth again, and they applaud Papacal's discomfiture.

There is the customary halt in the Grove of Thirst, half way to the Red Grottos, and the field where the somber rheki grows, the fern from which the centaurs draw the strength that is in their bones. Every two days, when Klevorak leads his people there, they never fail to stop in the grove. Not that his fatigued muscles command the halt; in spite of his age, he could follow the sun at a gallop for half its course without a drop of sweat pearling on his burnished brow—but he is a prudent chief. He knows that the young ones run out of breath and strength in a long ride. Most of all, he takes pity on the dolorous lassitude of the old females.

Scarcely have the oaks passed, the trunks more widely scattered and the eternal verdure of the holm-oaks mingles with the darker foliage of pines, than Sihadda's limp become worse and she begins to suffer from her old wound, while Hurico's hoarse chest begins to labor. With torsos streaming and foam on their flanks, both would gallop until they collapsed with exhaustion rather than confess that they are weary, but Klevorak call a halt.

The centauresses let themselves fall into the grass. Hurico lies on her side at full stretch; her tongue hangs out of her toothless mouth, and her rumbling flanks throb precipitately. Kneeling in front of her, Sihadda supports herself, holding on to the stunted trunk of a small oak; her eyes are closed and her lips taut, in order to retain her soul. It is as if, their effort having paused, the old ones feel the crush of fatigue all the more intensely. They have no voices with which to reply to the sarcasms of Hark, who mocks them, and pities the wolves whose teeth will son break on their bones.

The centaurs spread out in the clearing. They take turns to slake their thirst at the spring, and then glean berries from the bushes. The plums still taste bitter, but the black cherries and strawberries are already tasty. Hark spots a small tree whose fruits are hanging down above head height. He takes a step back, leaps into the air, but falls back with empty hands. Immediately, Haidar takes up the challenge, measures the distance with his eyes and launches himself in his turn. There is a crack; to the acclamations of all, he holds a major branch in his hand, laden with blood-colored berries. Laughing, the centauresses jeer the red-haired centaur, who clenches his fists and mutters that the greyhound with the white socks would quickly give in to him at another game.

The old females have recovered their breath; they follow the jousters with their eyes and sadly remember the distant times when, under different skies, similar young males made them mothers. They also gaze enviously at the shiny fruits, and the spring murmuring a short distance away, but their limbs are exhausted. They content themselves with raising a few soft and half-rotten acorns to their lips, the debris of last autumn disdained by the wild boars, the rancid taste of which deceives their thirst.

A voice makes them turn their heads. Kadilda the white is nearby. She leans over and hands them five or six branches with foliage speckled with red berries.

"Take them, Mothers," she says.

They seize the branches and eat avidly; and while the sour taste caresses their dry palates, they are astonished by Kadilda's action. Proud of their strength, the young centauresses do not think that one day they will be old, and willingly humiliate their elders with their sarcasms and the spectacle of their games. In revenge, the old ones do not stint in censuring them, and warning the males against their coquetry. Such is the rule. Kadilda has broken it. Because her action is benevolent, however, the centauresses are not scandalized, and they follow her with an approving eye as she moves from tree to tree collecting booty.

A burst of laughter crackles in the old ones' ears. They raise themselves up on their arms and search the bushes. Their noses denounce the laughter before their eyes; the breeze brings an odor of billy-goat. From the thicket where he was hiding, Pirip the faun has just emerged. His broad ruddy face with the big snub nose is joyfully split from pointed ear to pointed ear. Beneath his bushy eyebrows, his little round eyes are blinking comically. His short horns barely protrude from the thick shock of hair that covers his head.

In each brown hand he holds a fistful of cherries. From time to time he bites into one with beautiful teeth, and gluttonously swallows them, stones and all. Then the red juice starts running down his chin and all along his tangled beard, his tawny torso and his hairy legs, doubled up beneath him. He has stopped chewing; open-mouthed, he is looking at something in front of him; now he takes two steps; the loud sound of his full-throated laughter resembles the staccato beating of goats. He stuffs another fruit into his mouth and crouches down again, his eyes fixed a few paces ahead.

The centauresses try to make out what he is looking at. Very pale, Kadilda moves away from the black foliage of a juniper. Pirip follows every one of her gestures; a glimmer ignites in his eyes, frissons run down his broad back, and from time to time, he runs and appreciative tongue over his thick lips.

The old ones exchange nudges with their elbows, simultaneously shrugging their shoulders. Like all of his brethren, Pirip is incorrigible. On an empty stomach, he is idle, dreamy and gentle; he squats down for hours contemplating water in a stream, the forms of clouds drifting across the sky and the complicated maneuvers of insects in the moss. For hours on end, sitting motionless, he blows into a bizarrely-punctured reed, from which a shrill voice emerges. But his ordinary nonchalance is only equaled by his folly when, under the influence of the season or the juice of the berries that intoxicated him, his spirits rise.

In the autumn, when the fauns gorge themselves all afternoon on grapes, delirium puts fire in their veins. With grunts of lust, they chase after one another and males and females, in furious embraces, roll in the bushes. Scornfully, the centaurs turn their heads away in order not to witness their impudent frolics. When Pirip's salaciousness is roused, he is no longer capable of restraint, and there is no limit to the obscenity of the monstrous unions to which he might stray.

The centaurs do not deign to dwell on such thoughts, however, which are unworthy of sovereign animals.

On awakening from his escapades, Pirip is the first to deplore his folly; he bemoans his aberrations, berates his ignominy; he would punish himself if he could; his contrite face begs pardon for his sin; his mood becomes mild and indulgent again; once again he becomes the humble brother whose staccato laughter cheers up the woods and whose inoffensive ecstasies stop a fluttering butterfly or a gilded fish in its course.

And because they are aware of the goodness of his heart, the centauresses feel sorry for him when they see him trembling, his eyes full of Kadilda. In the violence of his desire, he is capable of forgetting all prudence, of throwing himself upon the one he covets. The anger of the centaurs will not spare him.

Obligingly, Sihadda calls in a loud voice: "Pirip! Pirip! Pirip!"

At the last and most sonorous call Pirip shivers, as if emerging from a dream, and perceives the old females who, their lower bodies recumbent, are leaning on one elbow, watching him. He scratches his forehead, wipes his hands on his shaggy thighs, and says: "Greetings, Dominatrices; what do you want?"

With the flat of her hand, Sihadda crushes a horse-fly on her flank and says, mockingly: "Rid yourself of bad thoughts, little brother. Instead of the centauress, look at Klevorak."

With a dubious expression, Pirip looks his adviser up and down for a few seconds; then, following her advice, his eyes seek out Klevorak. Motionless on his four feet, shod with hard hooves, the chief, with his head held high, seems to be challenging power of the wind in the clouds. With a negligent gesture, his arm is twirling a cudgel with which he could break the back of an ox. He is the image of strength.

Pirip's forehead darkens; his cheeks crease; the corners of his thick lips turn down, and a deep sigh elevates his bosom. The two old ones burst out laughing. Confused by having been found out, the crouching faun scratches the ground mechanically with his fingers, and murmurs: "Your speech,

Sihadda, is like the benevolent shower of a cascade. Thank you."

And, shaking off the fruit-stones, leaves and stems with which he is covered, he gets up on his cloven feet. At first he quivers and stumbles, but two or three bounds restore his aplomb, and he draws away with his hopping stride.

Hurico shouts after him: "Go find Sitta. Next to her you'll forget the white centauress." Sitta is the tawny fauness with whom Pirip already has eight loquacious faunillons, noisier than a herd of bleating goats.

But Pirip is no longer listening to the old ones. A short distance away, a clump of irises looms up in the grass, and now a ray of sunlight, cutting through the foliage, illuminates the velvety splendor of the petals. Magical corollas sparkle with violet, mauve and roseate glints.

Fascinated, Pirip approaches the flowers, caressing them with his delighted gaze, kneels down beside them, and a melodious whistling escapes his slightly-parted lips, celebrating the divine beauty.

The centauresses have followed him with their eyes; with identical gestures, they touch their foreheads. For an herb that could be crushed underfoot, Kadilda is forgotten.

The entire herd is standing up. Klevorak's thunderous voice has signaled the departure. On the dry slope the centaurs disperse at unequal pace. The majestic trunks of the oaks, beeches and chestnut-trees are succeeded by a more cheerful vegetation. The impenetrable dome of the high branches no longer maintains the humidity of the soil, no longer interrupts the vivifying rays of sunlight.

Beneath their fecund caress, almond-trees with stunted trunks and bright foliage bloom, speckled with the white of pink snow of flowers, orange-trees with gleaming palms, lentisks, pistachios and arbutuses, ripen their berries, green as yet, son joined y the silvery pallor of olive groves. A few tall parasol-pines and a few junipers with blue glints rise up here and there above the smaller trees. The stony ground is adorned with bright gorse, euphorbias and heather. In more sunlit areas, cacti expand their fleshy prickles, where figs, the wealth of autumn, are becoming greener.

Here and there, the earth is softer, alternating adorable meadows of violets and celery. Tangled vines climb up the blanched trunks of elms. The gusts of the breeze are charged by turns with all the scents of spring. And the centaurs, intoxicated by the perfumes, move at a slow pace, collecting a ripe fruit here and there.

But the weary sun is gradually descending in a sky that is turning pink. Klevorak utters a cry to step up the pace. The ground beneath their hooves is sandy now. The olive groves, vines, almond-trees and cacti become sparser; above the yellow and green carpets of gorse the twisted trunks of pines loom up, with dark foliage. The gusts of the breeze have freshened; if the passage of the herd were less noisy, they would surely already be able to hear the powerful sigh of the sea.

Again, Sihadda is out of breath. Her foot is hurting more than ever today. Age is weighing upon her. The time is long past when she could leap over the backs of four males with a single bound. Kadilda encourages her. Soon they will reach the bend in the river. The old female can cool her bad leg there. Then the bank can be quickly rejoined.

With a clamor of cries, the centaurs move into the sandy dunes, urging one another on and climbing them at the gallop. Their hooves sink in, slipping on pine-needles. Even Kolpitru feels sweat pearling under his belly. The old females' muscles stiffen; a kind of mist veils their eyes. Hurico's feet catch in a root; she stumbles heavily, and falls to her knees. The laughter of the young ones brings her to her feet with a thrust of her hips. Sweat inundates her meager flanks, sticking the sparse wisps of her hair to her temples. She does not want to fall behind, and braces her legs as best she can--but even Klevorak is slowing down, and voices fall silent in the general effort.

At the top of the hill, on the heath that is now deserted, the chief stops and, one after another, the centaurs wipe their brows with their horny hands, while their hairy chests dilate in the beneficent breath of the evening breeze—and once again, their large eyes fill with the splendor of the familiar horizon.

At their feet, the dune descends in a steep slope. Amid the black trunks of pines, the water of the river water gleams here and there, close by, subsequently making a detour to the right; its mouth is invisible because of the foliage, but facing them, beyond the last curtain of trees, the centaurs perceive the infinite splendor of the scintillating waves. The Red Rocks, where their brothers are waiting for them, stand up on the left.

An old tale, recollected since time immemorial, relates that the Red Rocks emerged from the sea and came to gather on the sand, like a monstrous flock. Or perhaps it was the Smoking Mountain from which the mysterious force projected them. Out there, beyond the sea, in the golden, purple and azure atmosphere into which the setting sun is sinking, the dark plume from which flashes spring by night overlooks the coast that limits the view.

Behind them, when they turn round, the animal-kings recognize, above the sylvan slopes that they have just traveled, above the darkness already extending over their flanks, the roseate summits of sheer mountains, which they once traversed when, chased by the menace of the cold, they followed the sun in its course in search of more clement climes.

"Hahahh!"

Klevorak utters the cry, claps his strong hands, and launches himself down the steep slope; in his wake, the entire herd precipitates itself chaotically. The descent draws them down as rapidly as the stones that the mountain pours forth. Piqued by self-esteem, even Hurico forgets her pains. They slip on their hind feet, get up again, and gallop harder. Pine-branches crack under the impact of torsos; gorse and heather are crushed under hooves; the sand scatters. Between the trunks, more widely-spaced, the water scintillates close at hand; a moist odor caresses the nostrils. One more surge!

The curtain of foliage vanishes; a little flat and muddy beach borders the bend in the river, which curves back on itself to reach the sea. In a few bounds the centaurs can cross it, in order to plunge into the final wood that separates them from the desired refuge of the Grottos.

Scarcely have they appeared on the strand, however, than a shrill cry escapees from the river. There is a seething in the water, and above the troubled waves rises the steaming torso of Gurgundo, the triton. Behind him surge those of his brethren. Instantly, the river is populated with flat faces holed by glaucous eyes and crowned with green-tinted hair, viscous torsos and flaccid bellies that terminate in sparkling tails. And the large hands whose fingers are linked by thin webs appeal to Klevorak, gesturing to him to stop.

The centaur hesitates. Every morning, Gurgundo hears some new lie, and believes it true until evening. His indefatigable tongue is as loquacious as the waves in which he was born. But today, a grimace of distress had lowered the corners of his habitually-laughing mouth. By his side, Glogla, his siren, is moaning restlessly, and when she sees the chief hesitate, she hauls her newborn, little Plax, out of the water, who screeches with all his might, frightened, struggling desperately and twisting his scaly tail without letting go of the dead herring that he is clutching in his webbed hand, on which he was sucking a moment ago with his toothless mouth.

Klevorak approaches the river. Glogla, who reeks of fish and whose twisted rump inflames Pirip with desire when he glimpses it through the reeds, is devoid of charm for him. But none of the living beasts whose offspring are nourished on milk demands the help of the animal-kings in vain. And above all, Fauns and Tritons have the right to the particular amity of their brethren. The blood-bond between the three tribes is indestructible.

Klevorak moves into the water, knee-deep—for Gurgundo, so supple in the waves, is as nimble as a snail on land. And while the centaurs squat down on the sand or bathe their weary feet, tritons and sirens cluster around their chief;

with broad gestures and loud voices, they harangue him all at once; the squeals of the sirens drown out the voices of the males, as sonorous as the breaking waves; the tritonneaux clutch at the centaur's legs, uttering shrill cries like those of seagulls. Impatiently, Klevorak whinnies and kicks out. The water splashes around him; the little ones fall over one another as they retreat, jostling. In the reestablished silence, the centaur tells Gurgundo that the chief must speak for them all.

In a plaintive voice, the triton relates the misfortune that has just fallen upon his tribe: Neboum, the handsome Neboum, Glogla's own brother, who is capable of out-swimming a trout or a salmon, Neboum with the torso more viscous than an eel and the tail more glittering than a dorado, with the fingers better-webbed than a cormorant, Neboum, the fisher of red mullets, is dead, having fallen victim to a frightful fate.

While he was resting on the shingle, bloodthirsty aggressors have thrown themselves upon him. Capable in the waves of wrestling a crocodile, or putting a shark to flight, Neboum, surprised on land, was unable to defend himself. In an instant, he had been killed, before the eyes of his wife Pouzouli; she had seen the murderers gorge themselves on his blood and tear apart his lifeless limbs.

A dull roar rumbles in the centaurs' breasts. Nostrils flare, fists clench and hooves make the sand fly. Tails whip fuming flanks—but Klevorak imposes silence.

He suppresses the anger that is choking him, and asks who the murderer was. Whether it was Raram the jaguar, or the carnivorous tribe of the wolves, or the voracious hyena, he will pay with his life for the sin of having violated the strict law.

But Gurgundo shakes his head with the glaucous eyes. No, the guilty party was not among the beasts who have sworn the truce; even the most insane would not have scored the sovereign animals' own brother with his claws.

Klevorak's eyes flash; was it, then…?

His lips refuse to pronounce the name of the Impure Ones—but Gurgundo understands him, and reassure him.

No, they were not the murderers. Undoubtedly, though, the centaurs remember the Wild Beasts who, on encountering the rest of the teat-bearers, refused to bow down to the pacific yoke of the Dominators. Colossal were their heights, multiple their species. Once they had wandered the mountains and the forests, in numerous troops.

Only few years ago, there had been occasional sightings of the Mammoth with the rounded tusks, or the toad-elephant. Now, their tracks are scarcely ever seen any more on damp ground. What has become of the monsters of old? Because of their indomitable ill-humor, the centaurs had massacred many of them; such had been the fate of the Lions that they had exterminated in the Red Grottos. Many have killed one another in furious combats, or had recoiled before the six-limbed people. And when, from time to time, a wandering faun happened to glimpse them in the woods, he noticed before fleeing how much difficulty the giants had moving their weary limbs. Their breasts were heaving as if the air were drying them out; they sniffed the fruits and foliage languidly; and, as if Nature herself had rejected them, one often discovered their whitened skeletons among dry leaves or in the densest thickets— gigantic bones like those of fully-grown birch-trees.

Recovering their ancient ferocity, two Wild Beasts have attacked Neboum. Gurgundo describes the brown pelts of the aggressors, their drooling mouths, the enormous strength of their limbs, their height, superior to that of the centaurs...

The murder was committed on the Shingle Beach, at the final bend of the river, where its waters mingled with the briny sea. Perhaps they are still there, with their victim...

That is sufficient. No more talk. Action is better than words.

In two steps, Klevorak is on the bank. He shakes himself, and says to Gurgundo: "Swim, brother, with all speed. Let those who want to see the blood of Neboum washed in the blood of his murderers descend the river breathlessly!"

And amid the joyful howls of his people, the old chief, his white hair bristling on his centenarian head, utters the war cry that once announced death to the Lions roaring in the caverns.

In a trice, the beach is empty. The gallop of the centaurs is swallowed up by the pines. Along the thread of water the tritons make haste in order to witness the punishment. Only the tritonneaux remain, under the guard of two old sirens. In the shallow water warmed by the last rays of the sun, they chase one another and roll around, with noisy laughter and loud clapping of their webbed hands, fighting over little crabs on the muddy bed.

Bearers of death, the centaurs hurtle forward. Only for a few seconds does one or another of them pause to uproot a young tree; in haste he rejoins his brothers, and all of them strip the trunks of branches as they run, fashioning clubs.

Haidar has remembered the carcass of a mastodon lying in a thicket of furze. He draws aside, rummages among the bones, and comes back brandishing a femur—a terrible weapon that several others envy. Kolpitru's gallop is heavy; in his hands he bears a boulder capable of smashing the carapace of a rhinoceros with a single blow. Hark the Rude disdains such assistance, though; with a great laugh, he extends his hardened arms and puffs out his bulbous chest; the power of his muscles is the only weapon he trusts.

The ground flees beneath the hooves. Only one more dune to cross, and they will reach the beach that Gurgundo specified.

In response to Klevorak's voice, the centaurs arrange themselves in battle order. In spite of his age, the chief is in the first rank, with Hark, Kolpitru, Papacal, Kaplam and Haidar, the most vigorous of the six-limbed people. Behind them come the other adult males, and then those whose limbs are weighed down by old age, or have not yet attained their full strength. The females follow them, under the guard of Tregg the Gray, Pocolo and Palkaval.

33

The nostrils of the young ones are quivering, and a frisson wrinkles their flanks. Since the defeat of the Lions, the centaurs no longer fight battles, so uncontested is their dominion; and the centauress Kadilda, when her nation took possession of the Red Grottos, was only four years old. So, while the old ones grind their teeth and the bellicose heart of their race quivers in their slender torsos, she is fearful of combat, apprehensive of the frightful odor of blood, and hopes vaguely that the approaching darkness might hide the murderers from the vengeance that is pursuing them.

Haidar utters a cry, and points with his finger at something on the ground. The centaurs stop, bend down, sniff and hold a discussion. Two sets of vast clawed footprints appear distinctly in the sand. Kolpitru's entire hoof disappears in the smallest of them.

One glance is sufficient for Klevorak to recognize the enemy tribe. Gurgundo was not lying.

By means of the tracks, the centaurs follow the Giant Bears, crossing the final dune on their trail and descending with them toward Shingle Beach. The foliage of the pines no longer blocks the views. The avengers advance into the open. Perhaps, by making a detour to the left, remaining masked by the woods, they would be able to take the enemy by surprise, but the six-limbed folk are scornful of ruses; they only deign to attack head on.

Eyes search the descending darkness...

A long whistle halts the clatter of hooves. The murmur of the entire herd replies to Klevorak's warning.

They have been seen. Their hearts are ready.

Some way ahead, two colossal forms rear up over the beach. At their feet, frightful shapeless debris is detectable. The giant bears had fallen asleep beside their victim; the approach of the avengers has awakened them. They give no thought to fleeing. They gather themselves, swinging their enormous heads, mouths open, monstrous paws raised, and a rumble of menace escapes their breasts. Perhaps they do not know their adversary, and imagine that they can intimidate him.

Klevorak's voice cuts through the silence. To the murderers, he announces death. Such is the law of the centaurs. And the clamor of his people repeats in thunder the inflexible formula that imposes peace on earth:

"Those who kill perish!"

Perhaps, at that moment, the Wild Bests realize the danger in their obscure souls and want to flee. It is too late.

"Harrah!"

Klevorak had uttered the cry. Like an avalanche descending a mountain, the herd races into battle. A single soul vibrates in the deep chests, in the knotted arms, in the steadfast legs. The whirlwind that uproots oaks is less irresistible than the surge of the sovereign people. Neither the mass of the mammoth, nor the armor of the Great Lizard can protect them against it.

Howling, bristling with fists, clubs and hammers, the wave of centaurs breaks upon the brutes. There is a cracking sound like that of a tree struck by lightning, confused cries, frightful somersaults. The bears' jaws are convulsively agitated; their heavy paws rise and fall, striking at random—but in vain. At the first impact the weaker of the two had fallen to the ground, and is struggling pitifully against the hooves that are pulverizing it. Its hoarse cries grow weaker, and fade way.

The other defends itself better. Clinging to the ground with all the force of its caws, it has withstood the initial impact; then, abruptly rearing up, it has let all its weight fall back on Papacal, too slow to disengage. As quick as a flash, however, Hark the Rude leaps at its throat and strangles it with his powerful arms, while Haidar, Klevorak, Sakarbatul and Kaplam hang on to its limbs, paralyzing its strength. And with all his might, with furious thrusts, Kolpitru smashes the brown skull several times with his stone hammer, which turns red.

Under the blows, the monster buckles, totters...

With one more effort, it raises itself up for the last time, and shakes off Hark's grip, but then falls back with a terrible howl, Old Babidam has slipped around behind it, and with a precise thrust she has sunk a pointed stone into its eye. Black blood gushes.

Blinded, the bear hesitates momentarily. That is its doom. One final time, Kolpitru brings the slab of rock down on its head. The skull fractures.

With a moan, the monster collapses. A blow from Haidar shatters its jaw. The herd utter cries of triumph, and scale the panting mass, trampling the limbs, which writhe, break, and then remain inert on the sand.

In the quaternary sky, the sun has set. Night descends upon the earth—except that, above the distant country beyond the violet sea, extraordinary bands of red are still aflame, projecting bloody gleams.

From the river bristling with heads, screeches of delight celebrate the victory. With clamors like the crashing of waves, the tritons jostle one another enviously. Climbing out, standing up, aiding themselves with hands and flippers, breathless and grotesque, they drag themselves over the strand to salute Neboum's avengers and mock the beaten strength of his murderers.

The bodies of the giant bears lie in dark pools that the sand is slowly drinking. In spite of the reek of blood, the sirens lift their heavy paws curiously, and push back their soft lips to display the length of the yellow-tinted fangs, clicking their tongues fearfully.

Scattered on the river bank, the intoxication of the combat having dissipated, the centaurs wipe away their sweat and interrogate one another. The victory has been costly. Hark the Rude has had his shoulder opened by the sweep of a claw all the way to his spine. Palkaval's left thigh has been cruelly lacerated; he will be limping for days. Motionless in the river, Kolpitru watches blood dripping from his scored sides and dissipating in the water in murky clouds—but he laughs, proud of his exploit. Many others have retained the imprint of teeth or claws; several have been painfully struck by the hooves of their own brethren. Nauseated by the acrid odor of the murder, they carefully wash their limbs. The rising tide has turned the river water salty; its salutary burn cauterizes the wounds.

Not far away from the remains of Neboum and the gigantic cadavers, however, another body is lying. It is that of Papacal the Joyful. In the attack, he lost his balance; with a single blow the paw of the giant bear broke his back. Lying on his side, he is panting terribly. His hands are digging in the sand; he is clenching his teeth in order not to cry out. The old ones gather around him, moaning. They fill shells with river water and gently bathe his wounds. On the deepest of them, Sihadda expertly places her lips, and alternately sucks the blood and spits it out, in order to ward off the evil spirit.

Papacal's eyes open slightly. A murmur of gratitude emerges from his dry mouth. Kadilda is kneeling beside him; she lifts up his hirsute head, supports it with one of her white arms and puts a shell full of fresh water, which she had fetched from a spring, to the wounded individual's lips. Papacal drinks long mouthfuls. Then, with a sigh of relief, he lets himself fall back on to the sand—but his feverish hand holds on to that of the centauress, who dares not refuse his grip, and remains crouched down beside him.

Klevorak's voice resounds: "Well, Papacal, did you mistake the wild beast for a centauress, and consequently threw yourself into its arms?"

Papacal raises his heavy eyelids and tries to laugh, but a grimace of suffering creases his cheeks. The chief's face becomes grave. He puts his hands on the sides of the wounded centaur and palpates them several times. Under the stout fingers, Papacal's limbs quiver, and in spite of his courage, groans escape his throat. With his gaze, Klevorak interrogates the old females; they understand his mute question, and sigh, letting their chins hang down over their meager breasts.

Then the chief gets up and calls for help. The centaurs gather silently around their stricken brother, and the solemn voice of the oldest male pronounces the sentence.

"Papacal, the six-limbed people fear nothing that lives, but death is more powerful than the centaurs. Prepare yourself, Papacal, to render to the sun the strength that you have received from your ancestors."

Papacal blinks. He has understood.

The tritons gather on the bank, blowing into their conches, from which they extract melancholy notes.

The air is still. Night has fallen. Silky flocks of bats flutter in all directions.

Klevorak asks: "What is your wish?"

With a great effort, Papacal pronounces: "Give me three days."

There is a murmur of astonishment. What! Three days of suffering rather than immediate great rest? But the law is definite. Papacal has exercised his right.

"The three days will be counted from tomorrow's sunrise."

And at sign from the chief, Hark, Kolpitru and two others lift up the body of the vanquished centaur, place it on their backs, and move off. Because of their burden, the journey will take a long time; but Gurgundo, doubling the cape, announces the victory in advance to the brothers in the Red Grottos.

Before the last centaurs have left the beach, gleaming eyes light up in all directions, and with grunts of joy, voracious shadow fall upon the cadavers. Today, the eaters of flesh owe a feast to the justice of the sovereign people. In the morning, the bones of the dead will be clean.

Beneath the black dome of the pines, the centaurs walk slowly, because of the fallen night and the heavy body of Papacal. In spite of their precautions, they cannot avoid every shock, and sometimes bump into a branch. Then a groan escapes his lips and he clings even more tightly to Kadilda's hand, which he is still holding in his own.

Obligingly, the centauress renders him an amicable pressure. She feels great pity in seeing the strength of Papacal annihilated thus by a single blow. She has forgotten the male's importunities and mocking jests. The terror of the imminent death obsesses her mind, and she is astonished that the laughter of her brothers rises up again in the darkness, and that the old ones have resumed their tiresome chatter.

The porters stop momentarily to get their breath. Then the white virgin feels the moist hand of Papacal drawing her toward him. She obeys the pressure, putting her ear to his mouth, and hears the halting words: "Kadilda, it's to continue seeing your face that Papacal will suffer for three days!"

But the effort has been too great; the centaurs' fingers relax, letting those of the centauress escape and fall away. He has lost consciousness. His groans no longer rise into the peace of the night.

In the east, the moon has risen, fully round. The wood is illuminated. The trunks extend harsh shadows along the ground. The foliage of the pines brightens. The pale verdure of the olive groves sparkles. The centaurs increase their pace.

The last dune is crossed. The sea breeze whips the hot torsos. Beneath the lunar rays, the idle waves are flecked with foam. At twice voice-range the protective mass of the Red Rocks looms up. In the distance, on the other side of the sea, the Smoking Mountain is crowned with a crimson glow.

Scarcely have the centaurs cross the edge of the wood when shouts greet them, and the silhouettes of their brothers are seen, coming across the sands to meet them. Gurgundo has carried the news. Enviously, Kreps, Perik, Klop and Hadda interrogate the victors, examine their wounds and have the episodes of the battle narrated. There is a great hubbub of voices. Everyone celebrates their exploits noisily. A bitter regret bites the hearts of all those who missed the battle.

Inside the Grottos, Papacal's body is set down, and while the old females arrange pillows of moss and seaweed under his limbs, the conversation warms up among the males scattered on the sand. The fight and the odor of blood have sharpened their bellicose humor. As Kolpitru attributes the merit of the victory to himself, Hark sniggers disdainfully; menacingly, the two giants face up to one another; in their rival souls the ancient fury revives that once set the jealous tribes of centaurs at odds throughout the world.

The thunderous voice of Klevorak stops them. They dare not infringe the chief's orders and separate, grinding their teeth. Crouching on the sand a few paces away from one another, however, they exchange hateful stares and provocative gestures.

Klevorak knows the way to calm overexcited minds and to reunite hearts in a single pride. His voice commands once again: "Let Pittina sing the song of the race to us."

The centaurs form a circle on the sand, and now Pittina, the old female, gets up. No one can count how many rainy seasons have bathed the discolored hide of her meager back. For as long as the memories of the chiefs go back, Pittina has been old. She knew the ancestors. She knows the things of old, recites them as they have been transmitted from age to age. Although it is many years since she has succumbed to the trials of the leap, the gallop and the struggle, no one demands the execution of the law against her As her tremulous limbs can no longer carry her far from the Grottos, it is the young ones who bring her fruits and nourishing roots every day, and those whose gifts she nibbles with a blackened tooth are proud.

So Pittina the ancient gets up, beneath the white light that makes her silvery hair gleam, emphasizing her fleshless thighs, her jutting ribs and the sinister emaciation of her torso. She holds a seashell in her hands, a magical gift from the tritons. When she blows into it, a voice more powerful than Klevorak's resounds.

Pittina fills her lungs and puts the conch to her lips. Three times a long roar drowns out the whisper of the waves. While the crouching centaurs lick their wounds silently, their hearts quiver in anticipation. And Pittina's song, frail, shrill, sonorous and formidable by turns, rises up to the stars.

First she tells how the divine sun put into the world the strong race of centaurs, and made them a gift of the Earth, in order that they might reign over it as masters, and cause sanguinary violence to disappear therefrom. Before the six-limbed people emerged from the mysterious cradle of the Orient, murder desolated the forests and the plains; anguish was the law of groaning animality. The centaurs reminded the beasts of the fraternity that they had forgotten; the menacing justice of the sovereign people forbade the eaters of flesh to kill; they only had the right to the cadavers of those that life itself rejected, by striking them down with old age and disease.

Thus it was that among the beasts—those, at least, whose new-borns were nourished at their mothers' breasts—fraternity was reestablished; they now formed a single family, whose leaders were the Centaurs, the Children of the Sun. In combination with the Fauns, the Children of the Earth, and the Tritons, the Children of the Ocean, they form the triple race of noble animals, the Three Sovereign Sibling Tribes.

Undoubtedly, that peace was not established easily, and has been troubled more than once. The ferocity of the flesh-eaters has revolted more than once, and it is only by means of terrible examples that the centaurs have imposed the law upon them. The Wild Beasts never recognized their empire; it was necessary to exterminate them. Between the populations of the six-limbed folk themselves, there have been fratricidal struggles for domination; the blood has flowed in floods, and the meadows have been covered with cadavers—but what would become of the flesh-eaters if all nourishment was refused them?

To make robust hearts and hard limbs, an idle peace is inefficacious. The new law does not exclude all warfare, but it forbids sly and futile killing; it suppresses the anguish that tortures the weak, destructive and immoderate appetites, universal insecurity. For the age of pitiless murder, it has substituted that of general peace, interrupted solely by combats without treachery, in which preeminence is the stake. Such is the benefit of the centaurs.

Pittina stops to draw breath. An approving murmur circulates on the white beach, and it is not only those of the tribe who thank her. At the call of the magic conch, the people with

41

the sticky limbs and scaly rumps have gradually emerged from the waves, and have drawn nearer to the singer, crawling over the sand. And from the woods where they play by night, under the fantastic rays of the moon, the capripeds too have emerged and have come quietly to sit down beside their brethren. Thus the Three Tribes fraternize, and all admire the powerful voice of the old female, her incredible memory, her knowledge of words and facts, and they rejoice with a single soul in the common glory of their race.

And the old female gets up again, and her voice recites the second song.

Having related the origin of the centaurs and the grandeur of their assigned task, she also relates their destiny.

Once, in time immemorial, the innumerable tribes of noble animals lived together in distant countries of the Orient, from which the sun took flight every morning. There, immense prairies offered the centaurs an abundance of rheki, the fern with the edible root, the mysterious plant that maintains their vigor in all seasons and that no nourishment can replace. But this is what happened. From the mountains that surrounded the cradle of the sun, terrible masses of snow descended, and swallowed up all life beneath their mass. The mortal north wind and the ice withered the trees that were the bearers of fruit, the edible herbs and the flourishing fields of rheki.

Then, chased by the cold, the six-limbed folk had abandoned the frozen deserts and, following the sun in its course, had rediscovered under other skies the splendor of green foliage, comforting warmth and the indispensable root. Galloping behind them across the plains and the mountains, the fauns had followed their older siblings. With them, the tritons had descended the rivers.

And thus it was that, in successive stages, the noble animals, so far as memory extends, have had that destiny: across the earth, from age to age, they have carried their pacific reign with them, beneath various skies; everywhere, their presence has been the signal for the fraternity of beasts, has coincided with the warm splendor of seasons; and when they have disappeared, they have left behind them the sinister reign of violence and cold.

Pittina falls silent. Recalled to the memory of their ancient amity, fauns, tritons and centaurs draw closer together. Beneath the pale radiation of the heavens, around the emaciated singer, there is a strange confusion of rigid torsos, projecting rumps, scaly backs and fleeces like those of billy-goats. At Pittina's evocation, the simple souls fill up with the majesty of the past, and are perhaps obscurely frightened by the possible mysteries of the future; and all of them feel a need for their flanks to touch, for their respiration to mingle, and to sense their communal strength.

Because they anticipate what the old female's last words will be, however, a frisson is already running over their limbs, and they huddle closer together, silently.

Pittina sings.

When, following the sun, in pursuit of the cold-sensitive nourishing plant, the centaurs have quit the regions invaded by cold, behind them there is not only the reign of the frost, but that of murder and violence. Why? Is it because, as soon as the Dominators have disappeared, all the beasts feel the ferocity they thought they had forgotten reviving within them? No; the flesh-eaters too obtain the benefits of the imposed law and have lost their thirst for killing. But the forests shelter guests deadlier than the Wild Beasts, which Nature seems to be rejecting, or the carnivores capable of yielding to the pacific yoke of the dominators. Everywhere that the centaurs have established their empire, they have been obliged to chase before them the filthy race of the Flayed; in all the regions that they have abandoned, it is said that the Flayed have replaced them.[7]

---

[7] The French word *écorché* [flayed] has a specialized meaning used in reference to a kind of anatomical diagram used in training artists as well as physicians, in which a body is represented with the skin removed, in order to display the musculature. "Flayed" cannot be a literal translation of whatever word

Between the three tribes, Nature has marked differences. The centaurs are the foremost because of their incomparable strength; alone among the living they possess six limbs. The fauns are distinguished by their hairy lower bodies and their feet, similar to those of goats. The tritons live in the waves, and have a tail equipped with fins. But they all resemble one another in the face, the torso and the arms, and especially in the intelligence that is in them, and renders them capable of thinking and acting together.

The Flayed too have the upper bodies of sovereign animals. But the livid color of the face, the weakness of their torsos and the thinness of their arms are pitiful. A blood so poor runs in their veins that they have been unable to cover themselves with fur, or to fortify their fragile skin—which is like that of a skinned animal—with a protective hide. In the lower part, their body is terminated hideously by the grotesque limbs of Ful, the macaque, but do not even have his supple tail. Naked, feeble, slow in running, unskilled in climbing, the Flayed have mores even more repugnant than their appearance.

With them, no treaty is secure. The word sworn today, the Flayed will violate tomorrow. Their voracity is insatiable. Instinctively, like Kronon the wild boar, they gorge themselves on all fruits and all roots, but their passion is for blood. Although they are lazy, the Flayed kill for the pleasure of killing. They devour palpitating flesh and, satiated, kill again. Their pleasure is to shelter their naked limbs in the skins stripped from their victims. Thus they can brave the mortal cold. Egotistical and imbecilic, they bury their dead, frustrating the flesh-eaters of their due. Pain wrings shrill screams from them and makes their eyes stream with impure water. Their lubricity is incredible. They rush to love in all seasons, and the consequence of that is that the race pullulates. Their minds are as rebellious to mildness as to threats. Stupefied,

---

the centaurs are using, because it implies the use of a knife, which the centaurs do not possess, but none of the obvious alternatives is any better.

they are isolated by their very nature from all other living things. Their malice, however, is incredible; they have obscure magic, strange ruses and incomprehensible practices.

The law of the sovereign animals is inexorable. It is permitted to spare even the Wild Beasts when they become inoffensive and remain in their lairs, but between the Accursed Ones and the teat-bearers. no point of alliance is possible. The Flayed have two brothers: cold and death. Where the centaurs are, their place is not; they have excluded themselves from the general peace.

And in a supreme effort, Pittina's voice intones, mightily, the centuries-old song of the six-limbed people:

"Of all living things, centaurs are the foremost, fauns and tritons their brethren. To them the sun, the earth and the waves. By their actions, joy enters the teat-bearers. Banish dread and death by murder. Kill those who kill! Peace between all!"

And with an immense rumor all the members of the audience rise to their feet. A host of arms is raised toward the pale sky, and with one voice, they all repeat the solemn refrain:

"Kill those who kill! Peace between all."

Exhausted, limbs weary, the singer has let herself fall on to the sand. Around her, all the bodies stir. Hands are shaken, amicable salutations exchanged. Joyfully. Hark picks up Titul the faun and shakes him; Titul kicks out. Around the sirens lying on the sand, Sirix and Puiulex press curiously. Klevorak, Pirip and Gurgundo swear a renewed amity. Centaurs and faunesses, fauns and sirens, tritons and centauresses fraternize noisily.

A large cloud veils the moon, however. The shadows blacken. The breeze is fresher. It is time for sleep. Gurgundo seizes his conch and raises it to his lips.

A roar signals the departure. Tritons and sirens jostle on the strand; they reach the foamy fringes of the waves, are swallowed up, and emerge again, already distant. Once again, their sonorous voices hurl a farewell, and then they disappear into the night. The last fauns plunge into the edge of the pines.

At a slow pace, the centaurs return to the shelter of the Red Grottos. Abruptly, fatigue has descended upon them. Their limbs are moving ponderously. Their eyes are sleepy. With delight, they penetrate into the spacious lair that shelters them from the wind and the rain, and they lie down on heaps of grass and seaweed. Soon the rhythm of respiration rises, echoing against the rocky walls, the snores louder than the infinite sighing of the sea.

Kadilda, the white centauress, has regained her customary place. Because of the strong odor exhaled by the scattered bodies, she lies down every night in an isolated corner near the entrance. She prefers to cover herself with fodder, and even to feel the bite of cold, rather than sleep with the other females.

This evening, however, it takes her a long time to go to sleep. Too many emotions are oppressing her at the end of such a day.

All the horror of the battle makes her hair bristle at the memory of the war cry, the crouching monsters and the furious charge that struck them down. The acrid odor of blood fills her nostrils. She remembers the moving mass that she felt, crushed beneath her hooves. The cracking of its bones echoes in her ears. She sees her legs again, red to the knees. Was a little salty water enough to wash away so much blood?

Against that horror, she would like to feel reassured and protected, as in the days when she was a two-year-old centauress who never quit her mother's side—but the rains have fallen many times since the bones of Paddiah, whose milk nourished her, have whitened. Who will caress the fearful Kadilda now?

Something gently flattered her ear today, though. Papacal had a word as sweet as the dew-soaked morning moss: "It's to continue seeing your face that Papacal will suffer for three days!"

Several times, Kadilda repeats those words in a low voice. They have a strange and delicious tone. Why do such phrases emerge so rarely from the rude throats of centaurs? There is a need for tender words that caress like melodious hymns...

Pittina's song was beautiful. At her voice, the dead awoke, distant countries came nearer, the things of the past were present again. When she heard the song, Kadilda relived the days of her childhood, the long journey through the mountains and the woods, traversing profound gorges, all the fatigues by means of which the tribe reached the shelter of the Red Rocks and the shore of the loquacious sea.

All those things had been dead in her for a long time. They awoke in response to Pittina's voice, like the inexpressible horror of the accursed race that soils the earth...

Kadilda's eyes have never beheld the Flayed, but their mere evocation makes her shiver, and she blesses the singer for not having designated the Impure Ones by their true name, the symbol of death. Among the centaurs, no one dares to pronounce the name Human without lowering the voice.

Kadilda shivers again—but sleep falls upon her, extinguishing her thoughts and relaxing her limbs.

Above the clouds, the moon has emerged again and is following a descending path among the paling stars. One by one, on the silvery beach, the eternal waves advance, singing their song of foam, and then return to sleep in the profound bosom of the sea.

In the distance, the Smoking Mountain glows red. Everything alive is asleep.

Part Two

From a heavy sleep agitated and interrupted by frightful visions, Kadilda awakes. She raises herself up on her hands and looks around. Shadow fills the cavern, but a yellow light at the entrance announces the dawn.

Worn out by the battle, the centaurs are still asleep. Their huge bodies are lying on the ground. Their powerful lungs are alternately aspiring air and exhaling it. A stink that scarcely dissipates during the day fills the atmosphere. A muffled plaint rises up in a corner, fading into a sigh.

Kadilda's thoughts clear. Soon, as there is every morning, there will be a tumultuous awakening: coarse laughter, the sonorous slapping of thighs, familiar jostling. Soon, Papacal will demand her presence. She will have to dress his wounds, watch him suffer, leave her own hand in the moist hand of the centaur; and although he is not dear to the virgin's heart, the claws of death that are already gripping him will hurt her too—and frightful things will penetrate her soul.

From these anticipations, a cowardice insinuates itself into her. Abruptly, an irresistible desire grips her to flee from the wounded centaur, and to flee from her brothers too, in order to wash away the impurities that are impregnating her in the open air and the nascent light.

Quietly, Kadilda lifts up her upper body, gathers her legs and braces herself. When Klevorak speaks, the law is to obey him, but the free centaurs are their own masters as soon as his voice falls silent. Without a sound, the centauress raises her hooves one by one, places them cautiously on the ground, and goes to the nearby opening. Across it lies the body of Kaplam, the nocturnal guardian of the threshold. His dappled flank is rising and falling alternately. In order not to brush him, Kadilda gathers up the white plume of her tail in her hand and steps over him without touching him. In three bounds she is outside.

She shakes herself to get rid of the sand and wisps of straw with which she is covered. She passes her fingers back and forth through her tangled hair. Then, throwing her upper body back, with her arms folded behind the back of her neck, she stretches, yawns deeply, and breathes the salubrious air delightedly.

Behind the eternally green curtain of pines, and behind the mountains that loom over them, the paternal sun has not yet surged forth. Already, however, an indecisive glow is announcing his advent. Opposite, on the other horizon, a similar roseate glow is reflected above the mists that are asleep over the waves. Entirely gray, the sea is murmuring in a low tone, as a new-born centaurin whimpers before awakening. Only a few nonchalant wavelets wrinkle the surface. The protective rocks are like stricken mammoths. The birds are asleep on the branches. The woods are silent. In all of Nature, only Kadilda has open eyes; for her alone the luminous beauty of daylight is reborn.

Suddenly, a frisson runs down the neck of the centauress, along her back and through her limbs, causing her hackles to rise.

Perhaps she is feeling the cold of the morning; perhaps she is troubled by a slight childish fear born of the surrounding silence, of her solitude, of the majestic calm of things. She shakes herself, leaps into the air, looks to the right and the left, bows her head, sniffs, shivers again, and suddenly, with an abrupt release of her leg-muscles, and with a cry like a seagull, she launches herself recklessly over the strand.

The blonde cloud of her hair and the white cloud of her tail float behind her. From time to time she looks back, utters another cry, and then increases her pace, devouring space.

As she gallops, warmth refreshes her limbs and gaiety is reborn in her heart. Where is she going? Instinctively, her course has drawn her southwards, in the direction opposite the one where the frightful battle took place...

Suddenly, she is enchanted by an idea. She will follow the coast as far as the River of Swans. Then she will go upriver, and plunge into the woods that envelop its sinuous course. For several seasons, the centaurs have not ridden in that direction. The white virgin will not be troubled in the day of solitude that she desires, and she feels an itching curiosity to explore that unknown territory. No fear of danger occurs to her; is she not the daughter of Klevorak the Dominator?

At a slower pace Kadilda crosses the stony cape that terminates the promontory of the Red Rocks. Carefully, she scales the blocks of granite, avoiding setting her hooves on the slippery algae, sometimes sinking up to her knees in saline pools carpeted with sea-urchins, multicolored weeds and strange anemones with nacreous gleams. The fish in the rockpools flee her footfalls. The water sizzles in the porous pebbles. The vivifying odor of the sea ricks her nostrils.

The rocky area is quickly crossed. Kadilda's feet tread on sand again. Now the southern beach extends as far as the eye can see. The River of Swans is invisible, save for an indicative silvery patch in the far distance.

Abruptly, the dazzling eye of the sun opens above the pines, setting the Red Rocks on fire and projecting massive shadows over the shore. Birdsong is awakened. Above the waves, gannets soar, letting themselves fall in sudden plunges, and reappearing with fish quivering in their beaks.

In front of her, the open space intoxicates the centauress. Again she utters a shrill cry, claps her hands, and sets off at a light gallop that scarcely brushes the sand, surprising snipe in the hollows of the dunes, which take fright and fly away. In the joy that inundates her, Kadilda laughs alone at the glory of the nascent day, and, in the manner of centaurs when they challenge one another to contests of flexibility, she bends her upper body back several times, so adroitly that she caresses her face with the plume of her tail, abruptly brought back by a kick; then, with a burst of shrill laughter, she straightens up and increases her speed, pursued by the cloud of her sungilded hair.

Placidly, the River of Swans mingles its slow waters with the every-swarming waters of the sea. The centauress, out of breath, stops on the sandy bank. In the distance behind her, the Red Rocks are no more than phantoms drowned in the morning mist. Kadilda rejoices in her solitude. To refresh herself, she wades knee-deep into the water, and then to the depth of her withers. Abruptly, she plunges into it entirely, and emerges streaming like a triton. At a stroke her fatigue is banished. The paternal sun will quickly dry her off.

Reinvigorated, she resumes her journey. Now the river will be her guide. It snakes lazily between the gentle slopes of its banks, sometimes gradually gathering two curtains of verdure about it. At a brisk pace, Kadilda trots alongside the clear water, peering around curiously, delighted by the flutter of dragonflies and the chirping of the birds. Soon, the maritime pines are succeeded by a less somber and more varied vegetation. Alders and willows tickle the tranquil waters with their tresses. The banks are covered with reeds and water-lilies. As the virgin passes by, water-fowl rise up heavily. Multicolored swifts zigzag in pursuit of butterflies. White swans swim majestically.

In the rich and calm life that surrounds her, Kadilda forgets the frightful images that were oppressing her. She rejoices in the gracile delicacy of the plants, the variety of the sparkling flowers, and the noble beauty of the forest species. Sometimes, she plunges belly-deep into the undergrowth, and hanging foliage forces her to lower her head. She is intoxicated by the perfumes that rise to her nostrils, sometimes skirting the river and sometimes, on a whim, pursuing an insect through the thickets, breaking through creepers and brambles, glad to surprise the flight of field-mice and to awaken in her abrupt course the loud cries of blackbirds and starlings.

Suddenly, a short distance away, on a mossy mound at the foot of an oak, she perceives the comical silhouette of a rabbit. He is sitting on his rear, alternately twitching his right and left ears. Kadilda calls to him with an amicable whistle, but Titul is born and remains suspicious. He shivers, leaps, and as soon as the centauress emerges his white rump disappears into his burrow.

Mischievously, Kadilda crouches down beside the hole, in such a way that neither her shadow not her scent will give her away—and as soon as the tremulous tip of Tutul's nose appears, she brings her hand abruptly down on his furry neck and stands up, laughing, lifting the coward up by the ears level with her face. Will he recognize the daughter of the dominators and realize that his terror is vain?

But Kadilda's attempts to calm Titul down with kind words and caresses are futile. The simpleton's tiny brain is panicked. His eyes roll in their orbits; his entire body trembles and struggles convulsively. He sees death. Kadilda takes pity on him. She passes her hand over his brown pelt and sets him on the ground.

"Be happy, then, my little brother."

Shock leaves Titul motionless; before he has recovered his spirits, the centauress has plunged into the thicket again. He follows her with his eyes, as if astonished to be alive.

Because of the ground she has covered and the sun that is rising into the sky, Kadilda feels thirsty and tired. When necessary, a centaur can go for three days without eating and lose none of his strength, but hunger nevertheless draws the virgin to the multicolored berries hidden in the bushes.

The fruiting season has barely begun; besides which, there are no olive-trees, nor vines, nor orange-trees with shiny foliage—all cherished by the centaurs—growing on the banks of the River of Swans. The red patches of strawberries bloody the moss, however, and currant bushes offer their glaucous berries within arm's reach. When she has gorged herself with pink and pale fruits, she yawns. The sour flavor has made her slightly drowsy. After a nap, her feet will carry her more lightly.

Kadilda takes a few steps into the ferns that rise up higher than her withers, and then, turning round two or three times to make her bed softer, she settles down, stretches out her limbs and goes to sleep.

Around her, the ferns straighten up again.

When Kadilda opens her eyes after the reparative sleep, she remain languid for a few seconds. Squirrels are pursuing one another along the branches overhead. Motionless, the centauress rejoices in the agile grace of their slender bodies, their tufted tails, and the gleam of their keen brown eyes. Suddenly, the squirrels stop and tilt their impudent necks, seemingly listening. Their eyes stare anxiously. Then, in a trice, as if in response to a signal, they launch themselves into the foliage, leaping from branch to branch and into the next tree. They have disappeared.

Without moving, Kadilda pricks up her ears. What is the wild animal whose approach has terrified the little russet folk? The centaurs' subtle hearing permits them to recognize almost all species of creatures on the move, without seeing them. Amid the confused rumors of the forest, the virgin perceives the distinct sound of approaching footfalls, treading down the vegetation noisily. Even though her ear is applied to the ground, however, she is annoyed not to be able to discern the family to which the walker belongs. It is neither the gliding movement of a feline, nor the clatter of full or cloven hooves, nor the thin trot of Lull, nor any of the beasts whose names come to mind.

Kadilda's attention sharpens with astonishment, her eyes widening. Either she is mad, or the unknown is walking on two feet. Now, his step is not that of Pirip, whose hooves resonate more sharply on the ground, nor that of Ful the macaque, who is more flexible and lighter when he chances to come down from the trees...

Now he is very close; in the ferns that surround Kadilda, she perceives an undulation. Curious, she gets to her feet, causing the foliage to rustle; she looks, and utters a cry of amazement.

Before her stands a being whose like she has never seen before. He is almost as tall as Pirip and his brothers. Like them, he stands upright on two feet, but his paltry appearance has none of the joyous strength of the fauns. A fur covers him from his shoulders to the level of his thighs. The rest of his body, the face and the limbs seem devoid of hair, having pink-ish-white flesh like that of sucking-pigs. Beneath the forehead, devoid of defensive horns, a mobile and wan face gives evidence of fear. Two eyes as pale as the sea confer a gentle sadness upon it. At the end of thin white arms are small frail hands, incapable of strangling an enemy or brandishing a club. His feet are not protected by hooves, but made of soft flesh that the brambles have bloodied.

At the sight of the centauress, the unknown has also uttered a cry, and jumped backwards in order to take flight. But as she remains motionless, only her torso emerging from the ferns, he stops, legs braced, hesitating, and considers her with a gaze that is simultaneously fearful and curious....

His right hand is desperately clutching a poor twig that Kadilda could break between two fingers; but, looming over the unknown from the height of her withers, she has no thought of molesting him. When the initial astonishment has passed, she is moved by his weakness and ugliness, and in order that he might cease to be afraid, she claps her hands and begins to laugh.

The unknown imitates her; he brings the palms of his hands together, and parts his thin lips, letting out a snigger.

Then, in a voice that she softens, the centauress interrogates him. What is his name? Where has he come from? Where is his tribe? Has he sworn Klevorak's truce?

The unknown listens attentively. His face remains stupid. He shakes his head, and begins to speak in his turn, but his language is harsh and confused. He utters unintelligible sounds that have something of the whistle of the blackbird, the howl of the jackal and the voices of many other animal people, all of which mingle in a ridiculous cacophony. By means of broads gestures, he indicates the Orient and then the west, waving his spindly arms; he shouts more loudly, with an astonishing volubility, and then seems to expect a reply.

At these insanities, the centauress shrugs her shoulders. In spite of his mental weakness, however, the unknown might perhaps be able to say his name. Directing her finger toward her own breast, she says: "Kadilda."

The biped has understood. He points a finger at her and repeats: "Kadilda." Then he turns it toward himself and articulates: "Naram."

After him, the virgin's voice, as sonorous as a buccina by comparison with his, repast: "Naram."

And in unison, both of them, several times over, point at one another alternately, repeating: "Kadilda...Naram..."

And being thus understood, they feel less distant, and burst into simultaneous laughter, clapping their hands.

Then Naram seems to ask more questions. The sounds trip so rapidly from his tongue that they buzz in her ears dizzily. Finally, as the centauress remains silent, he makes a sign that is less unintelligible. Several times, he lifts his head, sticks out his lower lip, and lifts the hollow of his cupped hand to it.

This time, Kadilda has understood. Naram is thirsty. She feels her pity return. Why, when the river is only two or three times voice-range away, has the unfortunate's sense of smell not revealed its presence? Feeble and stupid as he is, what will become of him?

The centauress parts the clump of ferns and currant-bushes with her lower body and makes a sign to Naram to follow her—but when she looks back, she sees him standing motionless, mouth open, eyes bulging looking at her from head to toe and breast to tail.

Kadilda laughs. Did he think that she was vacillating on two meager feet of soft flesh, like him? Beside the robust centauress, standing on her muscular legs and hard hooves, the unknown seems even frailer, and even paler.

Abruptly, however, he seems to make a decision. In a deliberate manner, he takes two steps forward, stretches out his arm, and places his hand on the virgin's flank.

Kadilda shudders and recoils. What effrontery does Naram have, in order for him to dare to touch a daughter of the dominators without being invited? Also, at the contact of his smooth skin, a bizarre disgust rises to the heart of the centauress, as if she had just touched flesh skinned alive.

Increasing the volume of her voice, she says: "Don't touch."

But Naram does not appear to understand. To the virgin's astonishment, his body suddenly appears, as bare and white as his limbs, and he swings in his right hand the fleece that covered him just now. And while, frightened by this prodigy, she directs her eyes alternately at the narrow torso and the stripped skin, searching for traces of wounds, the unknown draws closer, making inviting gestures. Such is Kadilda's astonishment that she does not draw away immediately when Naram places his hand on her flanks, patting them, and palpating her lower shoulder. Her eyes remain invincibly riveted to those of the unknown, the blue gleam of which fascinates her, and she forgets to reject the strange caress that runs over her limbs.

Suddenly, however, the indignant virgin jumps. Slyly, Naram has bent down, and with the fleece that he has taken off has wound it around the centauress' front feet, so singularly that Kadilda stumbles, feeling her movements impeded. With a kick, she frees herself. Anger blazes in her eyes. What is this runt, whom she could flatten with a playful thrust, daring to attempt?

Naram is undisturbed. He raises two fingers to his lips and emits a long whistle, then laughs in a reassuring manner and begins speaking again in his shrill voice, to which the virgin's ear is beginning to become accustomed.

Centaurs cannot bear prolonged mental tension. Kadilda's ideas become confused. Mechanically, her eyes remain fixed on the brown fleece, which the unknown picks up. She sniffs. Her amazement increases; Kadilda has never seen anything like Naram, and yet the odor of the skin that touches her limbs, and is his own, seems familiar.

The centauress raises her head and looks around. Whistles similar to the one emitted by Naram's mouth are now resounding in the woods. Doubtless his brothers are approaching. What is their intention?

Naram puts his fingers to his lips again, whistles and moves forward; from his arm hangs the fleece, of which Kadilda, neck extended and nostrils dilated, breathes in the singular odor.

Krooh!

The virgin has uttered a cry of horror and bounded backwards, her coat bristling. Death! Naram is carrying death in his arms! The odor that emanates from the suspended skin is the sinister odor of blood, of the blood of Ghali, the brown antelope, who has such a pelt on his shoulders. But then...then...?

Like ripples spreading over the water around the sudden fall of a stone, Pittina's terrible song is revived in Kadilda's ears. She trembles on her fetlocks.

Close at hand, the whistles redouble, and the foliage rustles. In response to Naram's summons, his brothers are coming at a run...his brothers with white skin, blue eyes, paltry limbs...his brothers, the Accursed, whose very name is a pollution...

With a howl, Kadilda launches herself into the thicket. The bushes crack under the impact, the branches break like twigs. A hectic course carries her through the thorn-bushes, where her skin is lacerated and entire clumps of her hair ripped out. No matter! One single thought illuminates her soul: Flee! Flee, at any price.

She thinks she can still hear the frightful signal of the Flayed ringing in her ears. She redoubles her efforts. The river is soon far away. The open shore is ahead of her. Kadilda races recklessly...

Out of breath, streaming with seat, her legs buckling, she collapses on the sand. A few voice-ranges away, the protective masses of the Red Rocks rise up, illuminated by the fires of the setting sun. The purple, yellow and pink horizon is cloudless. The sea smells good, singing softly, its waves moving back and forth monotonously; the breeze is sweet. All these familiar things bring comfort to the virgin's heart. The tumult of her thoughts calms down. One question comes to mind: what should she say to her brothers about her encounter?

A little while before, in the convulsion of the initial horror, no doubt brushed her soul. In response to her denunciatory voice, the centaurs would utter the war cry; a single surge would take them to the River of Swans in order to exterminate the Accursed. But now Kadilda hesitates. A kind of shame oppresses her at the thought of recounting her adventure. Questioned, a centaur cannot lie. The centauress suffers in anticipation of relating how she perceived Naram, how the two attempted to understand one another, and how the Flayed has placed his hand upon her. She is irritated in anticipation of the coarse laughter that will rise up around her story, the jests of Hark, Kolpitru and the other males.

Then again, in spite of Pittina's maledictions, pity grips her at the thought of the carnage for which her words would give the signal. Undoubtedly, the old woman was just in denouncing the filthy race of the Flayed—but Kadilda has seen their sickly limbs with her own eyes. The majority of the animals of the forest surpass them in strength and agility. All their malice cannot make them a danger to the sovereign people. The memory of the previous day's battle still saddens Kadilda's heart. It seems intolerable to her to scent the frightful odor of blood again.

Suddenly, with an abrupt gesture, she puts her hands over her ears. She has just imagined hearing the sound of the paltry Naram's bones cracking under Kolpitru's enormous hooves...

The virgin's decision is made. Her tongue will not demand the blood of the impure ones. She will not involve herself in their fate.

Satisfied, Kadilda gets up, washes her shanks in the waves, smoothes her hair and heads back toward the Red Rocks at a slow pace.

She crosses the rocky promontory again.

While Hekem has taken half the people to the rheki field today, the remainder have been idling in the pines all day long, Now that the sun is about to set, they have all come back down on to the beach.

Crouched on the sand, the centauresses are removing the tangled debris of bits of wood, leaves and brambles from their hair. By rubbing themselves with sand and water, they are effacing the patches of mud that are soiling their limbs and belies, and they are helping one another to hunt down their lice and snap them with their fingernails.

Among the males, some are devoting themselves to wrestling, jumping and racing, and the others, standing around the contestants, are admiring their prowess. Taking turns, Hark and Kolpitru have floored their brothers and now, confronting one another, they are at grips, their legs intercrossed, each one trying to throw the other on to the sand.

Several times, Kolpitru has made the red-haired centaur's back bend by crushing him with his bulk; each time, Hark has been able to escape from the hold and, rounding on the giant, has shaken him severely. Sweat is streaming over their pectoral muscles; the veins in their necks are swollen. Face to face, torso to torso, arms knotted, the wrestlers persist—and gradually, in the simulated combat, their tempers flare up, and it is with snorts of anger that they attack one another.

Klevorak's authority has to intervene. When his voice calls a halt, neither Hark nor Kolpitru dares to disobey. They draw apart, their glares die down, and, congratulated by everyone, they walk down to the sea in order to bathe before it is time to rest. Among their brothers, no one interrogates the virgin.

Paternally, Klevorak expresses his pleasure in seeing her return, but a centaur does not indulge in pusillanimous tenderness. He passes his hand back and forth through his daughter's blonde tresses and points her in the direction of Papacal, who has asked to see her several times during the day.

The wounded individual is lying on a bed of seaweed near the entrance to the Red Rocks; the centauress approaches him. In his fever and his pain, however, he does not see her. Raucous breath is escaping from his throat. Bloody drool is running from his mouth. His body is emitting a frightful odor of putrefied blood.

Gripped by revulsion, Kadilda watches old Hurico applying her lips to his wounds in order to such out the hidden venom. Her heart revolts and she moves away.

When night has fallen, Kadilda lies down in her usual place, apart from the rest of her people. As again, as on the previous evening, too many thoughts crowd in on her and dispel sleep. She dreams repeatedly of all the details of the encounter she has had. Before her eyes, there is the pale body of Naram and his frail limbs; the voice of the unknown still resonates in her ears, and her name as he pronounced it: "Kadilda."

And several times, the virgin's lips move and she repeats, in a low voice: "Naram."

She remembers, too, how the soft hand was placed on her flank while the sparkling pale eyes were fixed upon her.

And Kadilda shivers, doubtless with horror.

Three suns have risen and set since Papacal fell under the claws of the Giant Bear, so the legal delay has elapsed. When the fourth sun illuminates the moving tops of the pines and the back of the Red Rocks, the centaurs, as they do every morning, carry the wounded individual out on to the sand in order that he can respire the vivifying air and rejoice once more in the light. Then they remain around him, their visages pensive. Klevorak advances in the silence and says in a gravely interrogative voice: "Brother, pronounce your destiny."

Papacal raises his dying eyes to look the chief in the face, and nods his head. The law of the centaurs is as just as it is ineluctable. Anyone whom old age, infirmity or malady renders incapable of crossing the regulation distance in a given time, or satisfying the proofs of the leap and the combat, cannot remain a useless burden to his tribe or to the earth. Nature has announced that his time is over. Thus, after three days, if his strength has not returned, he intones his own death-song and accepts his destiny. Pittina alone, because of her knowledge, is exempted from the rule.

Papacal knows the law. A centaur knows no fear. The wounded individual closes his eyes to collect his vigor, and with a voice that does not tremble, he sings an account of his exploits. At each pause, the chorus repeats his final words and celebrates the generosity and courage of Papacal.

The final strophe has vibrated. After the dying man, the entire herd has repeated the centuries-old words that affirm, beyond the death of any individual, the perpetuity of the race.

In the serene joy of the morning, Klevorak prescribes, according to the ancestral rite: "Brother, state your will."

The centaur's eyes scan the immobile troop of his brethren one last time, stopping on the virgin with the blonde hair.

"Let Kadilda's face be the last I see!"

No one disobeys the desire of someone who is about to die. Although the idea of murder strikes a chill into the virgin's bones, she collects herself, and going pale, positions herself in front of Papacal, who contemplates her and smiles.

To the right of the condemned man, the ancient Pittina has come to stand. On the other side, Hark is standing, with the sacred club—the shoulder-blade of a mastodon—in his hands. All around, the circle of watchers is motionless.

"Sing the song, Pittina," orders the one who is about to die.

The old one extends her thin hands above Papacal's head and her high-pitched voice rises into the air. She blesses the sun that gave Papacal the spark of life, the earth that offered him its fruits and the water that slaked his thirst. Papacal has lived, he has eaten, he has drunk. His task is complete. Let his body yield food and drink. Let him return his life to the sun, the father of all life. Thus let it be.

With a supreme effort, Papacal braces his hands in the sand and raises up his upper body. A centaur does not die lying down. He parades his last glance around him, smiling to the right and to the left. Then, with his profound eyes staring straight ahead at the white virgin, without lowering is eyelids, he commands: "Strike!"

Hark's arm comes down, as prompt as lightning. Something warm splashes Kadilda's face; she utters a cry and flees. The skull smashed, the gray matter oozes out. Papacal lies on the ground, which drinks his blood.

The old ones lean over, putting their hands to his breast and to his lips. They straighten up, and clap their palms together.

Papacal's suffering is over. His life has returned to the sun.

Then, noisily, the males congratulate Hark for his skill, which they all envy, and they disperse to gather plants or to amuse themselves on the strand. Four of them, however, directed by Pittina, seize the cadaver and carry it to the edge of the woods behind the Red Rocks. All dead flesh belongs to the carnivores; it is only just that one who has lived should give life, instead of rotting uselessly...

Covered in Papacal's blood, Kadilda has raced toward the waves, which are splashing around her. With all her might she rubs her face, her arms and her torso in order to get rid of the stain. Might she not be able, at the same time, to wash her soul clean of the fright that fills it?

And when she has allowed the waves to cover her and lifted herself out again, alternately, she hears the centaurs' bursts of laughter, and sees them resuming their games. A kind of horror grips her at their resuscitated gaiety. A flock of vultures is describing circles above the trees behind the Red Grottos. No one but them remembers Papacal any longer.

A tremor shakes the limbs of the centauress: one day, she will serve as fodder for the beasts.

Kadilda remembers Pittina's song. Alone among the living, the Flayed do not allow the fangs of carnivores to tear their dead apart. Now, the thoughts of the centauress revolt against the old female's maledictions, and return to Naram, the unknown with the smooth skin and the bright gaze.

Kadilda has dreamed about the humans. For many days she has struggled against the secret instinct that pushes her toward the River of Swans on every morning when she does not accompany her brothers to the rheki field. For many days, she wanted to rid herself of the memory of her encounter, to forget the child Naram who called her by her name: Kadilda.

Eventually, her resistance was exhausted. One morning, at dawn, she left. She crossed the southern beach, and went up the course of the river. Eyes wary, nostrils dilated, ears pricked, placing her feet cautiously in order not to rustle the foliage, she went into the surrounding woods. She recognized the trails of the humans, narrower and taller than those of the wild boar. She followed them.

She knows now where Naram's people reside. In a clearing, in the middle of a wood of chestnut-trees, she has perceived, through the bushes, the singular Grottos that the impure ones know how to construct for themselves with branches, moss, fodder and mud. Around the huts, she has seen the males and females devoting themselves to their occupations.

Some are frightful. Horrorstricken, Kadilda has watched them cutting up dead beasts and eating their flesh. At other times, they devote themselves to labors with a surprising skill. With their marvelously slender and delicate fingers they assemble hides, shape wood and stone and make them stick together by methods that smack of prodigy. As she follows their subtle movements, Kadilda feels dazed.

For some time, the virgin felt disgusted by those bloodless bodies covered with detached furs, and their insipid odor gave her nausea. Gradually, she has become accustomed to it. Although the idea cannot occur to her of comparing the weakness of the Flayed with the divine strength of the centaurs, Kadilda does not deny them all merit.

Among them, the males disdain vague wrestling-matches. The skin of the females is incredible sleek. Next to them, Kadilda, so admired among her own people only has a coarse and common hide. As Kirri the bat combs his fur with his paws, in such a way as to divide it into two masses separated by a straight line, the female humans know how to smooth their hair with a bizarre instrument. At first Kadilda thought their conduct grotesque; one day she attempted to imitate it; she was obliged to give up, humiliated and discouraged because of the clumsiness of her stout fingers.

At first, Kadilda was also scornful of the human children, all of them similar, with their bare and ruddy skin and the writhing of their limbs, like big worms or plucked birds, but she has learned to look at them without repugnance. She even feel unknown stirrings in her heart when she sees them rolling in the moss, twittering, under the gazes of their mothers, who, from time to time, squeeze them in their arms. Instead of mocking their puerile frolics, the males join in their games too as evening approaches.

Assembled at the doors of their huts, the human males, females and children amuse themselves together, and the rattle of their precipitate speech, which once made them seem ridiculous, now does not seem to the centauress to be devoid of charm.

One warm night, when the fireflies were sparkling and the joy of the cicadas was singing in the grass, punctuated by the melancholy plaints of toads, Kadilda saw something strange by the nacreous light of the moon. Apart from their brethren, behind a bush, two pale beings, a male and a female, were lying side by side. Under the lunar caress, their juxtaposed white bodies stained the thick grass. Their arms were interlaced. Their mouths were murmuring very softly. Suddenly, their lips came together for a long time, and then they went to sleep, the female's head resting on the male's shoulder—and their placid faces were radiant.

Why had an obscure disturbance gripped Kadilda's heart at that spectacle? Among the centaurs, the males and females sleep separately.

The following night, before going to sleep in solitude, Kadilda had placed her lips on her arm, as she had seen the man and the woman do. A warmth had run through her veins.

Undoubtedly, the six-limbed folk are rightly ignorant of such a caress. No desire moves the virgin to press her mouth against the chubby mouth of one of her brothers. Such contacts are unworthy of centaurs. The mere imagination of them is more appropriate to a lascivious faun than a daughter of the sovereign people. More than once, however, Kadilda's thoughts have returned to the sleeping couple. One night, shivering all over, she woke up from a shameful dream: she too was lying on the grass, and on her lips were posed two lips, cool and burning at the same time, that were those of the child Naram.

For she has also dreamed about Naram. She knows which grotto of foliage he lives in; it is one of the largest, at the foot of a dead chestnut-tree. He lives with a male in the prime of life and a female, whom he obeys. Doubtless he was born of their entrails. And the woman is breast-feeding a white and pink nursling, who is Naram's brother.

One morning, Kadilda, on emerging from a clump of laurier-roses, found herself face to face with the little human. He uttered a cry of surprise and, smiling, called out to her—but with one bound, the centauress hurtled back into the bushes and fled as far as her legs could carry her. There can be no amity between her and the enemy of her people, and the mere idea that Naram's hand might touch her again distresses her. Sometimes, however, without him being aware of it, Kadilda, hidden in the long grass for hours on end, has lain in wait for the frail-limbed child Naram.

And when she returns to the Red Grottoes, Kadilda finds once again, without pleasure, the games, the quarrels and the noisy laughter of her brothers. And she responds angrily to the sharp words of the old females and the sarcastic remarks of the males. For, even though the sovereign animals are free in their actions, it is contrary to custom for a centauress to prefer solitude to the company of her people. The rule is that the joy and thought of each should be the joy and thought of all, and whoever affects to live apart is acting contrary to the spirit of the race. Because of that, Kadilda is an object of reproach.

She, however, does not care. Every day when the herd does not go to the rheki field, she makes her way to the River of Swans; and by night, when she lies down in the shelter of the Red Grottos, she is not among her own people, for she dreams of Naran of the bright eyes, whose caress is placed on her flank.

Stormy rain has been falling all day. Only toward sunset do cracks appear in the gray dome. A few pale rays of sunlight filter through the branches, making the pearly droplets with which they are covered glisten, and giving bright gleams to the copper beeches and yellow-tinted birches.

The centaurs do not like a rain, so their spirits are morose and the return to the Grottos is exempt from joyful clamors.

In accordance with custom, Klevorak's gaze wanders from right to left. Suddenly, he clicks his tongue, turns aside from the usual path and heads straight into the brambles. The herd follows him. He has stopped beside a body lying on the moss: that of Ghali, the russet antelope without a tail, with the white underbelly and ringed horns. Death is in the velvet eyes. His blood is flowing; tremors of agony are shaking his limbs.

Klevorak kneels down, raises he slender head in one of his strong hands and says, in an angry voice: "Who, then, has violated my law?"

The antelope passes his tongue over the protector's hairy arm. Then his neck slumps, inertly. He is dead. He belongs to the carnivores. A duty remains, however: to avenge hm.

Attentively, Klevorak examines the wound. Will he recognizes the imprint of the teeth of Raram, the jaguar with the supple limbs, or those of Herta, the she-wolf, or perhaps the mark of the furious horn of Bhor, the wild ox with the bad temper? In any case, the murderer will not escape punishment.

Klevorak's eyebrows frown. Something is lodged in the middle of the oozing wound; something is buried therein. The chief enlarges the wound with his broad fingers, grabs a stalk and pulls it toward him. At the end of the piece of stripped wood, impregnated with blood, a pointed stone with sharp edges is fastened.

The young centaurs utter exclamations. What is the name of the strange tree on which stones bud? With cries and laughter, they lean over to contemplate the prodigy, all asking questions at the same time.

As if by the effect of a sudden chill, however, Kadilda's teeth come together; a pain bites her heart. Has the blood ceased to warm her limbs? She has seen such morsels of wood before, which a strange magic attaches to sharpened stones, and she knows that it is not from a root-stock that it emerges but from industrious hands with slender fingers. Such a confused vortex of thoughts is agitated within her that her eyes are veiled and her muscles seem devoid of strength.

Klevorak turns the broken javelin over and over. He sniffs it and studies, alternately. His bronzed face creases with such terrible wrinkles that the young centaurs stop laughing. He hails Hurico.

"Do you know what this is, old one?"

The old one has no sooner placed the object in her palm than she hurls it away and screeches, in a strident voice, several times over: "The Flayed! The Flayed..."

Everyone shivers. With a common impulse, they rear up, their eyes aflame and their fists raised. Tails whip flanks, hooves stamp. Snorts emerge from lungs between clenched teeth. They jostle one another around the chief. Why is the blood of Ghali not being avenged already?

But Klevorak shrugs his shoulders and reprimands his people sternly. Should they launch themselves forward at hazard to reach the Flayed? Ghali, although wounded, is capable of having run for several days, and his tracks, so light, have been washed away by the rain. In vain the old centaur scrutinizes the bushes with his eye and his nose, aided by Hurico, Haidar and the most sagacious. Wasted effort. He stops and reflects. But such is the mental excitement that grumbles are heard. Are they going to stand still instead of taking action?

Hark gesticulates, as if drunk on the juice of grapes. Suddenly, because Haidar shrugs his shoulders and mutters while looking at him, he falls upon him. They each grab hold of one another and roll on the ground. Around them, among their brothers, some take the side of the red-haired giant, and others that of Haidar. Threats are exchanged. Already several challenges are being offered; but the best are ranged around Klevorak, obedient to his voice. He seizes the combatants and pulls them apart.

Covered with mud and twigs, the males get up. At the severe words from his chief, Hark feels reason returning. Confused by their lightness, the most impatient fall silent and await the chief's decision.

This is what Klevorak will do. Because the centaurs go to the nourishing fields every second day, and spend the other gathering fruits, they ceased making more distant excursions a long time ago, but Pirip is not constrained to such discipline. Thus, quite often, little groups of fauns travel the forests over considerable distances, such as would require several days to cross at a gallop. Perhaps, in the course of their expeditions, one of the goat-foots will have come across some trace of the Flayed. Before making a decision, it is necessary to interrogate them.

While the rest of the band go back to the Red Rocks under the guidance of Kreps the Prudent, Klevorak therefore heads toward the fauns' retreat. He takes Hurico with him, whose ingenious mind will be able to unravel Pirip's lies. He also permits Kadilda to company him, because, even though he has forbidden himself that sentiment, as a weakness not in conformity with the law, the old chief experiences a particular tenderness for the last-born of his blood, and enjoys feeling the virgin's flank beating beside his own.

At the edge of the great woods, not far from the region of olive groves, Pirip and his people live in great thickets of holly, lauriers and giant pelargoniums, which shade the domes of the tall walnut-trees. Such is the thickness of the superimposed foliage that the autumn rains never reach their refuge, any more than the tempests of the west wind. They are in close proximity both to the forests where they go to gather beech-nuts and soft corns and to the trees that are covered with tasty fruits in autumn: bright oranges, red arbutus-berries, crimson olives and, above all, black or golden grapes, which make the souls behind the horned foreheads merry.

Some time before they perceive Pirip's people, Klevorak and the centauresses realize that they are getting close. It is not only that the odor of billy-goat that pricks their nostrils becomes increasing acrid; soon, a tumult of songs and dances drowns out the chirping of the birds. In the autumn, when the last ardors of the sun glimmer, when the splendor of ripe fruits expands from the overladen branches of the trees, when the frequent threat of storms exasperates the nerves and announces the approaching sadness of the winter rains, the fauns get madly drunk on the juice of berries and perform hectic entrechats on the brown carpets of dead leaves, which terminate at night in furious embraces.

So, when the centaurs emerge into the clearing that neighbors the thickets in which the horned people shelter, they are not at all astonished by the spectacle that greets them. On the dead trunk of a walnut-tree, Sadionx, Fiforix and Pulk are crouching. They are holding pierced reeds in their hands, which they raise to their lips, and their cheeks, alternately inflated and slack, extract loud or melancholy sounds therefrom. Around them, the whole tribe of goat-foots is capering. From the youngest pot-bellied faunillons and faunillonnes to the ancients whose tangled beards hang down below their navels and whose thigh-hair descends to the ground, all of them are gamboling in cadence, their foreheads crowned with foliage, their eyes crazed, their lips and chins dripping with crimson juice.

At the head, Pirip is leading the dance. He is holding old Krita by the hand, who leaps over the bushes, out of breath, her toothless mouth drooling with joy, dragging Pilpilo, who is pulling Priu, Puiulex, Turlu, and all the rest. The horned heads leap up as far as the yellowing foliage, or suddenly appear lower down than the white bellies. The comical little tails, the majestic beards and the cloven hooves rise, fall and twirl, their voices mingling in inexhaustible laughter at the hazard of extraordinary somersaults.

The appearance of the centaurs does not moderate the orgy at all. With a gesture of recognition, Pirip wishes the dominators welcome, and then, leading the farandole behind them, envelops them with the sinuous serpent of the dance. Laughing, jostling, foaming at the mouth and streaming with sweat, fauns and faunesses file in turn before the visitors, passing behind them and passing once again, tirelessly.

Klevorak does not try to speak. He knows that when Pirip is overcome by the juice of the vine and the influence of the season, it is futile to hope for any reasonable speech. Until he has exhausted the ardor that is surging through his veins, his mind is incapable of focusing. Thus, Klevorak, his expression disdainful, remains motionless and waits; except that his two front feet paw the friable ground alternately, and he turns his nostrils away when the acrid odor of billy-goat offends him excessively.

But the foreheads of the musicians turn blue; sweat inundates their cheeks; the whites of their eyes roll in their orbits. With an abrupt gesture, Sadionx hurls away his pipe. Fiforix and Pulk follow his example. Breathless and hiccupping, all three fall down in the soft grass. Deprived of the rhythm of their tune, the farandole slows down; moist hands let go of one another; one after another the dancers fall to the ground, grunting voluptuously, gorged on movement, devoid of strength and the power of speech. Nothing can any longer be heard but the panting of distended chests.

Then Klevorak, escorted by the centauresses, draws near to Pirip. The faun is sprawling on the ground beside Sadionx, the musician. When he sees the dominators advancing he sits up, lifts his broad sweating face toward Klevorak, and welcomes him with amicable halting words: this sun is more beautiful than the others, which has guided the sovereign animals to their humble brethren.

Klevorak is scornful of long speeches. He takes the broken javelin from Hurico's hands and holds it out to the goat-foot. A little while ago the centaurs discovered the body of Ghali pierced by this accursed thing and they have recognized the work of the Flayed, but their difficulty is great, in knowing in which direction to pursue the murderers; that is why they have come to Pirip. Might he not, in the course of his wanderings, fund some indication of their presence?

Pirip and Sadionx examine the broken weapon in turn, sniffing it and handling it. Then they exchange sly glances and lower their eyelids. As their mouths remain closed, the centaur repeats his question. Then, Sadionx is the first to reply.

"No, Chief, we know nothing about the Flayed."

And like the echo of the docile voice, Pirip repeats, in a persuasive tone: "In truth, Chief, we know nothing about the Flayed."

No one calls into question the word of a centaur, but the soul of a faun is so easily inflamed that they sometimes lie without even being aware of it. So Klevorak frowned suspiciously and admonishes severely: "Pirip, Sadionx, be careful not to say what is not true."

The fauns slap their chests with the flat of their hand and take one another as their witnesses with a flood of speech. Once, no doubt, they had perceived the Flayed, but so long ago that even the admirable memory of the centaurs themselves cannot remember when. Besides which, is it certain that the javelin is the work of the Accursed? It is said that in a certain country, the trees have branches that terminate in pointed flints. No, Pirip has not seen them, but Sadionx knows about them. Perhaps Ghali was wounded in that way by accident while passing beneath one...

Klevorak shrugs his shoulders, and kicks up earth with his hooves angrily. He will get nothing out of Pirip this evening; whether he knows anything or not, the faun will not tell the truth. Perhaps he will be in a better mood another time.

Before retreating, however, Klevorak warns him, in a voice rumbling with discontent: "Pirip, I think that you have lied and that your eyes have seen the Flayed. And since you do not disdain contact with them, if your words are capable of reaching their obtuse minds, tell them this: let them flee as far as their stork's legs can carry them, for the justice of the centaurs will not spare them."

Having thus exhaled his anger, the chief draws away with his two females—and while he deplores Pirip's duplicity to Hurico, Kadilda feels a slight force vibrating in her bones. She is obliged to clench her teeth in order not to utter cries of joy while jumping over bushes. What a blessing Pirip's lying tongue is! Because of him, new blood will not be shed to atone for blood. And the centauress shivers at the idea that Klevorak might have interrogated her, and that she would have had to reply. Now, however, she blushes of her own accord in the falling darkness, for she has understood that, in spite of the law of her people, her tongue would have refused to say what is, and that she would have lied, like Pirip.

When the rumps of the centaurs have disappeared into the lauriers and the sound of their footfalls on the dry leaves has faded away, Pirip and Sadionx look at one another, and their faces split simultaneously into broad laughter, which inflates their chests noisily. In the dark night, the sound of falling bodies resonates in the undergrowth. Shadows pursue one another with lustful cries. It is the feverish hour when males and females rush to love. With a snigger of desire, Kirri, the blonde fauness, brushes Pirip as he goes past, slips away, turns back, makes an obscene gesture and flees, leaving a strong odor behind her. The males shiver, sniff, and bound after her.

Motionless, like the storm-saturated air, crouching down, their brown hands dangling in front of them, Pirip and Sadionx contemplate the sleeping woman and adore her sovereign beauty. White and naked on the moss, in the shade of a chestnut-tree, she is asleep, her head supported by her arm, her body relaxed, innocent and voluptuous. Beside her, her little child is also asleep, enveloped in a silky skin...

The slow, profound and naïve gazes of the fauns scan the grace of the face, the soft roundness of the shoulders and breasts, the inward curve of the waist, the elongated slimness of the legs. From that entire pale and pink form, a penetrating sweetness emanates, languid and so perfect that it abolishes desire. Pirip and Sadionx have forgotten the lubricious faunesses with the tangled hair. Nothing impure crosses their minds. They adore the frail and radiant grace of the woman, as they adore the splendor of corollas, the magic of rippling streams, the soft light of lunar nights. They could remain their contemplating her for hours, without dreaming of a sharper joy. The universe outside of her is abolished. If she disappears, the sun will die. The fauns' entire souls are drowned in ecstasy.

The branches rustle under the caress of the breeze. A brown leave is detached, whirls, and settles on the sleeper's cheek. She sighs, extends her arms, and brushes the importunate leaf away. And because of that gesture, a more precise emotion rises in the capripeds' hearts.

Before, the slumbering woman was an unreal sister of flowers, light and iridescent waters, an ungraspable image of beauty, an impalpable and chimerical form. Because her gesture has revealed that she is alive, a creature of flesh and blood, capable of giving and receiving sensuality, the fauns' dream takes flight—and suddenly, at a stroke, covetousness sets their mobile souls ablaze. Their ears prick; their eyes shine; they pass their tongues over their thick lips. A frisson runs along their robust spines. Their hands open and close convulsively.

A stronger gust of wind makes the dome of foliage oscillate. A branch breaks with a dry crack. The woman shudders, opens her eyes, and perceives the fauns crouching in front of her, contemplating her with their avid eyes.

With a strident cry of terror, she gets up and starts to run away—but with an identical surge the two males race after her. All other thoughts abolished, the furious desire that burns in their bone-marrow directs them entirely toward one sole objective...

The woman runs through the tall ferns, which part and stand up again. In a few bounds, Pirip has caught up with her. He brings his hand down on her shoulder. She strikes him in the face, trying to drive him away, but he knocks her down, laughing. She falls to the ground on the bed of crumpled ferns. There is a distraught howl of terror. Sadionx launches himself in his turn toward the undulation of the foliage, his tongue hanging out.

Heart-rending plaints rise into the sky. Frightened, the birds fall silent in the trees...

Bloody, her eyes crazed, careless of tearing her delicate skin on the thorns of the brushwood, the woman surges out of the thicket and flees, with long moans. Behind her, Pirip and Sadionx reappear. The fever in their eyes is extinct. Pirip has a long scratch on his face and two tufts of hair have been torn away from Sadionx's breast, but there is a sly satisfaction on their faces.

Suddenly, they look at one another, lowering their eye-lids at the same time, as if ashamed, raising them again, and looking at one another from the corners of their eyes, burst out laughing noisily. Then, taking one another by the hand, they set off on the return journey.

A comical mewling causes them to prick up their pointed ears. In the atrocity of her anguish, the fleeing woman has forgotten her baby. Woken up by the screams and the noise of the struggle, it is weeping and digging its fist into its mouth. Indecisively, the fauns stop and contemplate it. Their compassionate hearts are troubled with regret. The little creature is suffering from hunger, and its mother might perhaps be a long time coming back...

Suddenly, Sadionx has a benevolent idea. He picks up a few half-ripe chestnuts that have fallen to the ground, sits down with his legs crossed, and places the wailing infant be-tween his hairy thighs. Then he introduces the fruits, one by one, into the open mouth. Jealous of his good deed, Pirip also hastens to make a collection and offer it to the little man-child.

The nursling struggles with all the strength of its limbs; stifled plaints emerge from its throat, which strives in vain to reject the fruits; its face becomes scarlet. Entirely devoted to their pleasure, however, the fauns are amused by its disordered gestures and cries, and by the violet color of its face. Eagerly, each one tries to force another chestnut between the distended cheeks. The game is to see who can get the most in.

Suddenly, the paltry creature ceases to whimper. The bulging eyes are no longer rolling. The blackened tongue is no longer trying to eject the accumulated fruits. The limbs, which were agitating desperately a little while ago, tremble for a moment longer, and then become motionless. The swollen face is inert.

Triumphantly, the fauns force another two or three chestnuts between the soft gums and then, astonished, consult one another. Anxiously, Sadionx lifts up the little body, raises it to his ear and his nostrils. Pirip watches him do it, fearfully.

"It's dead!"

The fauns remain still, disconcerted. Desolation inundates their hearts. Sobs rumble in their breasts. Now, without meaning any harm, they have killed the little being. They lament, and pull hairs out of their beards forcefully. It is against nature to recriminate with regard to the past, though. Their regrets will not bring the little mass of flesh back to life. They are still sad, but their thoughts are already turning to another idea. Curiously, they manipulate the arms and legs, which are growing cold, and admire the minuscule pink fingers, so incredibly delicate...

A clamor fills the clearing. With a thrust of his legs, Pirip is on his feet. The Flayed!

They launch forth, brandishing sticks and clubs. At their head is the woman, who points at the faun with her finger and utters a howl when she perceives the corpse of her child.

Pirip is not bellicose. He calls to Sadionx and dives into the thicket. But Sadionx, hindered by the little body, loses a second. As Pirip turns round to call to him again, the most nimble of the Flayed, a young male with bright eyes, has already reached the faun, and between his two shoulders he sinks a rigid stick, in which a pointed stone is edged.

With cries of vengeance, the entire band falls upon Sadionx, sticks raised. Without wasting any time, however, his murderer runs toward Pirip, whom terror has nailed to the spot. The others follow him.

Then the faun senses imminent death, and with a moan of distress, he sets off through the thicket. The screeching mob of Flayed is on his heels. At every instant, Pirip thinks he feels the bite of the pointed stone in his back. Terror lends wings to his legs. He knows that his life depends on the agility of his muscles, and he flees recklessly through the forest.

The approach of the storm oppresses everything that lives. The dry and heavy air does not refresh the lungs. The flattened sea is as dormant as a stagnant pool. Not a leaf rustles. In the south, a black mass of clouds rises slowly, occasionally traversed by a flash of lightning. Thunder rumbles dully in the distance.

The motionless centaurs are scattered on the sand. Sometimes, two or three get up, go to soak themselves in the salt water, and then come back to lie down. Their nostrils sniff the torrid atmosphere anxiously. Words are rare. Between the nervous males, quarrels arise easily, but the oppressive heat suppresses bellicose humors.

"Hirrh!"

Sihadda has uttered a cry of alarm. Everyone listens. Who can be running through the pine-woods at such speed?

Drawn out of their torpor, the centaurs turn their heads. The silhouette of Pirip appears at the edge of the black foliage.

A murmur of astonishment ripples. What has happened to the faun? His face is more scarlet than the fruit of the arbutus-bush, or the setting sun. Sweat has stuck the hair to his legs, blood is trickling from his nostrils.

He lets himself fall on to the sand, coughing, without being able to recover his breath.

The centaurs surround him and interrogate him. Has a waterspout fallen upon his people? Has he encountered a mastodon in rut? Or is it his lechery that has got him into some misadventure?

Pirip's lips part, Raucous sounds escape them. He compresses his chest with both hands; his heart is beating as if to burst. It is not until he had emptied a conch full of water that his features relax and, in halting phrases, he is able to relate the catastrophe: how his misfortune and that of his brother took them toward the River of Swans, and how an infamous tribe of the Flayed took them by surprise and murdered the musician lamentably.

Sadionx will no longer delight the goat-footed people with the melodious sounds of the pierced reed. He has only escaped death himself by virtue of the vigor of his limbs.

Such is Pirip's story. A closer rumble of thunder underlines its conclusion. But the thunder disappears in the roaring of the centaurs. In an instant, all of them are on their feet. A single angry voice inflates all breasts with the war cry. Without any need to confer, the same determination sets fire in their veins: that before tomorrow's sunrise, the murder of Sadionx will be avenged. The flesh-eaters will have more than their hunger can absorb tonight.

As Pirip's legs are trembling beneath him, Hark slaps his withers and gives him a sign to mount up. In the blink of an eye the Faun is astride his shoulders. At Hark's heels the entire herd races away.

The rocky promontory is soon crossed. The whirlwind of centaurs pours on to the southern beach, and runs into the storm. Gusts of hot wind lift up the sand, stinging the faces of the dominators. Shaking their hair and their floating tails, however, they exasperate its bite and run more rapidly. Serpents of flame rip the clouds in front of them; momentarily, they close their eyes against the prodigy of fire, but they do not slow their pace and force their speed, careless of the thunder.

The fearful threat of the storm troubles Kadilda less violently than the tumultuous thoughts clashing in her heart. Galloping beneath the opaque sky, streaked by livid light, it seems to her that she is the victim of a nightmare from which she has only just awakened. Pirip's words sing implausibly in her ears; the death of Sadionx is only a dream devoid of reality, and surely it is not possible that the white bodies she has so often seen through the foliage—including the body of the child Naram, whose name she repeats every evening before going to sleep—will soon be lying crushed beneath the feet of the centaurs...

At the image alone, her brain vacillates, and she pants like the old ones trying to keep up with the herd.

Before reaching the river, the centaurs have quit the beach. They plunge into the stunted pines. Soon, the foliage becomes lighter. In passing, Kadilda recognizes the clumps of ash-trees, lindens and alders that she has so often skirted. Tonight they extend their thin branches in a sinister fashion.

The sky is completely black now. The sun has sunk into the distant earth. On all sides at once lightning-flashes burn the eyes. The nonplussed centaurs pause momentarily, and resume their march to the rumble of thunder. The storm will serve them. Betrayed by their miserable sense of smell, deafened by the thunder, the Flayed will not suspect the avengers' approach. The punishment will fall upon their heads unexpectedly.

In a flash of blinding whiteness, something atrocious appears at the foot of a tree: the mutilated corpse of Sadionx, entirely stripped of its skin. On his back, Hark feels Pirip shivering in every limb. Intoxicated by rage, the centaurs grind their teeth. Imprecations rise in their throats, but Klevorak commands silence. It is necessary to take the Flayed by surprise. Here is their fresh trail, distinct.

Leaning over the recently trodden ground, the centaurs advance more slowly, stifling the noise of their footfalls.

And Kadilda recognizes the route she has followed so often, that she could follow with her eyes closed. It is necessary to skirt a thicket of lauriers, go passed a little wood of lindens mingled with furze, and then, beneath the chestnut trees, there will be the group of scattered huts. In a few moments, it will all be concluded. At a mechanical pace, the centauress follows on the heels of her brothers. It will be impossible for her to speak or act. She is a slave of the unleashed force of her people. But a poignant suffering wrings her heart.

Now Klevorak has stopped, a finger on his lips. Avidly, his eyes strive to penetrate the darkness. The dark masses of the singular Grottos stand at the feet of the great trunks; paltry phantoms are agitating here and there. A lightning-flash illuminates the undergrowth. The centaurs make out the Accursed, who are trying to secure their shelters with lianas and stakes, so that they will not be carried away by the tempest.

Wasted effort. With a howl that drowns out the thunder, the irresistible force of the centaurs falls upon the clearing, Men, women and children fall pell-mell beneath the hooves. At the impact of powerful shoulders, the fragile huts of thatch crack and crumble, burying those who have already taken refuge there beneath their debris. With an indescribable clamor, howls of agony mingle with shrill screams of terror, roars of triumph, the savage plaint of the wind and, less frightful, the voice of the thunder.

The livid glare of lightning flashes illuminates a chaos of robust rumps, muscular thighs, rearing torsos and redoubtable hands. Most of the Flayed have fallen at the first impact and cannot get up again. A few have seized their sticks and are defending themselves desperately. Because of the darkness, however, their badly-aimed blows go astray. The centaurs seize them around the waist, breaking them with a single twist, crushing them underfoot, or whirl them around at the ends of their arms and smash their skulls against tree-trunks, where their sticky brains remain plastered. The insipid odor of murder rises into the air. Feet skid in pools of blood. The impure ones who try to flee are immediately overtaken and massacred.

Gradually, the rumor dies down. Inert white corpses strew the ground. Unsatisfied, fearing that some remain hidden, the centaurs search amid the debris of the collapsed huts. The whimpers of infants are rapidly stifled. One hut remains standing. Hark sticks his head through the entrance. He throws himself backwards with a cry of pain. A flash of lightning renders his bloodied face visible, along with a frail phantom that is bounding toward the bushes. Already the herd is upon the fugitive, clubs brandished and fists extended.

A more frightful racket descends from the splitting skies. The clearing catches fire. A sulfurous odor poisons the nostrils. Bewildered, the centaurs vacillate on their fetlocks. With a deafening crack, a flaming mass falls on the ground.

It is a giant chestnut that has collapsed, struck by lightning. At the terrifying sight of fire, the centaurs recoil. The red and yellow flames crackle, devouring the branches and rising toward the sky.

The silhouette of a Flayed stands out against the blaze. The fall of the tree has robbed him of his last chance of escape. The centaurs have only to reach out their arms to seize him. They advance, uttering victory cries.

But now, with growls of horror, the members of the herd snort and jostle one another. Scaling the trunk of the burning tree, the Accursed One, with a desperate effort of his thin arms, tears away two branches whose ends are alight, turns to face the dominators, and appears to the enveloped in the prodigious majesty of fire.

A double cry springs from the frightened herd: that of Pirip, who has recognized the murderer of Sadionx, and that of the white virgin, who has recognized Naram. The others remain motionless and silent, astounded. What, then, is the mysterious power of this pale being, who plays with the sparkling force of the sun?

Naram advances, whirling the flames around him. Before the feeble child, the mass of the six-limbed people recoil, lowering their eyes.

Suddenly, however, the foliage becomes noisy. A torrential deluge falls from the liquefied skies. Under the downpour, the flames vacillate. Naram takes a step backwards. With a violent gesture, her hurls the flaming brands into the midst of the centaurs, who flee—and bounding with a defiant cry, he jumps over the trunk of the incandescent tree, and disappears into the undergrowth.

For a few seconds, amazement nails the dominators to the spot. Then anger at the outrage exasperates their pride. With imprecations of rage, they launch themselves in pursuit of the insolent individual. But the opaque night, in which the lightning flashes are dying away, protects Naram's flight. The cataracts falling from the clouds obliterate his tracks.

After a few seconds, the centaurs realize that their hope is vain. Klevorak utters the rallying cry. Let the six-limbed people not persist. Alone and naked, the Flayed will succumb to hunger or fatigue, even if Herta's teeth and Raram's claws spare him. And if, by chance, he escapes death and rejoins some tribe of his brothers beyond the mountains, he will inform them of the terror of the centaurs and their ineluctable justice.

The signal for departure is given. Through forests, heaths and thickets, the herd retraces its route, returns to the river, reaches the beach and heads for the protective Rocks at a long-legged trot. The rain has stopped. Spirits are joyful. No doubt a secret anger subsists that the murderer of Sadionx has escaped, but the others have paid for him. The sovereign people have shown their strength. No one has received any greave wound.

Abruptly, the disk of the moon appears among the fleeing clouds. Under its rays, the beach gleams like snow and the grumbling sea sparkles. The sonorous voice of Hurico rises up, intoning the song of victory, and they all repeat her words in chorus, making the sand fly beneath their feet.

When they reach the Red Rocks, it is already past midnight. Groping their way, the centaurs go to their litters. Sharp words are exchanged because of accidental bumps, but their fatigue is too great to give rise to quarrels. Soon, the rhythm of even respiration rises up.

Only Kadilda has remained on the moonlit beach; the scene of the murder is still before her eyes. In the midst of rolls of thunder and cries of agony, she can still see the slender bodies falling under the blows of the centaurs. Horrible images crowd around her—and yet, one figure is superimposed on all the others: that of Naram, the survivor of the disaster of his people, brandishing the fire. When she closes her eyes, she sees him gigantic in the blaze. When she opens them, it is him that she sees looming over the silvery waves. Before him, all alone, the entire herd of centaurs recoiled.

At the memory of his strength, Kadilda shivers. At that of his weakness, she shivers again. Alone, wounded, lost in the darkness, can he escape the bite of the flesh-eaters, and that of the cold, and the exhaustion that will paralyze his weak limbs? And even if he triumphs over all the perils, Kadilda will never see him again. Never again will he raise his pale eyes to look at her, never again will she follow him with her eyes for long hours, hidden in the bushes.

The centauress' breast heaves. An unknown dolor grips her throat. Her head inclines.

A hand is placed on the white virgin's shoulder. Before going to sleep with his people, Klevorak has noticed his last-born standing alone on the beach. His heart stirred, he has come to her. At the sight of her moonlit face, the astonished chief recoils. Kadilda's cheeks are streaming with sparkling droplets such as never emerge from the eyes of centaurs, like those of the dew, like those that spring from the eyes of a wounded deer, like the tears of men.

Seeing his daughter weep, the old male is speechless, frightened by the prodigy; his heart is uncertain. Suddenly, indignation grips him. Is he to be humiliated by his own blood? Fist raised, he steps forward. The chief feels a warm droplet fall on to his rough shoulder.

Gently, his hand comes to rest in the virgin's hair. A great emotion seethes in his primitive soul. He hesitates...

And he searches vainly for words that he does not know but wants to say. With a slow gesture, he draws the blonde head toward him, and both of them, their hands enlaced, remain motionless for a long time, without speaking, in the pearly night...

Part Three

Several times, in accordance with the immemorial rhythm, the seasons have succeeded one another and have declined in their turn, to be reborn. Several times, the Three Tribes have seen the splendor of the autumn fade away into the sad grayness of the rains. In the denuded forests, the bitter winter winds have made the dead leaves whirl, and everything that lives has taken refuge in the evergreen thickets or in the woods where the holm-oaks, the pines, the olive-trees and the orange-trees retain the durable shelter of their foliage; and the centaurs ride forth beneath the bare crowns of the great oaks, beeches and chestnut-trees, no longer hearing for weeks on end anything but the raucous cries of rutting wolves and wild boar, or the valiant song of the robin and the obstinate chaffinch.

Then the air has warmed up again. Warm breezes have put joy into the hearts of beasts, have sown the renascent meadows with florets, put buds at the angles of branches. And a few rays of sunlight have caused the perfumed glory of spring to blossom. The forest has dressed itself once again in its renewed green beauty; in the midst of songs of delight, the birds have built their nests; gamboling through the tender foliage, the quadrupeds have rejoiced in the rebirth of everything. On carpets of new grass, the fauns have renewed their dances.

Under the vivifying caress of the paternal star, the hearts of the centaurs have dilated, and at the approach of the summer solstice, when a more generous sap rises in the insensible trunks of the trees, when the fragile grace of flowers is succeeded on all the branches by the flavorsome maturity of fruits and berries, the dominators sense the fire passing through their veins that they receive from the sun and the sacred instinct of reproduction quivering in their loins. Sparkling, the eyes of the males remain attached to the rounded forms of the female, who shiver beneath their gaze.

When the herd of the six-limbed folk comes back from the rheki field in the evening, couples voluntarily deviate from the accustomed route. With nervous laughter, the female launches herself into the bushes; the male bounds after her. For a long time they chase one another, drawing apart and drawing together by turns, until the moment when, breathless and consenting, the female allows herself to be caught and abandons herself...

Side by side, both of them return to the refuge of the Grottos at dusk. The benevolent gazes of the elders welcome their return.

This year, however, with discontented shakes of the head, Kreps with the snowy hair and Hurico, trotting after their brethren on returning from the nourishing fields, remember the olden times and complain about the decline of the ancient ardor of the race.

Once, around the solstice, it was in dozens that the couples drew apart from the herd and sought thickets to shelter their impetuous amours. No male would have been satisfied whom the most beautiful of centauresses had not approached every season. And the latter would have been ashamed to draw away without their loins had sensed the precursory shudder of a birth the following spring. The custom, all the old ones could attest, was to give birth one year in three, or four at the most. Thus the tribe was perpetuated. Hurico, for her part, has brought eight centaurins into the world. Two were born of the love of Kreps; smiling, the old ones reawaken the memory, even though many years have gone by since then.

Now, everything has changed.

To be sure, at the advent of summer, the fire of desire still burns in the marrow of the centaurs. They seek the company of the females more frequently, challenge one another to violent games, and come more easily to blows, anxious to prove their preeminence. But there are no longer the formidable furies of yore to force the favors of the beauties.

Hurico remembers how, on a whim, or because she preferred the caress of Klevorak, she had once refused herself to Kreps, and run away across the heath. With what range the male had launched himself on to her warm trail! For several hours she had fled his pursuit. When, breathless and exhausted, she felt her legs buckle, she turned round, struck him in the face with her closed fists and bit him hard—but Kreps' enormous hand had clamped over her mouth, twisted her arms, and thrown her down on to the moss, panting. It was from that embrace that Kaplam the Valiant had been born.

Now it is no longer the same. When the capricious centauresses disappoint their desire, the centaurs can no longer contradict them. Instead of conquering them by violence, they employ vain words: they beg, they become sad, they wait, they forget. Once, it was more for the sake of amusement than timidity that the virgins pretended to refuse themselves; they had blushed to resemble faunesses, whose salacity is always alert; but in their hearts they had desired the approach of a male, and, in spite of the swiftness of their course, they had soon allowed themselves to be overtaken. Nowadays they are often sincere; they remain obstinately in the midst of the herd and disdain the ardent invitations of their brothers.

Kreps and Hurico shake their heads again and sigh. In the radiant afternoon, in which the joy of living sings, in the forest impregnated with perfumes and cries of love, no couple has drawn aside. And the gazes of the old ones go toward a group of centauresses huddled around Kadilda.

There are a dozen of them, the most beautiful in the tribe; their slender and robust torsos loom over the lustrous coat of their lower bodies; the undulant plumes of their tails brush their fetlocks. Eyes mistrustful, masked in a sign of refusal behind the drawn curtain of their hair, hands armed with sticks, they draw close together and move side by side without turning their heads. Haidar, Hark and Kaplam, the most vigorous of the males, cluster around them in vain, mounting assaults with smiles, warm words and gestures of promise. At the mere sight of their desire, Hurico feels her old marrowbones crackles again—but the young females do not deign to listen to them.

"Kadilda is responsible," Kreps opines.

She is the first, for many years, who has refused herself to love. It is without precedent for a centauress of her age and beauty still to be a virgin. Now, every summer, with the same obstinacy, she rejects the handsome Haidar—who, humiliated by his failure, scorns any other and gets thinner. And as if Kadilda's fault were contagious, several others, following her example, behave likewise.

And the damage has been considerable. Once, capering at hazard on their long legs, their thin arms always moving, pirouetting and capering relentlessly around their elders, centaurins and centaurines would be the hope and the glory of the six-limbed folk. Now—it is incredible when one thinks about it—two seasons have gone by without a single centauress giving birth. Whereas on the other hand, since the death of Papacal, four centaurs have nourished the flesh-eaters; most recently Pittina, the ancestor, was found dead one winter morning.

And Hurico, whose mind is still alert, reasons: "If the females no longer give birth, and if one of the six-limbed folk is claimed by death every year, our strength will be diminished."

The justice of this thought strikes Kreps forcefully, and he passes his hand through his hirsute beard several times. Running his gaze over the multitude of gallopers, however, he is reassured. One day, Klevorak wanted to make a count of his people. One by one, he had called his brothers, raising a finger for each one, and when all his ten fingers had been lifted, Hurico lifted one of hers, and Klevorak continued his calculation in that fashion. Now, all ten of Hurico's fingers had been lifted before the herd had finished filing past. A people that is counted at more than ten times ten is innumerable.

The old female cannot contradict this memory, but her mind remains anxious. If the young females persist in their folly, a day will come when the least clever will be able to count the people on his fingers. It is necessary for Klevorak to give an order. Kadilda is his own daughter. He has a double right to command her. If he instructs her not to refuse Haidar, the others will imitate her. And instead of only Mimitt being pregnant, as at present, next summer, many centaurins will open their troubled eyes to the sun.

The Red Rocks appear. The old female's irritated gaze scans the ranks of the males and females. They are all there. Disgustedly, Hurico blows into her cheeks and spits on the ground.

Klevorak approaches her. The passing years have left the immutable vigor of his torso intact—but his hair is whiter and his beard hangs down further over his muscular chest. Hurico's eyes light up as she gazes at him. He laughs and claps her on the shoulder.

"Why are you angry, old Hurico?"

With an irritated thrust of her chin, the old female directs his attention to the centaurs dispersed on the beach. The young females are all crouching together to one side. Among the males, some are bathing; others are lying idly on the sand; the most ardent are competing at jumping or wrestling. They have all forgotten the glorious duty of the solstice.

"Klevorak," the old female says, "I'm grieving because the young ones have lost the taste for fecund caresses."

The chief's face darkens, and he scratches his sides mechanically. Emboldened, Hurico gives free rein to her complaints; she moans about the hostile reserve of the females, the meekness of the males, the obscure menace suspended over the race. And when the chief does not reply she shakes her bony head and declares: "Take care, Klevorak, that the strength of your people does not decrease, and that soon, like the Wild Beasts, the last of the centaurs will be wandering sadly in the forests, until the day when his solitary bones whiten there."

The dominator becomes irritated and shrugs his shoulders; what can he do? No law left by the ancestors prescribes the duty of love.

The old female whips her threadbare flanks with her tail to chase away the tenacious flies and ripostes hotly that all the evil stems from Kadilda. She was the first to reject the males. Let Klevorak break her pride; when she has given in, the others will submit likewise and the dark fate will be avoided.

And when the chief still remain silent, Hurico adds: "What will be your shame, Klevorak, if, because of you, the weakened people of the centaurs succumbs one day to the multitude of the Flayed?"

A glint of anger appears in the chief's dark eyes, and the old female understands that she has gone too far; but she has only insisted in order to stimulate Klevorak's determination, and he knows it. He reflects profoundly, and then, suddenly, as if talking to himself, murmurs: "You have thought wisely; I shall command."

And that evening, while the males, scattered on the sand, indulge in their usual games, he approaches the solitary Kadilda and says to her: "Child, listen to what I have to say."

She inclines her head meekly. The chief speaks. The words emerge from his throat with difficulty. Perhaps that is because of the somnolence that descends upon the centaurs not long after dusk. Perhaps, however, he would have even more difficulty if he had to sustain the virgin's gaze.

He reports what Hurico has said and approves her wisdom. It is contrary to nature for a centauress obstinately to flee the approach of males. Haidar, the most handsome of all, has been seeking her for several seasons. If, by some caprice she does not want him, she may choose another, but it is necessary that the future chief of the herd should be born from her loins next year.

Klevorak feels his daughter's flank shivering against his own, and the virgin's indignant response flies into the darkness: "Never!"

Anger rises to the king's face. Does she who was born of his loins dare to disobey his voice? It is painful for him to command, but his commandments must be without appeal. In a tone of menace, he asks "Do you intend to resist me? Tomorrow, I shall not lead my people to the rheki fields, but the day after, either on the way there or on the way back, you will leave the path, and Haidar will follow you."

Softly, without looking at her father, her expression calm, the virgin replies: "So long as she lives, your daughter will not disobey your order, but Klevorak does not command the dead. At dawn on the day after tomorrow, rather than submit to Haidar's caress, I shall climb to the summit of the Red Rocks and hurl myself to the ground."

Amazement closes Klevorak's mouth. So far as his memory goes back, such words have never emerged from the mouth of a centaur. Death is the natural terminus of life when the individual's strength is exhausted, but that a virgin in the dazzling flower of youth should invoke it is an action as inconceivable as rending living flesh with her teeth would be.

Klevorak's spirit is wearied by such meditations. He feels dizzy. He quits the virgin without speaking and returns to the shelter of the Grottos.

Among the six-limbed people, a delight is born at dawn. Whinnying, the piebald Mimitt is writhing on the sand. The old females, assembled around her, examine her, and recognize by certain signs the first dolors of childbirth. A few moments more, and the sun will live again in a new being. With jealous sniggers, the males congratulate Hark the Rude, whose caress has been fecund. And although the red-haired giant affects insouciance, a joy that is anxious and proud at the same time softens his harsh breast.

Once, a birth was no great event, but Klop, the youngest of the tribe, will soon be full-grown, for the centaurins born after him have died before knowing pasture, and for two years none has seen the light of day. Thus, the entire herd awaits the solemn moment impatiently. From time to time, those who are playing on the strand approach the entrance to the grotto where Mimitt has remained in the charge of the old females; those who have gone to collect fruit have instructed their brothers to cal them. Klevorak scatters the sand under his feet and his gaze turns away, charged with wrath, whenever it chances to fall on the white virgin.

Alone among her people, Kadilda is indifferent. No curiosity stirs within her with regard to the expected child. Her thought goes to the embrace of which it is the issue, and disgust creases her lips. In her soul the determination she expressed the day before is still vibrant. She will die rather than submit to the approach of Haidar or any other.

In order to be alone with her thoughts, she has gone into the sea breast-deep, and unthinkingly, she contemplates her face, scarcely deformed in the calm water. An infinite sadness weighs upon her; she remembers the tears that flowed from her red eyes on the evening when she saw the child Naram for the last time.

The water splashes beside her. A cheerful face looms up above a streaming torso, and Oiotoro the triton laughs broadly, gurgling because the centauress has shivered; then he dives again, and heads off at top speed in pursuit of bewildered mullets.

From the depths of the inlet a cry of pain has escaped. The males assemble at the entrance. Klevorak is on his feet. Even Kadilda comes out of the water and moves closer.

Old Babidam appears, a finger on her lips. Soon the newborn will see the light and Klevorak will receive it from Hurico's hands in order to present it to the sun. The centaurs wait in silence.

Mimitt's groans succeed one another without interruption, punctuated with sharper cries. Suddenly, a distressing howl raises all heads. Satisfied, old Kreps approves; he has recognized the mother's supreme plaint. Soon, the astonished centaurin will try his vacillating legs on the sand. He will be called Karam.

The silence becomes more serious. Necks extend. A murmur rises. In the shadows, Hurico, the mother of the people, appears. She is holding an elongated form. Loud laughter breaks out among the centaurs. Hands applaud. Hark pushes his brothers aside and bounds forward...

He recoils with an exclamation.

In the thin arms of the old female, an inert corpse is lying. She lays it on the ground at Klevorak's feet, and says in a quavering voice: "Strengthen your heart, Klevorak. The newborn's eyes will never see the sun."

Distressed and pensive, the centaurs contemplate the paltry form of the centaurin: his little red face, his little arms with creased hands, his ridiculously bulbous torso and his long legs, which will not carry him. Klevorak raises the curly head in his palm and lets it fall back on to the sand. Distraught, with his face in his hands, Hark moans indefinitely, and his dolor resonates in the hearts of his brothers, who do not have the words to console him. From the grotto, however, another lamentation replies to his own, and Babidam appears again, wringing her hands, her face grimacing. Of what misfortune is she the messenger?

"Fortify your heart, Klevorak. Mimitt's eyes will not see the sun again."

Behind her, mournful, come the other centauresses. They are carrying the body of Mimitt; they deposit it in the ground beside that of her child.

A stupor chills the entire tribe, and Klevorak's soul is gnawed by a great suffering. But Hark shoves the group of females out of the way; he kneels down beside the two cadavers and sniffs them. Then, abruptly, he gets up, and, fists clenched, pawing the ground, burst out in imprecations. He curses the old females who cared for Mimitt; he curses the new-born; he curses Mimitt herself; he curses love. The oaths flood from his lips. He threatens to strangle Hurico with his own hands. His insults go as far as Klevorak. Madness inflames his brain.

The males prepare to defend the old females against his violence, but all of a sudden, his fury changes its object. Formidable, rearing up to his full height, his fists raised, Hark insults the sun, and, rising and falling alternately, he picks up enormous stones and, with all the taut strength of his muscles, he launches them at the star, vomiting a torrent of blasphemies. Then, foaming at the mouth, tearing at his hair and beard, he hurls himself on the sand and rolls over and over, biting the stones.

Such conduct is unworthy of centaurs respectful of the ancient order of things, but in the melancholy that envelops them, no one attempts to recall Hark to reason. Sadly, four of the most vigorous lift up Mimitt's body; two others take that of the centaurin; and they go to abandon them on the edge of the wood, in order that, in accordance with the rule, the dead might serve to nourish the strength of the living.

When he sees them lay down their burdens, however, Hark launches himself toward the bearers and chases them away. Wildly, with all his hair bristling, he lies down beside the two cadavers. In his hands he holds a club, and his inflamed eyes scan the surroundings. By virtue of the effect of the delirium that is burning in his veins, Hark scorns the order of the eternal law; with frightful imprecations, he declares that while he is alive, no flesh-eater will lay a tooth on Mimitt or on Karam. So terrible is his grief that it has steeped the centaur's soul in the vile passions of the Flayed.

Klevorak orders that his rage should not be opposed. Tomorrow, Hark will recover his senses and will incline before justice. The carnivores can wait twenty-four hours for the feast that is due to them.

Throughout the day a dark cloud hangs over the souls of the sovereign people. The conversations lack their customary gaiety. The games are abandoned. The ripening fruits seem to be tasteless. Only a few curt words are exchanged in muffled tones.

Until the sun has set, Klevorak remains alone, lying on the strand, his face rigid, his eyes staring into the distance, as if his intelligence were striving to pursue his thoughts beyond their ordinary limit. Then a voice speaks in his ear.

"Father and chief, is it really your order that tomorrow, on returning from the rheki fields, I obey the desire of Haidar?"

The virgin says nothing more, but her tone is grave, and Klevorak grasps the meaning of her words. His heart sinks, and without replying, he hides his face in his strong hands. His strong shoulders tremble convulsively.

The white centauress kneels down beside her father, puts her arm around his neck and places her head on his shoulder. Their hearts are beating so close together that neither of them knows any longer which is their own. And thoughts, so formidable that their minds are impotent to conceive them in their entirety, rise up around them and project a cold shadow over them.

The old centaur, all of a sudden, feels age weighing heavily upon his white head, and he wants soon to fall asleep in the great sleep of death, as Mimitt has done, as the centaurin has done, as all the others will do one day—and then there will be no more centaurs...

And that thought, which seemed to him to be monstrous yesterday, Klevorak envisages now, and can no longer put it out of his mind...

He makes an effort. "Never, Kadilda, will I command you to love against your will; and you, until the wolves have devoured my flesh, will never repeat the words that my tongue refuses to repeat. But explain this to me: why does the desire of males horrify you?"

There is no longer anything harsh about the chief's tone. Even Kadilda feels a tender distress at the unaccustomed sorrow of his voice. She presses more closely against him and tries, with stumbling words, to make him see, to voice more clearly herself, so many confused things that dwell within her and which she is impotent to contend.

She talks about the repulsion inspired in her by the jovial brutality of the young males, their coarse and hairy limbs, their rough skin and the odor their bodies emit. Certainly, she does not hate them, but the mere idea of their embrace horrifies her more than the pursuit of Wild Beasts. And indeed, the old chief feels the virgin's entire body shiver against his own.

He shakes his head and sighs. Never have such statements emerged from the mouth of a centauress. Certainly, Kadilda has the right to reject the love of anyone. By the fact that neither Sakarbatul the Beardless or the fat Kabalop pleases her, no one would be astonished, but others are better made to please her, to whatever extent her beauty elevates her above others...

Her beauty? With a sour laugh, Kadilda shrugs her shoulders. And more bitterly than she has spoken of her horror for the males of her race, she jeers at all that the centaurs admire in her: her blonde hair is as coarse as the fur of an old fauness; the skin of her face is tanned by the sun; her arms are as stout as a pig's thighs; her hands are as plump and awkward as those of tritons; what could be as grotesque as the conjunction of that massive lower body and a slender torso? And besides, people with six limbs constitute a monster of Nature, which has only given four to all other living things.

Ugly: she is ugly and deformed, more than any being in the world, and in her eyes, the males of her people are all the more hideous more coveting a creature like the one whose image the water reflects when she leans over the waves...

And suddenly, Kadilda hides her face. She bursts into sobs, and the old centaur sees tears streaming between her fingers.

This time, it is not anger but a mysterious fear that grips his mind, not only at the hitherto-unknown prodigy and his daughter's thoughts, so strange that, in spite of his efforts, he cannot contrive entirely to grasp them, but also at the many frightful omens surrounding his people.

He is silent. In the distance, savage howlings testify to the combat of Hark the Rude as he disputes their prey with the flesh-eaters.

In the morning, as she has done so many times before, Kadilda, before her people are awake, has run away, muffling the sound of her footfalls. The centaurs rejoice in living side by side, in galloping together through the forest and exchanging frivolous words. Kadilda's pleasure is the opposite. In every season, but especially that in which love excites the males, she seeks solitude. Every second day, it is necessary for her to follow the herd to the rheki fields, but the following day, she flees at dawn and wanders all day in the woods, in order not to return to the Red Grottos until drowsiness has extinguished their desires.

And in the placid splendor that surrounds her, she savors a sweet and melancholy joy. Among the plants, the centaurs only seek out those whose roots and fruits are appropriate to nourish them. From afar, they recognize the slender fronds of the rheki, the silvery foliage of olive-trees, the twisted stems of vines, plums, sweet acorns, beech-nuts, arbutus-berries and all the varieties of edible mushrooms; but they are indifferent to species that are not useful to them, trampling them underfoot and breaking them without a care.

Kadilda cannot distinguish any of those plants by their names, for no memory could retain their infinite number, but she envelops them all with the same love. It is not only to seek her nourishment there that she roams the forests; there is for her an incessantly-renewed pleasure in mingling with their multiple life. She knows when the buds begin to show green, in what order the flowers succeed one another and the date at which the berries mature. She recognizes the mosses, the grasses, the slightest florets carpeting the undergrowth, rejoices in their birth, admires their blooming, mourns their death. The varied splendor of corollas gives her delightful joys. Rigid, tortuous, supple, hard, slender or massive, the stems of all the plants delight her eye. Velvety, smooth or harsh, elongated or short, tripartite or integral, all leaves are simultaneously dear to her, each one because of its particular charm. And she will contemplate indefinitely the play of the sun on all the foliage, from the dark green of the larch or the juniper to the silky gleam of citrus trees or the pallor of olive trees.

And the beasts, her sisters, are even dearer to her heart. To all those whose young are nourished by milk, the centaurs have given peace, but, robust and joyful, they have no great respect for their timid souls; and some dread is mingled with the confidence that the dwellers in the woods afford to them. More than once, with fearful clamors, the centaurs by way of play, have forced Pilta the timorous to run, and the long ears of Titul have been subjected many times to the contact of their rough hands. But all the beasts have learned to know Kadilda. The virgin has never molested them or amused herself with their naivety.

So, as soon as her white silhouette is profiled in the underwood, they all hasten to meet her. Confident, Axor and his hinds, the roe deer and their young, come to offer her their black muzzles, and the fawns with the speckled hide bound delightedly around them. The great white cattle that are ruminating raise their heads when she passes by and salute her with their bellowing. Titul and his little ones with twitching noses do not run for the burrow at the sight of her, but continue to yawn, dawdling to the right and the left, smoothing their fur with their paws; or they chase one another with sudden rushes, even under the legs of the obliging centauress.

The flesh-eaters themselves, who do not usually like to get close to the six-limbed folk, look at her without hatred. When Kadilda passes close to her lair, Herta, the gray she-wolf, does not raise her hackles and does not bare her teeth, but remains lying down and swishes her tail. And the wild aurochs follows her with his eyes without anger.

That is because they all know from experience that Kadilda's soul is devoid of malice. She speaks to them in a soft voice, and her hands are always full of caresses. Although they do not understand everything she says, they know that her heart is with them. "We love you. It is good to live. The woods smell good. You are with us. We love you." Such is the language of their eyes. Kadilda has never deceived their expectations. She knows how to bring help to everyone, according to their race.

When, in the rutting season, the red deer engage in furious combats, their antlers sometimes become interlocked, and in spite of their efforts, they cannot disengage them. That is certain death for them. More than once, Kadilda has heard their desperate belling, and has patiently liberated them from the fatal grip. She has often constrained Volp, the thief, to decamp from a den usurped from Kraan, the badger. She has indicated to Mumm the ponderous the purest springs in which to calm his thirst.

Even Raram, the jaguar with the green eyes, has soothed his bad temper for her. Raram suffers cruelly from thorns that penetrate the satined skin of his paws. One day, when he was limping badly and leaving bloody footprints behind him, he collapsed on the moss, mewling in pain. Without being intimidated by the swishing of his tail or his nervous spitting, Kadilda examined his paws one after another and pulled out the poisoned darts; and Raram had been surprised to discover suddenly that he was purring.

Kadilda extends her tenderness beyond the teat-bearers, all the way to the chirruping birds. How many naked and screeching chicks she has picked up from beneath the bushes and replaced in the soft shelter of their nests! How many times she has put to flight a voracious weasel, stoat or polecat! In spite of the cracking of the plants beneath her heavy weight, the winged guests of the trees have learned not to flee at her approach, and it is a strange spectacle to see the centauress passing along the forest trails with her arm around the neck of Axor, with Herta the she-wolf on her other side, and then the escort of her cubs, and, bringing up the rear, the little people with the long ears, while the squirrels and the macaques launch themselves from tree to tree in her wake, and a multicolored flock of warblers, robins, blue-tits, wagtails and all the other forest songbirds flutters around her head, sometimes settling on her rump or her shoulders.

There is one place, however, to which the centauress' legs take her as if in spite of herself.

For long months after the terrible evening when the centaurs exterminated the tribe of the Flayed, Kadilda did not return to the clearing in the chestnut-trees. When, by chance, she perceived that her wanderings were bringing her near to it, she stopped and changed direction. That is because time, which covers everything with a gray mist, left within her too vivid a memory of that nocturnal battle: of the death-rattles, of the bodies trampled by hooves; of the blood spurting from everywhere, of Naram, pale and naked, brandishing the fire, and then plunging into the darkness under the cataracts of the splitting skies...

All those images rose up so clearly before the virgin that the mere idea of seeing the place of so many catastrophes again wrung her heart as if to make her cry out.

Then, one day, without knowing how, she found herself close to the River of Swans. And suddenly, at a decided pace, she headed for the clearing, astonished to have been able to live so long far away from it. Without hesitation, traversing one by one the clumps of willows, alders and hazels, which had changed their foliage and become green again since her last passage, she parted the bushes and ferns with her breast, and stopped at the place where the industrious Grottos of humans had once stood.

Under the chestnut-trees, the following spring, the plants had grown taller; here and there, however, between the stems, mounds of branches and thatch were still discernible. The desiccated, half-charred trunk, over which Naram had bounded as he fled, was still lying there. At her feet, Kadilda noticed all sorts of debris that reminded her of the past. Bones strewed the thick grass; initially gnawed by the carnivores, the ants had finished the work of stripping them, and then the winter rains had washed them. They lay there, polished and shiny, among other objects: half-rotted fleeces, flints embedded in staffs, clubs, pieces of stone and carved ivory, strange pieces of bark, lianas that do not exist in the undergrowth—all products of the complicated artistry of humans.

At first, Kadilda did not dare to touch those things, for it is said that everything that comes from the Flayed is impure. As she returned more frequently to the clearing, however, and became increasingly detached from the customs of her people, she forgot her fears. Soon, it became a joy for her to search among the luxuriant verdure, and sometimes the ruins of the huts, for all the debris that Naram's brethren had once handled, and which his own fingers might have touched. In the hollow of the felled chestnut, she has gradually assembled a small treasure of the objects that seemed to her the most precious, and it is with a tremor of pleasure that she picks them up, one by one, considers them, and carefully puts them back in place.

Among the inventions of humans, there are many whose subtlety disconcerts the mind of the centauress, but she never wearies of running the round beads threaded on a string through her fingers. She has also found sculpted pieces of wood, bracelets, leather sandals and vases that shine in the sunlight. She takes delight in passing a little wooden comb through the tangled tresses of her hair, as she has seen the pale females do.

The jewel of her collection, however, is a dazzlingly white piece of bone on which impressions are engraved. For a long time Kadilda did not realize its true value, and loved it merely because of its polished gleam, but one day she made a marvelous discovery. When she holds it in a certain manner, the grooves hollowed out in it offer two figures: one is that of a Flayed with thin limbs and the other that of a centaur. Kadilda did not discern that prodigy right away. Many a time, she has been unable to rediscover on the piece of bone the silhouettes she thought that she had seen there, but now her eye has grown accustomed to it. At the first attempt, she holds the ornament in the necessary position, and contemplates the lines engraved there by the skillful hand of a Flayed—in which the virgin attempts to recognize her own image and that of Naram—indefinitely. So, every time she comes to the clearing, it is the sculpted bone that she takes from its hiding-place first. It is that object she rejoices in anticipation of contemplating today.

A surprise awaits her, however, when she emerges beneath the chestnut-trees. Another visitor has preceded her. He is sitting with his back against the stump of dread wood. At the noise of rustling leaves he looks up and Kadilda recognizes the face of Pirip.

Pirip has passed the age of maximum strength. His beard is long and gray. Between his horns, his bushy hair is speckled with white hair and the wrinkles in his face are deeper. On several occasions Kadilda has noticed his tracks in the vicinity of the river, but she has not imagined that she might meet him one day in the very place that has become a sacred retreat for her.

Suddenly, an angry flush rises to her cheeks. Between his hands she perceives the precious fragment, which he has dared, impudently, to remove from its hiding-place.

In a menacing voice, she says: "Pirip, give me that image!"

His eyes dreamy, the faun replied: "Many times, Kadilda, I have perceived you on this path. You and I can meet here. Don't be sad. Together, if you wish, we shall make the dead things live."

The faun's voice is very soft. Age has diminished his passions, and Kadilda feels the suspicion that initially put her on the defensive ebbing away.

As if talking to himself, the goat-foot asks: "What are your thoughts on the subject of those who lived in this place?"

The centauress looks at him indecisively. It is difficult to reply to such questions. At first, mechanically, she repeats the formulas that the centaurs have transmitted down the ages to curse the Flayed. Then, suddenly, she stops. A centaur does not lie; in this matter, the tradition of her brethren speaks in one manner, but her own mind suggests other words. But how can she explain to Pirip what is happening in her heart, which she cannot conceive clearly herself? She falls silent, reflects, and finally comes to a decision.

"Pirip, I am only an inexperienced centauress. What does your wisdom inspire in you?"

The faun tilts his head over his shoulder several times, scratches his thigh, looks around, and says in a whisper: "I shall tell you a great secret. These people are more powerful than us. They will live and we shall die."

Kadilda thinks that she is about to fall over in surprise. She remembers Naram's frail stature, and how, since time immemorial, the strength of the centaurs has been sovereign. Is it the vilest of living beings that will be capable of defeating them? Has Pirip lost his mind? But the faun goes on. The population of the Flayed is infinite. Beyond the mountains, in the valleys where the noble animals once lived, their tribes are crowded. No one can imagine their number. Standing beside one another, they would cover all the space that separates the Red Grottos from the River of Swans. And in other regions there are even more of them. And so on. Their females give birth in all seasons. Protected by the skins with which they cover themselves, they brave the cold and the heat with impunity. Because they eat anything, any country is propitious for them. In all the places that the centaurs quit, they appear and pullulate; and the subtlety of their intelligence is incredible.

But Kadilda, full of the pride of her race, replies: "Of all living things, none has a heart more robust and a mind more ingenious than the six-limbed people."

With his finger, the faun points at the polished bone on which the forms of a centaur and a Flayed are engraved.

"Which of your siblings knows the art of tracing such signs?" And when the disconcerted Kadilda says nothing, he goes on: "Believe me—the intelligence of the Flayed is the keener. It penetrates that which appears obscure to us, and remarks that which we do not perceive. When yesterday is dead, the sovereign animals pay no heed to it; they are only occupied with today—and who thinks about tomorrow? But the intelligence of the Flayed is triple. He sees yesterday, today and tomorrow. And a day will come when he will be king, above the sovereign animals.

Anguish grips Kadilda. Pirip's statements resemble the thoughts that often occur to her. Oppressed, she murmurs: "Are you not afraid, Pirip?"

But Pirip raises his head again and passes his hand through his beard. His eyes shine, and broad laughter opens his mouth.

"Why should I be afraid? Pirip is Pirip. The things of tomorrow do not belong to me. My thoughts are like bright butterflies that come and go, fluttering. The pleasure of my people is in blowing into reeds, getting drunk on the juice of the vine, dancing wildly on the grass and rejoicing in all beauty. What does tomorrow matter, if I enjoy today? And do you know, Kadilda, that the females of humans are very beautiful. One day, Sadionx and I saw one of them who was asleep...and our desire was satisfied. Because of what we did, blood was shed. Kadilda, I would like to see the females of humans again. I tell you this in confidence: the females of my own people offend my delicacy."

Kadilda starts to laugh, but instead of being scandalized by the faun's repugnant tastes, she feels a kind of secret joy. Blushing involuntarily, she allows her thoughts to return to the child Naram. Which of the centaurs has his melodious voice, his delicate hands and his blue eyes? Pirip's words have never touched her so much, and she would like to interrogate him further, but the faun's attention has fled. His eyes raised to the sky, his head nodding, his arms folded around his pointed knees, he is singing.

Alternately, in incoherent phrases, he celebrates the beauty of the meadows and the woods, the brightness of the sun, the flavor of olives and that of grapes, and the faunesses with tawny breasts and lascivious caresses; but human females are more beautiful than the countryside in flower, more radiant than the sun, sweeter than the vines and more voluptuous than the faunesses. Pirip shifts his weight in cadence on his goat's legs, intoxicated by his own song.

Kadilda refrains from tearing him out of his ecstasy. In any case, by virtue of having concentrated her own thoughts, she feels weariness overtaking her. She abandons Pirip and quits the clearing.

In the days that follow, however, she often takes the same route, and on several occasions she finds the faun beside the fallen trunk. They examine the precious objects together, touch them and exchange ingenious remarks at length. And thus, gradually, an unusual amity is born between them, because a secret sentiment unites them.

Meanwhile, the seasons succeed one another and flow by in their turn, and everything that lives proceeds, according to the obscure will of becoming.

It has been raining for four days: not the fine, light rain, the benevolent caress that makes the ground verdant again and brings it into flower; nor the tumultuous, brief and violent rain of the storm, like a brief fit of anger that can embellish it; or even the angry and unequal rain with which the west wind is charged, in the fast-moving clouds they carry; but an enormous, heavy, formidable rain. One might think that it were falling from somewhere higher than the sky, so crushing is its mass, as if unknown and inexhaustible reservoirs in the beyond have burst under some mysterious impact.

Beneath the deadening fall of its waters, branches are crushed, grass and brushwood are minced, the ground is furrowed, and living things are struck down. The very air is thickened and weighed down by its frightful, expansive humidity, becoming almost unbreathable. A dense, oppressive, mortal cold penetrates the bones, chills the lungs, and fills hearts with secret anguish. It rains all day, and it rains all night, with a monotonous and inexorable din.

Taking refuge in the Red Grottos, the melancholy centaurs huddle together. Several times, driven by hunger, the boldest have attempted to go into the woods in order to gather a few fruits there. Scarcely have they emerged than they have been suffocated by the deluge, and have retreated in haste to their protective shelter. The young have no memory of such catastrophes, but confused images rise up in the memories of the old.

In whispers, Klevorak, Kreps, Hurico, Babidam and Sihadda attempt to remember how, in times past, the centaurs were expelled from the shady valley they inhabited between the mountains. Frightful falls of water were the precursory sign of the cold that precipitated the tribe westwards. Gravely, the eyes of the old ones contemplate the uncrossable sea before them. There is an ancient prophecy: one day, everything will sink beneath the waves. Hunger tortures their entrails. No one complains. Who can struggle against destiny?

On the fifth morning, however, Trigg the Gray, the first to awake, utters a loud cry and hurtles out of the grotto on to the sand ploughed up by the water. It is no longer raining. They all follow him, becoming steadier on their uncertain legs.

The air is still cold, but the dome of the sky is disjointed. Between the dispersing cloud, luminous patches are growing larger. A pale sun rises over the forest. With a clamor of joy, the centaurs extend their arms toward the luminous father, creator of all life. The hour has not yet come when the land is to sink beneath the waves. Sinister thoughts fly away. The will to live is reanimated.

For four days hunger has been torturing their stomachs. Without conferring, in a single band, the centaurs quit the beach. Fruits, herbs and edible roots will calm the initial appetite, and will provide the strength they require to reach the rheki field, but only the incomparable fern will render all its vigor to the race of dominators. Pressing their pace as much as their lassitude permits, they hasten through the pine-wood.

As they progress further, however, a new fear overtakes them. That is because the masses of water that the opened skies have vomited forth have sown disaster and death. The stripped trunks extend their bare branches in a sinister fashion, when they too have not succumbed to the cyclone. A layer of broken branches, smashed fruits, drowned plants and miry debris covers the ground. Hooves fall upon it dully. Sometimes, legs sink to the knees.

Ravines have hollowed out the dunes, laying bare the roots of the trees. Innumerable torrents are racing. In all the valleys, muddy marshes extend their turbid waters, on which formless substances float. A humid odor of decomposition and death fills the nostrils, chilling the living to the bone.

There is no sound but that of the rippling waters. All life seems to be extinct, submerged, annihilated. No birds are chirping; the furious rain has killed them; their little bodies are rotting in the mud. All the quadrupeds that were able to flee have taken refuge on higher ground, but many have been taken by surprise. Their cadavers are scattered in lamentable groups. Tutul's entire tribe has drowned in its burrows. Their long ears will no longer stand up in search of the breeze. Inoffensive forever, Volp, the fox, lies in their midst. No one can count the inert little red bodies of squirrels.

The more robust have not been spared. On a linden floating in the middle of a pond, Raram seems ready to pounce, but his tensed muscles can no longer relax. He remains perched on the stump to which he was desperately clinging. In the thickets where they normally seek shelter, the red deer, their hinds and the roe deer have all died. The water invaded their retreat too rapidly; they tried to save themselves by swimming, but their strength gave out.

The white cattle had their preferred pasture and their habitual camp in a green valley where, beneath the scattered walnut-trees, around a small babbling spring, the grass was tender and perfumed. Climbing the hill that borders it, the centaurs are astonished not to hear the customary bellowing, but when they arrive at the summit they utter a long cry of amazement; the valley and the wooded slopes that overlooked it are no longer anything but a lake of troubled waters, where great white masses are floating here and there, swollen, unrecognizable and grotesque. The entire herd has been taken by surprise in the depths of the valley, struck down without having been able to reach a refuge. The calm lowing of the oxen will no longer salute the approach of the dominators from afar.

Distressed, the centaurs contemplate the liquid mass that extends before them. They can see no end to it, either to the right or the left. Mysterious and disquieting, it stretches away in front of them beneath the foliage, without it being possible to tell where the land recommences. They huddle together and click their teeth. A large gust of wind ripples the waters. Enormous clouds have risen in the sky, seeming to weigh upon the treetops and over the heads of the living. Terror makes their limbs tremble.

What if the rain, the terrible mortal rain, is about to fall again, overwhelming the centaurs too, before they are able to get back to the Grottos? What if their own bodies are soon to be floating, gigantic and lamentable, like those of the slaughtered cattle? In strangled whispers, several of them propose retracing their steps, in order to resume the expedition when the terrain is drier and the sky less threatening.

But Klevorak scolds the fearful. The chief's prudent intelligence deems that his people will not be able to do without the nourishing roots. The few half-spoiled fruits that they have been able to gather here and there are incapable of repairing their reduced strength. If the sovereign animals want to live, it is necessary for them to reach the field of rheki as soon as possible. Klevorak, his face cheerful, encourages his people. The torrential downpour will not come down all at once, and the centaurs, even if taken by surprise, will be better able to defend themselves than the imbecile oxen.

A ray of sunlight slips between the clouds, setting the dormant water alight, and restores a little confidence to the timid. With a rallying cry, Klevorak throws himself into the water first. Hark, Haidar, Hekem, Kadilda and Hurico—the bravest and the wisest—follow him. One after another, all the rest do likewise. So strong is the instinct of the race that none dares to be separated from his brothers at a moment when peril might be close at hand.

The black waters open beneath the impact of breasts. With powerful strokes, the centaurs swim across the marsh. From time to time they close their eyes, turning their heads away when they pass close to the bodies of dead oxen, surrounded by foam that emits a frightful odor.

Soon they have crossed the hollow of the valley and reached the curtain of trees. The entire hillside covered with giant olive-trees is flooded. Once the centaurs amused themselves licking the gum exuded by the split bark; now the nourishing trees are rotting where they stand. The swimmers support themselves on the trunks that remain and hanging branches. Sometimes, they feel the ground under their hooves, but then lose their footing again.

There is even more anguish in making their way through the devastated forest than beneath the open sky. Their legs are impeded by floating branches, creepers and uprooted bushes. From time to time, a cry of terror rings out. Perik struggles against sunken vegetation that has trapped him. They hasten around him, free him as best they can, and the herd resumes cutting through the deep water. The odor of corruption poisons the lungs. The cold paralyzes the muscles.

Suddenly, Kadilda, who is striving valiantly to keep up with her father, goes pale and points at something floating among the olive-trees. A long murmur of horror spreads. A colossal brown hairy mass is bobbing in the marsh; the wooly fleece that covers it is hooked on to low tree-branches. Everyone has recognized the cadaver of Phall the mammoth. His trunk is oscillating behind him like a great serpent. His prodigious strength has been useless.

The centaurs sense death floating around them. Klevorak makes a detour in order not to touch the cadaver, and they all grieve in silence in the somber waters.

Finally, the chief utters a cry of joy. His torso emerges, and then his back, his powerful rump and his mud-covered legs. He regains his footing, shakes himself and climbs a steep slope. Behind him, his people jostle one another, impatient to get away from the hideous pond, avid to traverse the high forest as quickly as possible in order to reach the coveted field. To the surprise of some, however, instead of taking the most direct route, through the Grove of Thirst, Klevorak veers off to the right. When Hekem interrogates him, he explains his plan in a loud voice: which of the centaurs dares to satiate himself before discovering the fate of their little goat-footed brethren?

In spite of the hunger that is twisting their entrails, no one raises a murmur. The task of the centaurs is to protect the teat-bearers, first and foremost the fauns. Stiffening their weary limbs, they head for the thickets that shelter the people with the horned heads. Only the hungriest gather a few leaves or fragments of bark in passing and chew them in order to deceive their appetite, but the aqueous flavor makes the stomach rise.

They reach the oaks. For the first time, for as long as they can remember, there is no verdure on the branches. Here are the white branches of the walnut-trees. But no sound rises from the thickets of holly and lauriers, from which the fauns ought to have heard their brothers' footfalls. Have all the goat-footed people perished too, then?

Klevorak steadies his voice. "Pirip! Pirip!"

In the lugubrious silence, a plaint is heard. The centaurs approach and bend down. Beneath the devastated lauriers, they perceive a heap of hairy bodies, shivering limbs and frightened faces.

In response to the reiterated appeals of their brothers, one by one, the fauns drag themselves on their hands and knees, daring to leave the thicket, to see the sun once again, which they thought had fled forever. They try to stand upright, stagger, and fall down again. Terror floats in their eyes. Their cheeks are hollow. Their muddy bodies exhale a frightful odor. The centaurs hand them a few rotten berries. They devour them avidly. But several bodies have remained motionless. Never again will the two last-born faunillons, Sukit and Prill, nor old Stypax, nor the joyous Tirril, leap in cadence on carpets of dead leaves.

When Pirip has calmed his initial hunger, he tells the story.

For four days and four nights the terror of the rain weighed upon his people. The first day, they all remained still, waiting for it to stop. In the night, the damp began to stream through the bushes in spite of their thickness. The next day, because of their hunger, a few attempted to go out. Stunned by the fall of the water, they all came back precipitately. But the branches no longer protected them. All night long, the glacial rain inundated the unfortunate folk. They could only find warmth by huddling together.

When, on the third morning, a livid dawn rose, it was still raining. The underwood was no longer anything but a pond, where they remained crouching, their limbs frozen. Torrents were bounding all around them. Exasperated by hunger, Bibik tried to gather a few fruits. He disappeared into the furious waters. All their intelligence was extinguished. Immobile, silent, too discouraged even to chew a few leaves, they had waited to die. It was then that the two faunillons had succumbed. Thus, they had not witnessed the ultimate horror.

In the terror of the last night, the ground itself, the old father ground, had suddenly oscillated. The fauns had rolled over one another pell-mell. From the depths of the earth an immense rumbling had risen up, and suddenly burst forth in such a frightful thunder that, when it died away, the noise of the precipitated water and the howls of distress had been like silence.

Pirip no longer remembers anything thereafter. Now he is not sure that he is alive.

Klevorak has listened gravely to his story. Today, Pirip is not altering the truth. Terror is still shaking his limbs.

"Where did the rumbling of which you speak come from?"

Pirip shrugs his shoulders. It was the voice of the entire earth. Perhaps, however—the faun points with his finger—it was roaring more loudly in the Orient. The ears of the living are not made to endure such clamors.

Tales that have been handed down through the ages tell of catastrophes. Fire has been seen, it is said, to spring forth from the earth, continents have surged from the waves and others have plunged into the depths of precipices. Perhaps some such event has occurred. Out there, to the east, the rheki field covers a small low plain at the foot of the mountains, separated from the edge of the forest by a ridge of rocky ground where only mosses, lichens and saxifrages grow. Perhaps, from the crest overlooking it, the centaurs will be able to see some indication of the prodigy.

One thing is certain; the herd is famished. The duty of the chief is to nourish it. Cheered up by the pale rays of the sun, the fauns have the courage to go in search of nourishment. The centaurs can think about themselves. With cries of farewell, they resume their progress.

But once they are among the oaks and beeches of the high forest that it is necessary for them to traverse, the spectacle becomes more terrible. It is not only the force of the waters that could have convulsed the centuries-old forest in this manner. It seems that an unknown power has shaken the ground all the way to its foundations. Ancient oaks, whose trunks three centaurs holding hands could not have embraced, are lying on the ground, having crushed smaller trees and bushes in their fall. Their twisted roots are in the air, like desperate arms. Potholes full of water have been hollowed out. All life is extinct.

A sudden fear softens hearts; an obscure desire to turn back causes legs to vacillate—but hunger is stronger.

At every step, the chaos increases. Now the forest giants are piled up in inextricable heaps. Gulfs into which the entire herd might disappear are gaping in the disemboweled earth, and new hillocks loom up. Come from who knows where, enormous blocks of stone, each one taller than Kolpitru, have fallen in the midst of smashed vegetation. A glacial breath is blowing in the face, as if powdered snow were filing the air and making it opaque.

The anguished centaurs move on. They no longer recognize the things of old. The terror of the unknown grips them. At times, even Klevorak pauses, pensively. In a low voice, Hurico pronounces incoherent words; perhaps diffuse memories of ancient catastrophes are rising in her soul.

Nevertheless, going around the precipices and insurmountable piles of rock, swimming across the black pools, climbing the hillocks where gravel slides beneath their feet, climbing over fallen trees, clearing a passage through accumulated branches, the centaurs continue their route. They should already have reached the rheki field some time ago, but, because of the many obstacles, their progress has been slow. So complete is the universal upheaval that even Klevorak's instinct has sometimes hesitated. But a murmur of relief lifts up their breasts. The nightmare of the ravaged forest is coming to an end.

The foliage disappears. On the far side of a heath covered only by meager grasses, heather and moss, the well-known barrier of the black rocks looms up. They have not changed. In the valley that separates them from the misty slope of the mountains, the centaurs will find the root that renders confidence to their hearts. In spite of the oppression paralyzing their respiration, they launch forward after Klevorak.

The chief, stiffening his legs, is the first to reach the crest of the hill—but instead of disappearing down the opposite slope, he rears up, throws himself backwards and utters a stifled cry. Sensing a new misfortune, his brothers hasten after him. One after the other, they join him and stop in amazement.

What they see surpasses what they were able to imagine.

Four days ago, from the ridge where they are assembled, a steep slope led to the valley floor; there the beneficent fern grew in abundance. The vigorous plants covered the ultimate foothills of the mountains, which then elevated their bare flanks much higher. High up, in the distance, the white patches of glaciers, which only disappeared in the fiercest summer heat, were visible on clear days.

Now, there is no longer a valley. A few paces in front of them, the centaurs perceive a strange and chaotic mixture of mud, clay, fragments of rock and dislodged earth, the mass of which has collapsed over the rheki fields, burying the forever. And facing them, on the bare flank of the mountain, in the wake of the destructive landslide, the glaciers have also launched themselves forth. Only four days ago, they were in-offensively dormant, in the far distance, neighboring the summits. Now their white tongues are only separated from the herd by the breadth of the landslide. Their breath is exhaling death.

Nothing that lives, nothing that they know, is capable of frightening the six-limbed folk, but confronted by the disaster that surpasses their imagination, the bravest of them feel their teeth chattering and their limbs quivering beneath them. Four days of rain, and fracas of one night, have sufficed to turn the nourishing field into a sinister chaos, to devastate the protective forest, to create around the centaurs a hostile, unfamiliar nature, in which they sense, obscurely, that destructive forces are lying in wait for them.

The breath of the wind stiffens their limbs. Enormous clouds are drifting in the sky, like monstrous birds of prey that will soon fall upon them. A dull sun is shining in a sinister fashion, which is as unrecognizable as the ground. If a further cataclysm unleashes the hostile powers, all that remains of the forest will be swallowed up tomorrow, and the deadly glaciers will extend all the way to the sea, to the Red Rocks them-selves—and that will be the end of the sovereign people.

Terror is the stronger now. In their bewildered brains it, abolishes all thought. With a long, despairing plaint, the cen-taurs turn round and take flight. Even Klevorak does not try to hold them back. His courage too has foundered in the general panic.

Through the scattered blocks, the gaping gulfs, the twist-ed and uprooted trees, the rocks, the brushwood, the stagnant pools and the torrents, and all the atrocities of convulsed na-ture, the centaurs race, bounding, jostling one another, falling and getting up, hanging on to one another, hurtling forward again, galloping madly, alternately climbing and swimming. They have forgotten the hunger that is tormenting them. One single instinct spurs them on: the furious need to cross the chaos, to find themselves once again among familiar things, to escape the nightmare that has descended upon them.

Without a second's respite, they flee, and leave behind them, in turn, the oaks and the beeches, the pool in which the mammoth and the cattle are floating, the flooded slopes where the fruit-trees are rotting, the dunes and pines ravined by the waters. Not one of them thinks of pausing to collect a few fruits; fear gives a renewal of strength to the legs.

At the end of their hectic course, the invariable sea offers itself. But the beach does not seem to them to be a safe refuge. Exhausted, streaming with fetid water, covered in mud, their torsos and arms bloodied by thorn-bushes, their knees skinned by falls, the centaurs jostle one another at the entrance to the Grottos. Only the solid vault of the rocks will be a sufficient shelter for them.

They huddle together and then, exhausted by fear, suffering and fatigue, they fall into a heavy sleep, to the eternal murmur of the sea.

The days that follow render them more sensible of the consequences of the disaster. Because the instinct of survival is stronger than that of fear, the centaurs emerged from the Red Grottos the day after the frightful discovery, and spread out into the surroundings in order to calm their hunger at any price. And for long days, in all directions, through the woods, the heaths, the dunes and the valleys, to the north, the east and the south, they have searched for nourishment.

Here and there, under holly-bushes and lauriers, they have found a few clumps of vegetation. They chew tender leaves, fragments of bark, and the bold buds that are trying to sprout again in the hollows of branches. Aquatic herbs, young reeds, the stems of water-lilies, a few rare water-melons have not rotted. The dominators gather them and crush them with their teeth. Here and there, on the highest hills, where the tangled crowns have formed a thicker barrier to the violence of the rain, they collect a few handfuls of half-ripe olives, figs, arbutus-berries and sweet acorns, miraculously preserved. As the rotten taste of foliage sickens the hungriest, every item of fresh verdure or intact berry is fiercely disputed. Several times, males have come to blows. The most vigorous, abusing their strength, deprive the old and the females.

Babidam disinterred a few stray rheki plants in a thicket of gorse. She was ambushed and half-strangled by Hark and Kolpitru, who tore the roots from her mouth and trampled her meager breast beneath their hard hooves. In the universal distress, Klevorak senses the soul of his people escaping him; egotistical passions are embittering hearts, putting hatred on faces, clenching fists and jaws.

That is because, no matter how far they pursue their research, they cannot discover sufficient resources; nowhere does the rheki fern exist other than in rare and meager clumps. In all directions, the rain has ravaged everything, and in any case, nowhere is the vegetation richer than in the woods to which their sure instinct guided them on the first days—and as soon as the onset of dusk, the cold chills the limbs and chases the dominators toward the Red Grottos.

So, redoubtable meditations agitate the soul of Klevorak every evening. For a long time, while the young ones sleep, he confers with Kreps, Babidam, Hurico and Sihadda, the elders of both sexes, and they exchange the reflections that the present circumstances inspire in them, the memory of past misfortunes and the all-powerful anxiety regarding their race. Gradually, the same thought has arisen in their minds to sharpen their distress.

Against the peril that threatens them, what can the wisdom of the ancients do? For a long time, their minds strive to come up with impossible remedies, but gradually, the truth appears, and when they have understood it entirely, almost at the same time, they understand the duty that is imposed on them.

In the darkness that bathes the sleeping Grottos, the voice of Klevorak, grave and calm, explains his plan to the elders. When he falls silent, everyone approves simultaneously with a single murmur. They shake hands in the dark. Then, serenely, they go to sleep.

When, in the whitening dawn, the centaurs wake up and prepare, with the customary jostling, to go into the woods, the roar of the magic conch stops them. They gather anxiously around Klevorak, who is surrounded by Sihadda, Kreps, Hurico and Babidam. And as peril cannot chase away all gaiety among the young, when they see the old ones thus assembled, they amuse themselves at the expense of their decrepitude and point, laughing at their toothless mouths, their gray hair, their protruding ribs, their stiff backs, their jutting knees and their worn hooves.

Motionless, the old ones remain silent. Then Klevorak speaks, and the faces immediately become serious.

In a slow voice, repeating his words several times over in order that what he is saying should penetrate all minds, he describes the misfortune that has just struck the six-limbed folk, and the imminent misfortune that is threatening them. The danger is twofold. At the price of arduous research, the centaurs are having great difficulty finding the nourishment they need. And even if they succeed, how will they endure, weakened and exhausted, the imminent rigors of a crueler winter? If no remedy is found, therefore, when the flowers are reborn next spring, the sovereign people will have disappeared from the earth.

The young centaurs look at one another fearfully. They cannot contradict the wisdom of the elders. The terror of death chills their blood; they press around Klevorak, waiting for him to give a salutary order. In the first rank, Kadilda searches his face with her avid eyes—but the old chief avoids looking at the virgin and continues in a calm voice.

Once, when Khrepnor was chief, before the cold chased the centaurs from the luxuriant valley where Klevorak was born, the autumn rains spoiled all subsistence. It was impossible in that advanced season to cross the snow-covered mountains. Then, on Khrepnor's orders, Palkar, Klevorak's own father, who was the strongest of the tribe, picked up a mastodon femur, and in order of age, Khrepnor summoned the elders. Each of them, in turn, lowered their heads before Palkar, who struck each of them a mortal blow. Thus half the people perished. Khrepnor, by his own order, was the last to be immolated, and because Palkar's arm trembled, he was obliged to strike twice. Then Palkar was named chief. Because their number was fewer, the centaurs were able to nourish themselves during the winter. In the good season, they crossed the steep slopes of the mountains and reached other climes. Thus was the race saved. The example of Khrepnor and Palkar would not go to waste.

The chief pauses for breath. The frightened centaurs remain silent. Have they grasped what he was saying?

Klevorak's commanding voice says: "Hark!"

The red-haired centaur comes forward. It is the first time the brethren have seen him shiver.

With his finger, Klevorak points to the mastodon bone that is lying on the sand at his feet.

"Pick it up."

Mechanically, the giant bends down, picks up the weapon and holds it up at arm's length.

Then the king's gaze settles on the group of old males and females, and he opens his mouth to speak—but his voice catches in his throat and, changing his mind, he orders: "Me first. The others afterwards."

And, taking two steps forward, he kneels in front of Hark and gives the order: "Strike!"

Hark the Rude turns his head away, drops his club and covers his eyes with his broad palms. An immense groan escapes all throats. With hoarse plaints, the centaurs put their hands together and plead with Klevorak to renounce his plan. Kadilda has thrown her arms around her father's neck and is hugging him desperately. Better for all to die together than to kill one another: such is the cry that emerges from all mouths. But the irritated voice of the chief ruses above the tumult. What! Have the centaurs lost their valor? If Palkar had had a heart as soft, his people would never have reached the shore.

Threateningly, Klevorak commands once again: "Hark, pick up that weapon. In the name of the race, I command you to strike.

And with serene faces, the old males and females, standing on their thin legs, repeat with one imperious voice: "Strike, in order that the six-limbed race will not disappear, and that the life we surrender up will be fortified in our descendants."

Perhaps, subjugated by the will of his chief, Hark's arm would have accomplished the sacrifice, if Tregg the Gray had not slapped his forehead with a shout of joy.

"Listen! Listen!"

And in the universal anxious silence, he recalls something that Gurgundo has said. The triton has often travelled across the sea, to roam along the shore overlooked by the Smoking Mountain. Several times, he has boasted about the richness of the other shore's fruit trees, the opulence of its rheki fields, and the mildness of its climate. Why should not the centaurs, guided by their brothers with the webbed hands, attempt to cross the strait? In any case, in spite of the murder of the elders, the most robust, if they remain, cannot endure the winter cold and shortage of food.

Because they have accepted death, the old ones protest. Who, then, dares to trust Gurgundo's tales? But Hark, Kolpitru, Haidar and all the young ones compete in giving their approval.

In the face of all the supplications, Klevorak renounces his obstinacy. He makes a concession: escorted by Trigg and three or four others, he will go to find Gurgundo. If, after the triton has spoken, the voyage is recognized to be impossible, Hark will strike without further delay—but the centaurs will attempt the supreme adventure together if the people with viscous skin will collaborate in it.

Such is the decision made. Among the dominators, the hope has reappeared that perhaps the murders can be avoided, and spirits rise again. Meanwhile, their pensive gazes sometimes stray toward the other coast, and the bravest feel their hearts weakening at the idea of braving the salty waves. Many, however, in spite of the remonstrances of the elders, would rather that they all sink together than see the blood of their brethren running over the sand.

Part Four

One day's gallop north of the Red Rocks, the isle of the tritons is visible, separated from the coast by an arm of the sea that is fordable at low tide. To bad weather the large island imposes a high barrier of granite; gulls have built their nests on the highest summits. On the landward side the land opens a placid bay. The waves die away gently there on the fine sand. This is the preferred refuge of the children of the sea. It is here that they come to rest after their hectic swimming games. The strand is covered with seaweed, dead medusas, wrack, half-eroded fish-bones, the carapaces of crabs and empty mollusk-shells. An acrid odor of fish and brine fills the air.

Today, the entire tribe of the web-handed has gathered. Assisting themselves awkwardly with their short limbs and tails, the tritons have climbed up in somersaults from the calm watery basin and have reached the shade of the rocks that frame it. Their yellow-tinted bodies are stretched out lazily; their emerald eyes are gleaming in their polished faces. The sirens are scattered alongside them. A few are asleep. Others, leaning on their elbows, are watching their children play some distance away. Turbulent and noisy, tritonneaux and tritonnettes wriggle around on the debris-strewn sand, unearthing edible crabs, sea-urchins and tiny fish from beneath stones at the water-line and squabbling over them excitedly.

Crouching in the mud, Glousk, the old siren, is holding little Phloum in her arms, who is struggling, red in the face. Voraciously, he has tried to swallow a cuttlefish whole and the animal's tentacles have stuck in his throat. He is choking. Gravely, the old female puts her hooked fingers into his mouth in order to pull out the cephalopod.

On seeing them thus, lazy and ponderous, no one would suspect the agility of the tritons when, intoxicated by the wind and the sea, they ride the tempests. That is because their unstable humor is alternately delighted by inertia and demented excitement.

For three days, the west wind has been blowing. Swollen and howling, the sea is crashing its unleashed waves against the shore. For three days, the tritons and sirens have been intoxicated by furious life.

With gurgles of pleasure, all of them, pell-mell, have precipitated themselves into the waves. Adroit and supple, they cross the breakers, gain the open sea in a few strokes, their streaming torsos alternately surging out of the waves and plunging back in. When they are far enough away from the shore, they cease to struggle and abandon themselves to the gallop of the waves, which balance them on their monstrous backs. Gradually, the glaucous mountains rise up and thin out, and he elongated bodies are outlined in the transparency of the waters. Soon, borne away by its surge, succumbing to its weight, the liquid mass folds up and its crown of foam curves over. Just as it is about to unfurl, the flat faces of the tritons giggle at the summit, and all of them, in unison, utter a cry of wild joy, which dominates the din of the waters. Then the wave collapses. Their tails sparkle in the turbulence. It seems that their bodies are going to smash on the rocks. With incredible skill, they slide, dive and flee. Beyond the breakers their viscous upper bodies reappear. They burst out laughing. The same game recommences on the next wave.

The charm of the sirens, above all, is incomparable, multiple and mysterious. Like flowers, they allow themselves to be nonchalantly cradled on the surface of the waves. A soft and monotonous song escapes their lips. Their hair shimmers around them. Their nacreous and silvery splendor, ablaze in the sunlight, illuminates the mobile mass of the waters. And suddenly, with a supple twist of their hips, they adopt a vertical stance; they raise their strange heads, their slender torsos, their tresses and their streaming arms above the green transparency. Momentarily, they appear, marvelous queens of the Ocean, and then they sink again until, a little further away, the sea catches fire and sings, and their curvaceous bodies shine and disappear into the swell by turns.

Sometimes, at a whim, they swim up rivers, making the waters resound under the repeated flaps of their tails. And then, in the shelter of willows, or among the reeds, they hide away and celebrate in chorus the undulating beauty of the sea. And slyly, they amuse themselves watching the fauns attracted by their melodious voices creping under the foliage. Spurred by curiosity and desire, the fauns advance, muffling their footfalls, and suddenly their horned heads appear. Then, with loud cries and laughter, the sirens leap into the water, making it splash around them; with two strokes of their tails they are out of range, mocking Pirip's disappointed lust.

Often, however, when he has gone away, the teasers return to the bank to rest there before returning to the open sea—and then, it sometimes happens that the cunning Pirip takes his revenge. More than once the sleepers have been surprised by him on a bed of moss and have not escaped his lascivious embrace. But they do not talk about those adventures. When they have emerged from the faun's arms, the sirens purify themselves in the bosom of the waters, whose current chases the memory away from their fickle minds. And Pirip does not boast about his good fortune, which has left him disappointed and ashamed, for the flesh that fascinated him by its admirable form and scintillation has a briny odor of the sea and slides away slickly under his caresses.

Today, though, fatigued, the tritons and their females remain sprawled on the sand. An occasional growl reprimands the turbulence of the tritonneaux, and then silence falls again among the people with the webbed hands.

Old Glousk utters a shrill warning cry. "Look!"

Lazily, the sleepers raise their heads, and, immediately coming fully awake, agitate one another with exclamations. At the entrance to the bay there are torsos that are not those of their people. The centaurs are recognized at the first glance. With laughter, the clapping of hands and comical efforts of their entire bodies, the tritons race dementedly over the sand.

Valvor is the first to dive and, pushing through the young ones splashing around him, launches himself forward to meet the dominators with cries of welcome. Gurgundo, Paphlongix and Oiotoro follow him, gamboling and shouting with all their might; as a sign of joy, Plax leaps out of the water, turns a somersault and falls back with a splash. Curious, the sirens dart their green gazes toward the swimmers, and, in spite of the awkwardness of their movements, utter admiring exclamations regarding their powerful stature. Excited, the tritonneaux are squealing all at the same time, holding up the crabs that are squirming in their little viscous fingers to the newcomers.

Somewhat out of breath, Klevorak, Hark, Hurico, Tregg the Gray and Kadilda find their footing, take a few more steps, and shake themselves. The tritons follow them and sit down beside them, curling up their tails. Coquettishly, the females remain half-hidden in the water, lying down, as if somnolent, but they listen to the conversation and their glaucous eyes flash from time to time. Hark and Tregg, distractedly, sometimes allow their eyes to stray toward her veiled splendor of their supple bodies with the magical scales.

In order not to humiliate his hosts, Klevorak has squatted down on the sand. Around him are Gurgundo, Borboroum, Phlanenor, Paphlongix and Oiotoro; the others crowd behind them.

Without wasting time, the chief explains the objective of his visit. He describes the catastrophe that has befallen his people and concludes that, if they cannot find new food supplies, only the death of the ancients can give the tribe the means to survive.

Noisy sobs break out among the tritons. Gurgundo's race is quick to be moved, and even quicker to forget; with great gestures they place their palmate hands on the chief's arms and proclaim their amity. They would consider it a honor to provide for their friends' needs themselves; every day, if they wish, they will give them half of their catch. There is a flood of speech and exclamations, punctuated by sonorous slaps.

When the loquacious flood has abated, Klevorak resumes. The centaurs cannot nourish themselves on algae and fish, but perhaps their marine brothers might be able to lend them other assistance. They know the distant land where the Smoking Mountain rises; might the centaurs not find the nourishment they need there?

Gurgundo strikes his breast with both hands and inflates his cheeks; his brethren imitate him, trying to outdo one another. Their vanity is excited by the fact that the sovereign animals are appealing to them. Certainly, they know all lands and all seas. They have gone up the rivers all the way to their sources and have swum much further than the horizon. They have approached shores the color of blood, battled crocodiles, put giant bats to flight. They know the detail of everything that is, and nothing can escape their clairvoyance. All at the same time, they talk to one another, interrupt one another, and resume their stories with bursts of laughter. Between Paphlongix and Borboroum there is a competition as to which of them can drown out the other. The sirens mingle their shriller voices in the hubbub. Excited, the tritonneaux wail competitively, and boast about their exploits in the mud.

Klevorak waits for a moment's silence and continues. What do the tritons know about the distant land? Does it contain fruit trees? Have the tritons perceived the dark and serrated foliage of rheki there? Do they think that, by swimming, the centaurs would be capable of reaching the other shore?

Their green eyes half-closed and their lips slack, Gurgundo, Borboroum and Paphlongix make no reply. In spite of their good will, their fickle thoughts slip away and wander. Why do the centaurs not sample gutted herring? If they lived in the water, they would not know cold; would it not be more agreeable to see their brothers with the webbed hands racing one another in the limpid basin? Or perhaps they would prefer to hear all their conches blown at once? Incoherent and nonsensical, the words of the aquatic people mingle at hazard...

Klevorak sighs and gets up, discouraged. He will get nothing out of Gurgundo. The triton's mind is more tumultuous, and his tongue more loquacious, than the sea. But Kadilda persists. If it is necessary to renounce the last hope, Klevorak will put the club in Hark's hands again tomorrow. She takes Valvor to one side and speaks to him quietly, interrogates him, presses his flaccid hands in hers.

Mouth agape, the triton reflects, makes an effort, and suddenly claps his hands. Light has dawned in his mind. Yes, certainly, during the summer, he has swum as far as the distant land, and while he rested on the beaches, he has admired the richness of the woods that cover it; and one by one, in precise terms, as if the landscapes were still alive before his eyes, he describes the shiny foliage of orange trees, the powdery pallor of olive trees, the powerful stature of oaks and entire fields of rheki with the somber and serrated foliage. And as he speaks, the others remember, and one after another, they relate what they have observed. And as they see the joy illuminating the faces of the centaurs, their benevolent souls rejoice too; their memories become sharper, and they increase their explanations.

But one question is serious. Gurgundo, Valvor and Oiotoro know their six-limbed brethren. They know that they are mediocre swimmers. Will the centaurs have the strength to reach the shore on the far side of the salty sea?

Gurgundo squints. Why would the centaurs quit the Red Rocks? A murmur of astonishment passes through the damp folk.

Impatience whips the blood of the sovereign animals. But it is a matter of life and death. Klevorak explains again.

The tritons all listen attentively. This time, they understand. A great chagrin creases their cheeks, lowers the corners of their broad mouths. What! Will the tritons have to live far away from their protectors? All together, they lament and wail.

"Why should the people with the webbed hands not follow the centaurs?" Klevorak suggests.

The tritons look at one another; suddenly, a mad joy exalts them, communicating itself from one to another, lifting all their bodies in comical capers, drawing gurgles of pleasure from all throats. Yes, of course they will go. They will serve their brothers as guides. They will support their unsteady swimming. Since the fall of the diluvian rains, the sea has a bad taste and the fish are becoming scarce. In the vicinity of the distant land, they will easily find a refuge a hundred times preferable, in healthier waters, and more abundant prey. Will the centaurs be able to cross the narrow strait? Nothing is easier. Half way across, a sandy islet will serve as a resting-place. Gurgundo knows the tides, the currents, the quarters of the moon and the winds. He will choose the propitious day and time.

The viscous bodies quiver and palms slap one another. The idea of the imminent departure uplifts the tritons' spirits, and they are all astonished that they have been able to remain for such a long time on this sterile coast, far from the marvels of the benevolent land.

Klevorak and Gurgundo confer. Penetrated by the grandeur of his task, the triton meditates profoundly, calculates on his webbed fingers, looks in turn at the appearance of the clouds, the south and the west. Finally, he speaks. At the third dawn, the entire marine tribe will be opposite the Red Grottos, ready to guide their illustrious brothers. Several times, Klevorak and Gurgundo repeat the same words in their turn. They have reached an understanding.

The centaurs resume swimming. The tritons caper around them. Tails, torsos, arms and heads emerge and disappear with vertiginous rapidity. Soon, the dominators find their footing again, and grip sticky hands in theirs. Then, shaking their coats, they launch themselves along the beach at the gallop. For some time, the clamor of the children of the sea accompanies them along the shore, but their speed is too great. Soon, the tritons are far behind.

While pursuing their course, the sovereign animals repeat Gurgundo's assurances to one another. When their minds envisage the future, they are frightened by the redoubtable crossing and the unknown land, but when they look into the past, they rejoice in the avoidance of murder and hope is re-born in their hearts. And because they have remained concentrated for too long in exhausting thought, they chase away their preoccupations and fly on, insouciantly.

Tomorrow, at dawn, the tritons will present themselves in front of the Red Rocks. At their summons, the centaurs will emerge from the Grottos, and throw themselves into the sea behind them. As far as tradition goes back, stage by stage, the sovereign animals have followed the sun, driven from the Orient by the invading tide of cold. Cheerful and placid years have been succeeded, stage after stage, by diluvian and glacial rains destructive of all life, primarily destructive of the indispensable root, rheki. In pursuit of the precious plant, the centaurs, for generation after generation, have moved westwards. So it is not only the horror of the necessary murder, it is the entire instinct of their race that is drawing them toward the distant land, and causes them to envisage the solemn exodus with serenity.

Joyful to have made a decision, confident in the future, they spend their last day resting, gathering new shoots—which, the disaster having passed, have had the courage to grow again—and chewing a few fruits that have escaped the inundation. Only Kadilda separates herself from her people, wanting to see the places where she has lived since her earliest infancy, separation from which makes her heart bleeds, one last time.

So, as soon as the sun rises, she quits the Grottos and, following the shore, goes to the mouth of the River of Swans, which she follows upstream. Since the diluvian rains she has not returned to the clearing in the chestnut trees. Now, as she approaches it, a more penetrating sadness descends upon her.

Here too the catastrophe has done its work. Swollen by the rainfall, the river has overflowed its banks and devastated the woods. When it returned to its bed, it left behind a muddy desert. Beneath the stinking mire, all life is extinct. Instead of the familiar groves, thickets and trails, there is nothing but sinister mud, full of vegetable debris, in which a few lamentable groups of leafless trees stand up at intervals.

The clearing itself is unrecognizable. The young saplings have been torn away by the torrent. The old trunk has been carried away with all the cherished treasures it contained. If the virgin did not remember the disposition of a few immutable stumps that have withstood the effort of the waters, she would think that she was in a strange place. The entire past is dead.

And Kadilda, in her grief, experiences a bitter joy. She will not leave behind her anything that she has loved. Without turning round, she draws away and goes into the woods. An odor of putrescence weighs in the air. Instead of going back to the beach, however, she will say a last farewell to the beasts who cherish her, and to her little brothers the fauns.

But her friends have fallen victim to the frightful rain in large numbers. Mad with terror, most of those who survived have fled the inhospitable forest. For several days, however, life has begun to regenerate in the underwood. The centauress has scarcely taken a few steps when there is a loud noise in the undergrowth. The antlers of Axor rise up above the bushes. Several hinds follow him. The warm muzzles rub the virgin's hands. A few rabbits hop in her wake. Kroon, who is digging in the mud with his snout, greets her with a grunt. With mewls of satisfaction, Spirr the panther rubs against her legs. Gorged on cadavers, she is in a good mood. The flesh-eaters have profited from the disaster. They have never had so much forbearance in their cleft irises.

With amicable vocal inflections, Kadilda passes her hands over the backs that are extended toward her, and bids all of them farewell. Doubtless the beasts do not understand the exact meaning of her words, but something of it arrives in their obscure intelligence. They all press against her, more numerous at every step. Around her head, chaffinches, bullfinches and blue-tits flutter. They perch in the bushes, calling to one another with their chirping, and when she has passed by, they fly off to catch up with her. Undoubtedly their little souls, alarmed by the catastrophe, have need of the virgin's protection.

At the approach to Pirip's camp, Kadilda's escort stops and allows her to go on alone. The fauns too have seen the dissipation of their initial fright, but gaiety has not returned to their souls. Oppressed by the humid atmosphere of the forest, they are occupied all day long in the difficult search for their nourishment.

When he sees Kadilda, Pirip utters a cry of joy and runs toward her. Since their meeting in the clearing in the chestnut-trees, an amity has arisen between the faun and the white centauress. Together they remember the Flayed, and have conversations that would astonish anyone else. When the virgin first told him about the emigration of her people, Pirip's face became earthen and his hands began to tremble. What would become of him far from his illustrious brethren? How would the goat-foots tread the forests, deprived of their protectors? He has had Gurgundo's words repeated to him several times, and the day on which the dominators will brave the briny waves.

So, when Kadilda perceives him, she feels distress, and rejoices in the opportunity to talk, for Pirip's anticipatory grief both pains her and consoles her; it is pleasant when a friend suffers for us.

Contrary to the virgin's expectation, however, the capriped's face reflects no sadness. Has he, then, forgotten what tomorrow will bring? With a kind of indifference, he listens to the centauress' farewell, and briefly bids her adieu. It is as if his mind is elsewhere, occupied by a strange thought that puts an occasional gleam into his brown eyes.

Her heart heavy, Kadilda draws away. The faunillons pat her legs gaily, and she lifts her feet carefully so as not to knock them over. The faunesses scarcely reply to the signs she makes to them. As she is about to plunge back into the lauriers, she darts one last glance backwards, and her heart is squeezed; Pirip is performing a jig in the grass, and the faunillons are capering around him. Is that really the sum of her horned brothers' tenderness?

But the beasts press around Kadilda again, and do not leave her throughout the time she spends making her way through the devastated forest. When the pines thin out and the sea sparkles in the light of the setting sun, they stop, for they dare not venture on to the beach to mingle with the jovial herd of centaurs.

Kadilda caresses them one by one and draws away. Their eyes follow her. From some distance away, she can still hear the stag belling and Spirr's lamentable mewling.

The centaurs are lying on the sand, in a strange rapture, and watching the sun sink behind the distant land, for the last time. To the south, the north and the east, a vault of black cloud oppresses everything that lives, so close that the treetops seem to the bending beneath its mass, but the bright star is descending in the midst of a pink, blue and mauve splendor. The centaurs feel their hearts quiver. Tomorrow evening, their feet might be treading the new continent. Their breasts, oppressed by cold and damp, will perhaps be breathing that light, mauve, blue and pink atmosphere, warmed by marvelous radiance.

Perhaps...

That is because the dominators are measuring the extent of the choppy sea. Very gently, mauve waves are succeeding silver waves. Others will come, and then others still. Tomorrow, all day long, it will be necessary to struggle against the profound strength of the sea. The thought of that effort renders the most courageous grave. But one can only die once. No one is the master of destiny. It will not be the fear of peril that troubles the sleep of the sovereign animals.

The sun disappears. Blacker, the fearful vault descends further. Is it not going to crush the heads of the centaurs themselves? An icy breeze is blowing from the land. Everything is sinister. At a sign from Klevorak, however, Hurico puts her lips to the magic conch. Its roar cleaves through the ponderous darkness, and, guided by an infallible memory, the old female's voice intones the verses of departure, which have not vibrated for a generation. And when she falls silent, they all gets up and extend their arms, and, with a single invocation blasted into the darkness, they summon to their aid the sublime strength of the sun, the father of al life...

The dawn whitens. One by one, the centaurs emerge from the Grottos, stretch their limbs and look around silently. The entire sky is dark. Only a faint indecisive glimmer vacillates in the Orient, as if the stifled sun were buckling under the heavy mass of the clouds. The sea is gray. An opaque mist lies upon the choppy waters, hiding the smoking mountain all the way to its plume. Anguish grips their hearts. Will it be necessary to attempt to reach an invisible land through cold and fog.

A sound of voices distracts their thoughts. Are Gurgundo and his brethren ahead of time? No. The centaurs all raise their arms in astonishment. Silhouettes are emerging from the still-dark woods, prancing as they approach. The entire cloven-footed tribe is there. Pirip, who is at the head, advances toward Klevorak.

The old chief clasps the capriped's hands in his. The dominators are happy, before their hazardous voyage, to see the beloved faces of their brethren again...

Pirip shakes his shoulders. It is not to bid a final adieu that the fauns have got up before the sun. From the day when the centaurs' decision became known, theirs was similarly made. Soon, when the six-limbed people take to the sea, their little brothers will throw themselves into the water with them.

An emotion ripples through the stolid centaurs. Their rude hearts are touched by such great affection. But Klevorak is anxious. His people, good swimmers, will have difficulty reaching the foreign shore. How can the weaker fauns, who have only four limbs and whose long hair will weigh them down in the water, possibly avoid death?

Pirip looks the chief in the face with calm eyes. Undoubtedly, many will die during the crossing, but the death of some is preferable to the death of all. When the centaurs have gone, in accordance with the ancient and ineluctable law, it is not cold alone that will strike down the fauns. Everywhere from which the sovereign animals have disappeared, the Flayed have arrived along with the snow and the ice; although the north wind might spare them, the Flayed will not. So, the fauns will attempt the adventure. Even if none survive, they would rather perish beside their brethren than under the blows of the impure ones.

His heart troubled, Klevorak says no more. A loud clamor goes up from the waves. In a trice, they are bristling with pug-nosed faces, bulging thoraxes, extended arms, undulating rumps and quivering tails. The entire tribe of tritons is assembled there. They are uttering acclamations and clapping their hands frantically. The little ones are performing their hectic somersaults on the surface.

For Gurgundo's people, the crossing is nothing but a game, and their mocking sense of humor is excited because their large brethren, so robust on their four legs, will soon have need of help.

Klevorak and Pirip advance to the edge of the water and hail Gurgundo. The waves come to lick their hooves. Involuntarily the faun takes a step backward. The old centaur explains to the triton the chimerical idea that has taken form in the horny heads, and begs him to dissipate it. Even though he is shivering under the damp caress, Pirip reaffirms his immutable determination.

Perplexed, Gurgundo clicks his tongue and falls silent in order to reflect. Suddenly, he imagines vividly how bleak the riverbanks will be if the fauns no longer cheer them up with their capers, and is afflicted by the idea of abandoning them on this inhospitable shore. And with an instant determination, he agitates his chin, claps his hand and lends enthusiastic support to Pirip's plan.

The tritons are surely more numerous than the centaurs and the fauns put together. In their element, they do not feel fatigue. They will be there to sustain their brothers.

Klevorak does not persist. His heart has been saddened by the thought of abandoning the cloven-hooved people. The joy is general among the noble animals that there will be no separation. Moving at the surface of the water the children of the sea explain what it is necessary to do to cleave through the waves and not swallow salt-water.

Daybreak has arrived, however. A warmer breeze is blowing from the west, rippling the waves. The sea is calm. The sky is still veiled, but the sun shining on the waters would tire the swimmers more. On the occidental horizon, the mist has dissipated and the distant land appears more welcoming beneath an azure strip of sky. Everyone, resolved, awaits the signal to depart.

Gurgundo has become serious. Now his mind is concentrated on the magnitude of his task. He speaks in a low, meditative voice, looks alternately at the sky overhead, to the east and the west, and checks the form of the clouds to the south. He also looks at the sea, the direction of the currents marked by changes in the color of the water. It is necessary that the emigrants reach the islet in the middle at the moment when the sun is at its zenith. Then they will have time to rest, and still reach land before nightfall.

The moment has come. Gurgundo claps his hands. Borboroum, Oiotoro, Paphlongis and Phlancnor imitate him, noisily. The centaurs and the fauns assemble and listen to the triton's instructions. He repeats them several times, in order to be sure that everyone understands. A unanimous murmur approves them. Today, Klevorak and Pirip are only second in command to him.

Then, one last time, Gurgundo places two fingers on his forehead, reflects, considers the horizon and makes a sign. The roar of conches fills the air. The Ocean splashes under the surge of the tritons. The most robust, Gurgundo at their head, form the vanguard. Their task is to break the waves and to guide the emigrants, taking advantage of favorable currents.

The centaurs follow them. They race forward, issuing exhortations to one another. First they are hock-deep in the water, then belly-deep, shoulder-deep...

They lose their footing and start swimming. Because they have six limbs, they can rest one pair at a time, and their torsos alternately emerge, when they are swimming with four legs, and sink when they are assisting themselves with their arms.

The fauns are behind them. At a signal from Gurgundo, Pirip has thrown himself into the sea, along with the bravest. At the supreme moment, however, the females, and even some of the males, are afraid. It requires every encouragement from their marine brothers and the fear of being abandoned to make up their minds. The tritons surround them, holding them under the armpits, carrying the faunillons on their backs, coughing, spitting, sneezing and uttering shrill cries of terror. Now, in its entirety, the triple race has left the ancient soil and is bound for new destinies.

After a few strokes, Kadilda turns round to look at the land she will never see again, and a strange spectacle strikes her eyes. The beach is crowded with the entire population of the forest beasts. Motionless on their massive legs, the aurochs are bellowing as they gaze at the sea. Among them, the red stags and the roebucks are prancing, their muzzles extended toward the water. Open-mouthed, Herta the she-wolf is howling mortally. The red coats of the foxes, the coarse bristling silks of the wild boar, the yellow bodies of the jackals and the slender silhouettes of the hinds and fauns are agitating, jostling one another, running along the shore, alternately advancing into the water and recoiling. Undoubtedly their simple souls, by some marvelous divination, have been forewarned of their misfortune, and an immense distress has descended upon all the teat-bearing races on witnessing the flight of those who have protected them—who have established peace among them, who are brothers and not pitiless masters—and doubtless divining obscurely the evil destiny that is suspended above their heads...

Compassionately, Kadilda, a few lengths behind the splashing of the fauns, distinguishes above the waves the antlers of Axor, who placed his muzzle on the neck of his great friend only yesterday. He has not been able to reconcile himself to the separation, and is desperately swimming after her, anguish in his eyes. A flock of birds takes off, noisily, into the air.

Kadilda feels her heart soften, and her limbs lose strength. A wave surprises her, covering her head. She sinks, struggles, throws back the water, and raises her upper body. When she turns around, he beach covered with sorrowful beasts is already far away, and she can no longer make out Axor's antlers rising above the surface. But the swell is becoming stronger because the promontory of the shore is no longer protecting the swimmers, and each of them puts heart and soul into the effort on which their lives depend.

Thus, across the murmurous sea, under somber skies, the triple race pursues its heroic migration. Against the threat of destiny, the noble animals have stiffened their hearts, and with a single will, they fight it. Cruel is the departure, dolorous the task imposed, doubtful the success, obscure the future, but no one has shirked the duty. Those who must will perish. Perhaps a few will escape death, and perpetuate the life of the species under other skies.

With sonorous bursts of laughter, the vanguard of tritons, moderating their ardor, trace out the route over the undulating plain. Attentively, Gurgundo does not lose sight of his reference-points, in order to spare his brethren, as much as possible, from any needless excess of fatigue. Around him, Paphlongis, Oiotoro and Borboroum, to give them heart, sing the marvels of the sea or indulge in astonishing acrobatics that make the foam fly.

Valiantly, the centaurs try to smile at their guides' jokes, but their hearts are saddened by having to travel through the perfidious water. The salty odor of the sea fills them with anguish. Their hooves are disturbed by not resting on a solid surface. The soft medusas floating around them cause them an invincible repugnance; they are frightened by the fleeing fish; and when sticky algae suddenly fold around them they struggle convulsively. Then again, their limbs, which carry them so rapidly across the grassy meadows, are beginning to hurt. Their lungs are breathing more rapidly. They clench their teeth in order to control their breath.

At first, in order to perceive the new land sooner, and also to distance themselves from the indescribable horror of the waves, they swam with their upper bodies out of the water. Now their weariness obliges them to help themselves with their arms. As a result, the waves frequently cover them. They choke beneath its bitter mass, and remember the cheerful beauty of the meadows, sadly.

The fauns are suffering more. Their weaker limbs are terribly weighed down by the weight of sodden fur. They are moving with difficulty, poorly defended against the swell. At intervals, frightened by the eddies, they lost their heads, splashing randomly, their eyes bulging and their faces convulsed. Around them, however, swarm the people with webbed hands. Tritons and sirens compete in cheerfully encouraging the less weary, and holding those whose strength is exhausted above the surface.

But the hours go by, and gradually, the fatigue becomes more dolorous among the sovereign animals too. Several times, in a hoarse voice, Klevorak, Hekem and even Hark have asked Gurgundo whether he can see the desired islet. The chief has reassured them, promised them an imminent rest— but in front of them, the centaurs can see nothing as yet but the splashing waves.

Their limbs are made of stone, blood is throbbing in their temples; their eyes are misting over. Several times, old Hurico has been borne away by a wave; with a desperate effort she has reappeared, succeeded in raising her meager head, to which the last wisps of her hair are clinging, out of the spray, but her gaze is vitreous and a gray pallor covers her face.

Even Kadilda feels distress invading her. Gurgundo is undoubtedly mistaken. Or even, who can tell whether, by virtue of a whim of his fickle intelligence, he might be leading them at hazard over the moving plain? Besides which, will the centaurs find the means to survive in the new land? What is the point of so much vain suffering? Instead of struggling against death, why not accept it now? The centauress lets her muscles relax, half abandoning herself, but the salt water that fills her mouth chokes her, and wakes her up in spite of herself. She struggles and fights again. It would be sweeter to die in the underwood on a summer evening.

The conches roar. Gurgundo utters a long cry. Oiotoro, Borboroum and Valvor shout as well. Kadilda straightens up. Within a single voice-range in front of the tritons she perceives a beach covered with wrack and the foam of waves that are breaking on it. A few strokes will carry her to solid ground. But the sticky waves paralyze her vigor. The waves grow as the coast draws nearer. The undertow drags the swimmers backwards just as they think they are about to reach their goal.

Finally, the virgin's hooves touch the ground. A wave lifts her up once again, but the following one carries her forward. With all the strength of her tensed muscles, she braces herself. Hark and Kolpitru are already on the shore beckoning to her.

When the water is down to her flanks, she makes one more effort, leaps forward conclusively, escapes the wet grip, and collapses on the dry sand.

One after another, the centaurs find their footing and let themselves fall, breathless, on to the strand, which is covered with scattered bodies. The fauns are close behind them. Pitiful, exhausted, lamentable and shivering, their faces distraught, their hair stuck to their thighs, they scarcely have the strength to take a few steps and then collapse, unconscious. A few of them vomit salt water continually. Helpfully, the tritons who have pulled them out of the water cluster around them, rubbing their stiffened limbs vigorously.

Gradually, the goat-foots recover consciousness—except for Priul and Paianx, whose bellies remain flaccid, their teeth clenched, their lips pinched and their faces swollen and blue-tinted. It is two cadavers that the tritons have pulled out of the sea. Priul and Paianx will not see the foreign land—along with how many others, perhaps among their brethren, who are contemplating them with clenched jaws?

But the sun has pity on his children. He is reaching the summit of his course; his rays pierce the white sky, coming to warm up the emigrants, perhaps preserving them from death. Vanquished by fatigue, the fauns and centaurs have fallen asleep on the sand. Their brothers with webbed hands related the incidents of the voyage to one another, while crunching crabs and washed-up medusas with their beautiful teeth.

But Gurgundo remains vigilant, and as soon as the star begins to sink in the sky he makes a sign to his companions, who inflate their cheeks and blow into the shells.

The sleepers complain and stretch their limbs. The triton scolds their idleness. The time has come to cross the second stage.

But when the centaurs perceive the Red Rocks, very tiny, shining at the foot of the mountains, and in the opposite direction they see, equally distant, a similarly abrupt and inhospitable shore, their hearts vacillate again. Klevorak, tugging his long beard, interrogates Gurgundo. Why leave the protective islet so soon? A night's rest will reestablish everyone's strength.

Exceedingly irritated, Gurgundo frowns, spits on the ground and clicks his tongue disdainfully. The cold of the night would numb the sleepers instead of relaxing them, and what is even more decisive is that the entire islet disappears beneath the waves at high tide. Now, at midday, the triton points out the yellow-tinted clouds that are rising. The sea will become more violent toward evening. It is necessary to go. Besides which, the second crossing is easier. The swimmers will be aided by the current.

The old centaur inclines his whitened head and repeats what Gurgundo has said to his people. Such is their lassitude that some, without doubt, would prefer to run the risk of spending the night on the islet and being swept away by the tempest, but no murmur of protest goes up. All of them are on their feet, ready to do battle again.

The fauns are not so easily resigned. At Pirip's order, they wail and lament, putting their hands to their heads. Their strength is exhausted. If they have to die, they would prefer to expire on this strand rather than sink in the bitter gulf. And when the centaurs grab them by the hand and try to drag them away, they let themselves fall passively to the ground, refusing to move forward.

The difficulty is great. The sovereign animals will not leave their brothers behind.

Gurgundo conceives a ruse. A soft song rises up. It is the melodious choir of sirens, who sing the praises the splendors of the foreign land. In the transparent waves, their slender bodies will glisten, and their nacreous tails will glitter. With their charming voices they will appeal to the fauns; they will extend their arms to them, allowing them to glimpse new sensual experiences.

Desire is stronger than fear. Fascinated, the most ardent of the goat-foots throw themselves into the water. The others follow, groaning. The sea whitens under the bodies that are precipitated into it, coming to life. Oiotoro and Valvor blow into their conches furiously. The sirens sing with all their might.

The islet is empty. The three tribes are following Gurgundo toward their unknown destiny. Soon, those who look back can no longer even see the pale strand. Only the wheeling sea-birds indicated the place where Priul and Paianx found final rest. But the noble animals do not waste time in futile lamentations. Their hope is directed toward the other land, and they concentrate upon it entirely, in a supreme effort.

Gurgundo has told the truth. If they had the tide and the current against them, even the most valiant would renounce the struggle, but feeling their assistance renders a kind of confidence to the best, aiding them to combat the distress into which the weak gradually sink.

Kadilda has placed herself between the two old females, Hurico and Sihadda, and encourages them, but they make no rely. When a wave lifts them up, their anxious gazes fix themselves on the shore that they are approaching so slowly, and their nostrils seek the odor of lush land in vain. When they sink into the profound gorges that are hollowed out between the watery mountains, they eyes roll and they choke. Amid the din of the waves, panting breath is audible.

In the rearguard, the goat-foots' courage has run out. Already, they are no longer allowing themselves to be distracted by the tricks of the tritonneaux who dive into the waves and reappear with fish in their hands and offer them to the swimmers, laughing. One after another, they abandon themselves to despair, and cease to struggle. Only four or five tritons have remained by Gurgundo's side. All the rest, summoned by loud cries, have come to help their brethren support the fauns overcome by fatigue in the water. They shake them, make jokes at their expense, insult them and encourage them by turns. Wasted effort. The children of the forest can do no more. They let their heads slump upon their breasts and their limbs remain inert. Tritons and sirens take turns to prevent them from sinking beneath the surface.

From time to time, Gurgundo's torso, as smooth as the skin of a porpoise, looms up above the waves. As the sun sinks, he shades his eyes with his hand in order not to lose his way, and his voice sounds the rallying cry repeatedly.

Now, however, the centaurs' strength is running out. Their eyes are bloodshot and clouded. Cold is afflicting them, their joints are stiffening. Their movements are becoming convulsive. Their breathing is unsteady. The din of the sea is roaring mightily in their ears. A briny odor is filling their nostrils and mouths. The swell is increasing by the minute. The waves crash, passing over heads that emerge with increasing difficulty. When they descend into the wet precipices, the centaurs lose the hope of seeing the sun again, and sense below them the death that is tugging at their feet.

A hoarse sound escapes Klevorak's throat as he is struck down by a thrust of the sea. With an effort, he disengages his muddy face.

"Are we getting near?"

Gurgundo turns round, his eyebrows frowning. The old one's agonized tone has touched his heart and renders him grave. He has words of encouragement ready. Let him look and listen from the top of the next wave. Here it comes.

The enormous green swell reaches the centaurs and lifts them up. Kadilda, Klevorak and Hark raise themselves up; a few strokes further on they perceive black rocks over a frightful seething of foam on which the sea is breaking furiously—and they hear the racket of waves unfurling and the harsh groaning of the surf.

The wave moves on. Behind it, they sink into the gulf. The spectacle they have glimpsed, instead of reassuring them, increases their distress. Gurgundo is evidently mistaken. Soon, their bodies will be broken against the granite barrier.

Why persist? Death is howling in a hundred thunderous voices. The swell has broken up the procession of swimmers. They feel that they are lost in the immense sea. It is the end.

But Gurgundo's conch rises above the tumult. With great gestures of joy, the triton cries more loudly than the ocean: saved! everyone is saved! Oiotoro has gone on ahead, has identified the channel that opens between the reefs and will lead the centaurs to a placid beach. One more effort and the new land—the warm, rich, perfumed land—is theirs.

And in their exhausted muscles, the centaurs find what they need to fight on. Teeth clenched, eyes vitreous, the fight body-to-body against the salty death that assails them relentlessly. They can no longer think, but, with all the energy of their race, they stiffen themselves furiously against the supreme spasm. Uselessly, no doubt, for every time the crest of a wave passes, they find themselves drawn backwards, and in the racket of the waves, who can dare retain any hope?

Side by side, brought together by chance, there are Klevorak, Hurico, Hark, Kolpitru, Kadilda and Sihadda, but they cannot even see one another in the vertigo that has drowned their thoughts. The fog of death envelops them. Robust hands seize their arms and shake them, while shrill cries force them to raise their heads. Is it necessary to live on, then?

The hilarious faces of Gurgundo, Oiotoro, Valvor and Borboroum appear to them as in a dream, descending with them into the black abyss, rising up again with them to the top of a seething mountain where they suddenly find the sun...

What's that?

A last clamor of anguish escapes their throats. In the mist of the surf the brown heads of reefs loom up in all directions—and like two monsters, two enormous reefs lie in wait for the swimmers, waiting for the wave that will carry them to break their fragile bones against the flanks of inexorable granite. The stinging water fills their mouths and nostrils. Eyes close, limbs go limp. The centaurs are vanquished.

"Keep going!"

Gurgundo has grabbed hold of Klevorak. With an agonized grip, Kadilda is clinging to Borboroum's shoulder. With both arms, Oiotoro is holding up Hurico's inanimate torso and advancing, with furious thrusts of his tail, into the roaring channel.

"Keep going! Keep going!"

A mountain collapses; with an irresistible force, it drags the swimmers away like wisps of straw and turns them upside-down. A plaint is lost in the tumult. They are dying.

And then, abruptly, bewildered eyes see the sun again.

Kadilda perceives that she is alive, finding herself projected on to her knees on a bed of gravel. An odor of earth embalms her nostrils. The rocks and the whirlpools of foam have been crossed. In front of her, a narrow strand rises up in a gentle slope. She gets up painfully, stumbles, takes a few steps, and, as if on the softest couch, lets her bloodied limbs collapse on to the pebbles.

Without saying a word, Klevorak collapses beside her. Hark and Kolpitru emerge at the same time. They have had the strength to support Hurico between them. With great murmurs, however, the tritons lay the body of old Sihadda on the sand. Just now, in an eddy, she slipped out of Valvor's grip. Her head struck the rock. The old centauress will not see the new land.

Without wasting time in sterile regrets, the children of the sea plunge back into the waves. They go in search, beyond the reefs, of the rest of the six-limbed people, in order to help them through the channel.

In spite of their weariness, those who have reached land raise themselves up, gazing with terror at the foaming torrent between the granite banks, wondering how they were able just now to allow themselves to be drawn through it without being smashed, and how their brethren will escape that fate.

The seconds go by, interminably. Have the rest of the sovereign animals succumbed, then?

No...there, in the midst of the eddies, are the upper bodies of tritons. With their indefatigable arms they are guiding centaurs, whom the marine turbulence sometimes drags toward one of the rocky walls and sometimes toward the other.

At the sight of their siblings, Kadilda, Hark, Kolpitru and Klevorak get up, advance to the water's edge to met them, and receive them, one by one, from the webbed hands of their saviors. Haggard, streaming with blood, unrecognizable, their legs exhausted, the centaurs find footholds one after another and collapse on to the pebbly strand, where they lie panting, their bodies too worn out and their souls too weary for them to rejoice in having escaped death.

Soon afterwards, the seething river is populated again, and tritons and sirens reappear, disputing with the waves over the inanimate bodies of fauns.

Very few of the grape-eaters still have the strength to help themselves. Most of them have lost consciousness. Their faces are green, their limbs floating at the whim of the waves. The centaurs think that they are receiving cadavers in their arms. When Klevorak sees Pirip, he calls out to him. The faun tries to smile, but his mouth twists and he falls back like an inert mass.

Until the moment when everyone is laid down out of the water, the tritons never cease diving back in, going to the other side of the barrier of rocks to lend assistance to those who arrive there. And as they are landed, the first to be brought ashore, who have already recovered their senses, rub the stiff and icy limbs and shake the inert bodies to make them vomit up sea-water, and drag them into the sunlight that will warm them up.

Before the rays of the star are extinguished over the new land, the triple race of noble animals is assembled in its entirety on the strand, and, successively, Klevorak and Pirip call each of their siblings by name. Several of the centaurs and even more of the fauns do not reply, however, because the waves have wrenched them from the grip of the children of the sea. Some of them have sunk silently into the watery gulfs, and will never be seen again. Others, whose bodies are lying on the new land, will not tread it underfoot, devoid of strength forever.

Sadly, Pirip contemplates the deformed cadavers of four faunillons. And Klevorak, after having hailed him without result three times, becomes convinced that he will never again see Kreps, who was born in the same year as himself, nor Sihadda, nor others still.

But when it is a matter of the life of all, the life of each individual is a small thing. What does it matter that a few have disappeared, since the race has been saved? There is no victory, except at the cost of blood. The sovereign animals have vanquished death; although it is appropriate to celebrate those who have succumbed, it is not appropriate to bewail their destiny. Already, hearts are becoming more serene, and all heads are raised in the same gesture of pride when Klevorak's voice commands: "Let the ancient Hurico sing the song of mourning and victory!"

For the first time, however, the old centauress does not respond to the chief's order. Astonished, Kadilda approaches her. She has remained where the tritons laid her down a little while ago on the beach, lying on her side, her legs stretched out, her ribs protruding from her threadbare flanks and her meager torso, teeth clenched, eyes vitreous and gray hair scattered over the stones.

The virgin places a hand on her arm, and snatches it back with a cry. Hurico is dead. Her voice will sing neither for the dead or the victory.

Disconcerted, the noble animals draw closer together in order to warm themselves by mutual contact. As one single people, centaurs, fauns and tritons lie down pell-mell, their limbs entwined.

And like the enormous respiration of a single individual, the breath of the triple race rises over the conquered land, in the silence of the first night. Here and there, large heavy clouds, dappled with and gray, draw apart, and in the black gaps, a few stars twinkle high above.

Part Five

Several times, in accordance with their customary ritual, the seasons have succeeded one another. The centaurs have established their empire in the Occidental land. The times of aguish have been effaced from their memory. They have recovered the joy of living, confident pride, and the assured sentiment of their might.

Gurgundo had not lied. Limited on all sides by the waves, the new land to which he has guided his brethren is a fortunate abode. To the east and the south it bristles with sheer peaks. Above them all rises the Smoking Mountain; because of the flames that sometimes illuminate its summit, the centaurs dare not approach its arid flanks, but the subterranean fires it conceals warm the climate, and its foothills bar the way to the icy winds from the Orient. Thus, the rest of the island is one vast woodland, alternately sunlit and shady, where the majesty of forest trees alternates with the richness of fruit trees and the verdant grace of meadows.

In spring, in the light air, the perfume of flowering almond-trees, orange-trees and olive-trees is so strong that the centaurs can lose the trail of a faun or a polecat at fifty paces. All the flowers, foliage and grasses make the entire island a single perfumed garden. In summer, when the sun chars the heaths and the rocks, superb forests of oaks and chestnut-trees offer their shade to the sovereign animals. In autumn the splendor of the fruits is radiant. The orange-trees are bowed down by their burden. Olives overload the branches. The cactus-figs turn yellow at the ends of the fleshy stalks. From one tortuous trunk to another, the vine-stems snake, their branches laden with grapes. Even winter is enveloped in so much verdure and so many scents that it is not until the daisies and

146

singing birds return that the centaurs notice that autumn has ended and that spring is being reborn.

For some time, they wandered at random over the island, smitten in turn by all its magnificence; then, finally, they settled near its western extremity. The nights are so warm that they have not needed to seek the shelter of caves. They sleep under the foliage of lauriers, shaded here and there by old olive-trees.

Close by, in the midst of lentisks, tamarisks, carobs and vines, is the refuge of the fauns. Since they have been united in frightful peril, the three tribes have maintained a closer relationship. The tritons too have established their camp at the mouth of a river with tranquil banks, covered in reeds, bullrushes and water-lilies, where the centaurs come to refresh themselves on summer evenings.

In a single season, the sovereign animals have informed the beasts of Klevorak's law. On this blessed earth, flesh-eaters are rare and timid, and they have submitted without difficulty to the imposed rule. And peace reigns between all who live beneath the azure sky, in the embalmed air.

The enchantments of the marvelous isle have not only chased away the memory of terrors past and rendered joy and confidence; in the midst of the exuberance of life that surrounds them, the centaurs have felt the fire of their blood revive in their veins; with a rejuvenated ardor, they have known the sensualities of love, and the belies of the females have trembled under the fecund caress of the males. Comical tritonneaux are swarming on the muddy strands. A dozen newborn faunillons are gamboling in the gorse. Two centaurins have seen the light of day and lived.

And the aging Klevorak rejoices in seeing the strength of his people increase. Almost every evening, before sunset, the three tribes assemble on the beach and play games while watching the star descend in the mauve air and set it ablaze with its bloody fire. It does not even occur to them to wonder what refuge there will be for their race if, in accordance with

147

the obscure destiny that pursues them, the menace of the cold falls upon them once again.

Once only, Kadilda questioned her father pensively in a low voice. The old chief placed his hand on her blonde head and replied gravely: "Any individual who wants to concentrate thought on the terror of the past, the sufferings of the present and the anxieties of the future is mad. Only today exists, my daughter."

Kadilda recognized the old chief's wisdom, and fell silent. More than once, however, her mind has returned to the concerns of the past, or launched itself toward those of the future.

More than once, in spite of the torture of the frightful migration, in spite of the horror of the diluvian rain, the devastated forests and the ice, her thoughts have returned to the places where she lived, when, in the times that cannot be erased from her memory, she watched the Flayed, and the child Naram among them.

Kadilda has retained her taste for solitary excursions. She often steals away from the noisy contact of her brethren and wanders around the perfumed island. As, because of the exceedingly mild climate, there is nothing to fear from the nocturnal cold, she sometimes remains far from the herd for three or four days in succession.

Thus, several times, traversing the entire breadth of the island, she has seen again the sinister shore where the centaurs landed. On the little stony strand, she has seen once again the whitened bones of old Hurico and those of the fauns that died during the crossing. Gradually, the wind has scattered them or covered them with sand.

Kadilda keeps coming back, however. She climbs the high cliffs; she contemplates the well-known silhouettes of the mountains on the other side of the sea, the somber mass of the forests and, on the coast, a few patches that the distance turns gray, which are the Red Rocks.

Frightful black clouds almost always gather on the horizon, and an icy wind lashes the face of the centauress. Nevertheless, she remains immobile for long hours, her eyes staring. Sweet memories rise up within her, and also numerous swarms of sad thoughts. The fortunate island is no more pleasant, more placid and more florid than the abandoned land once was. If, one day, the devouring rain comes to pursue the centaurs here, what will they do? Fearfully, Kadilda recalls the empty horizon into which the flamboyant star sinks every evening. Then the virgin remembers Klevorak's wise words and expels the superfluous imaginations from her mind. She shakes herself, warms her stiffening limbs up with a gallop and forgets her cares in the joy of the odorous woods.

Because, however, by virtue of an exaltation not in conformity with the habits of her people, the virgin's curiosity frequently extends beyond the island where her feet wander and her nourishment is found, she listens with a particular avidity to the tales of Gurgundo and his brethren.

The tritons have established their retreat in the river of water-lilies that skirts the thickets where their six-limbed brethren take shelter, but their humor is ever vagabond, and they are always joking about launching themselves at hazard into the sea, of struggling until they run out of breath against the force of the waves and visiting strange countries. They bring back tales from their voyages that they relate in the evening on the beach. Save for Kadilda, the centaurs shrug their shoulders and scarcely deign to listen to them. Their tongues wag at hazard and say what is not, and their minds are so sinuous that they can soon no longer distinguish very clearly themselves what they have seen with their own eyes and what their tumultuous imagination has invented.

On the subject of the abandoned land, however, they all say the same thing. When Kadilda questions them, they shake their heads sadly, spit and shrug their shoulders. It is the domain of cold and rain. The trees are rotting and dying there. The rivers carry the corpses of beasts in quantity. Only one race pullulates there now: the one that protects itself against the rigors of the climate by means of the fleeces of others.

Pirip's words were prophetic. The Flayed, brothers of cold and death, have taken possession of the ancient dwelling of the sovereign animals. Their puny forms, hidden beneath the skin of the aurochs or the wolf, wander through the forests. The other day, the loquacious Glogla approached the shore opposite the Red Grottos. Near the threshold, an entire pale horde was assembled, and the siren saw the females attaching palpitating flesh to sticks and presenting them to the terrifying heat of the fire, which they dare to look in the face. Glogla had turned her head away, uttering a cry of horror. Immediately, the males had got up, and, brandishing pointed sticks, they had hurled them with all the might of their arms. But the twigs fell into the water, impotently. For some time, Glogla had amused herself mocking their disappointed rage, and then, two or three times, as a sign of scorn, she had turned somersaults above the waves, making her scales shine—and, without looking back, had fled out to sea.

Several times, Glogla, proud of her adventure, has recounted it to the virgin at length. It is more difficult to add faith to Oiotoro's tales. At the end of last autumn, he left with three of his brothers and four females, and only came back to the river of the water-lilies in the first days of spring. In the course of his voyage he has seen strange things that he never wearies of relating. On the subjects of unknown shores, prodigious catches of fish, beasts of every sort and extraordinary plants, his chatter is interminable—but the most incredible relates to a country situated some eight days southwards, the route to which he would not be sure of finding again himself.

There, according to Oiotoro and his companions, live Flayed in infinite numbers. Their own hands have raised Grottos of magical artistry with stones and shaped trees, which they have filled with a profusion of disparate objects, of which no one can figure out the origin or usage. By virtue of their malignity they have established their empire over the beasts themselves—not, like Klevorak, in giving them the benefit of peace, but by terror and violence. Kahar the horse, whose lower body is similar to that of centaurs, has become their slave;

by means of a pointed stick and an unbreakable liana passed through his mouth, they have enslaved him to such an extent that they can launch themselves on to his back and guide him according to their whim, his lips ripped and his flanks bloodied. And they have attempted to ride upon the sea itself. Thanks to the vertiginous cleverness of their hands, they have so singularly gnawed and assembled tree-trunks, bark and branches that they have formed monsters capable of floating, of carrying their puny bodies, and advancing by means of thin pieces of wood that strike the water like flippers...

Such tales give rise to a general incredulity, and after some time, the voyagers themselves are unable to help laughing as they narrate them. Only one finds a welcome among the sovereign animals; that is the one in which Oiotoro relates how the Flayed were punished for their arrogance.

One evening, the tritons, hidden in the crevices of rocks carpeted with seaweed, watched the sun set behind enormous coppery clouds. Nothing was moving in the calm air, but already, sagaciously, the children of the sea were sniffing the imminent tempest and rejoicing in the fury of the waves. Suddenly, within a voice-range of the reef where they were sheltering, they saw one of the monsters laden with the Flayed gliding over the waves. Its wooden flippers were drawing it slowly through the choppy waves. Then, swimming just beneath the surface, the tritons had approached quietly, and from the crest of a wave the hair and the wet faces, sparkling eyes and smooth torsos of sirens had appeared, while the water lit up with the flamboyance of their tails. A murmur of amazement escaped the throats of the Accursed Ones. While a few hastened the movement of the wooden paddles, the others extended their arms toward the maidens, appealing to them with tender gestures and slyly preparing the pointed sticks with which they would soon strike them.

Nonchalantly, the daughters of the sea drew away by means of imperceptible flexions of the tail, while sometimes surging from the crests of waves and sometimes becoming scarcely detectable in the transparency of the waters, while their melodious songs and the lascivious grace of their gestures fascinated the futile human soul. Entirely inflamed with desire, they forgot the approaching storm, and allowed themselves to be gradually drawn into the midst of the brown heads of foam-fringed rocks...

Suddenly, a great gust of wind passed by, causing the waves to splash, and extracting a groan from the fragile wooden monster. At the same moment, Oiotoro and is brothers had appeared, roaring. At a stroke, the intoxication of the mariners dissipated. They saw the danger and plied their oars with a new vigor, attempting to escape. Too late! As rapid as a centaur's gallop, the tempest fell upon the frail skiff, shaking it with its angry hands, and suddenly allowed it to fall, with a fearful crack, upon the sharp crest of a reef.

Through the disjointed beams, the voracious waters had streamed turbulently. In a trice, nothing remained of the vessel than lamentable debris, to which the Flayed clung in vain. Then, with great outbursts of laughter, the marine maidens had thrown themselves upon the shipwreck-victims stupefied by their green eyes, and playfully detached their arms from the pieces of wood to which they were clinging, gripping them in a mortal embrace, and had dived with them, with a flip of the tail, into the depths of the sea. Soon, they reappeared, alone, smiling more broadly. Oiotoro and his brothers blew furiously into their conches. Thus perished, one after another, all the Accursed Ones who, thanks to their pernicious handiwork, had set out to tame the sea...

At Oiotoro's tale, a murmur of satisfaction circulated among the sovereign animals, happy in their strength and confident in the future. Nonchalantly lying on the occidental beach, satiated by the benefits of the nurturing island, they never wearied of watching the suns sink, one after another, into the ocean.

And that went on for several years. But one spring, the weather was rainy. An epidemic broke out among the fauns. The youngest lost their appetites and grew thin; their tongues swelled and became painful, and their eyes became gummed up. Several eventually died. There were no more births among the centaurs, and the previous season's last-born was found dead one morning. A malign fever did not spare the most robust. It was necessary to give death to Perik, who had become so weak that his legs could no longer support him. Even the tritons were not unaffected. They remained inert for hours on the sand, and complained that the sea-water tasted foul.

Heavy downpours fell. Many fruit trees perished. Even two or three of the most flourishing rheki fields were swallowed up by flooding rivers. Several times, gazing at the black clouds that were rolling across the sky, the centaurs remembered past catastrophes. The easterly winds crossed the protective barrier of the mountains for the first time. By night, the sovereign animals were unable to warm up their limbs under the foliage.

Klevorak wondered whether he ought not take his people to camp close to the Smoking Mountain in order to combat the chill, but when the dominators approached it, the rumbling of the ground frightened them, and they decided to seek another shelter. After having explored the island from north to south they came back, guided by the instinct of their race, to the western beach where the habitable land terminated.

On many evenings, nostrils flared, they wandered along the shore, whipping their flanks with their tails, going knee-deep into the water, sniffing the odors of the sea as if they were searching for the distant perfume of another land. At the horizon, however, the sky and the sea were confused. For three days and three nights, Gurgundc swam toward the setting sun, without seeing anything but the murmuring waves. Kadilda allowed sinister memories to rise up in her soul.

Then the evil days passed. The victorious strength of the sun dissipated the clouds, and cut off the deadly winds at their course. Under the warm caress, the splendor of the foliage became greener again, and the embalmed island was ornamented by flowers and succulent fruits. The hearts of the centaurs did not remain sad in the universal delight; they resumed their hectic races over the meadows and the hills. The turbulent fauns got drunk on grapes, sloes and juniper berries, and the tritons chased one another again over the surface of the waters. Even Kadilda felt her melancholy melt away and was obliged once again to rejoice in the beauty of things and the fact that death was far away from her.

But the joy of the triple race on the fortunate island came to an end.

It is late afternoon; the centaurs have been playing their games on the western beach. Taking turns, they have competed with one another in races, jumping and wrestling. Loud acclamations have celebrated the victors. Now, out of breath, covered in sweat and dust, they are heading for the sea to wash their soiled limbs there.

Klevorak watches them go, pensively, but does not follow them. A few days ago, he put his foot on a rabbit burrow that collapsed beneath his eight. Having damaged his pastern, he is walking with difficulty.

In any case, age is weighing heavily upon the old centaur's shoulders. His hooves are worn down to the crown. Long gray hairs cover his shanks all the way to the fetlocks. His legs have gradually become knock-kneed. His ribs jut out from his bare flanks; his back is concave and his thin torso leans forward. It is only with effort that he can still raise his head and scan the distance with his fading eyesight. His gums are exposed and his white beard hangs down beneath his knees. For at least two years, he would not have been able to satisfy the ordeals of running and jumping. So, in accordance with the old customs, he has asked for death several times over—but with a single voice, his people have begged him to endure the insults of age.

It seems that the humor of the centaurs has softened since they have been living on the fortunate island. When it was necessary for him to raise the club over Perik, Hark felt his throat tightening, and the mere idea of striking the old chief sets his pectorals trembling. Klevorak has not persisted.

As the centaurs no longer have to undertake long journeys, and there is abundant nourishment for all, his life is not a burden, so he has allowed himself to be touched by the love of his people.

He has confided to Hark and Kolpitru the care of direction, alternately. Over them, he still commands. Every day he takes a few steps to seek his provender and prevent his limbs from stiffening. Then, for hours on end, he remains lying on the beach, watching with a benevolent gaze the games that testify to the strength of his people, or contemplating the decline of the sun...

What's happening?

The centaurs, ceasing to roll around in the waves, have come together in the water in a single group. The unequal murmur of voices is audible. Arms agitate, and suddenly, Kadilda detaches herself from her brethren and hurtles toward the chief. The sand flies under her hooves. Although the flower of youth has passed, she is still the most beautiful of her people and the old male's wrinkled face splits into a smile as she approaches.

She stops, out of breath. "Father, come and listen to Glauvonde's words; we are in peril.

Painfully, the ancestor raises himself up on his heavy limbs and goes down the beach, hobbling, leaning on the virgin's shoulder. The centaurs draw apart in front of him. In their midst, a few tritons are crouching in the water.

Proud of having an audience, Glauvonde recommences his story. In a single surge, he has raced from the eastern extremity of the island to tell his brethren about the prodigy he has witnessed. Opposite the rocks that overlook the beach where the three tribes once came ashore, the sea was covered with monsters gliding over the surface. When he came closer in order to recognize their race, the triton was amazed to see the silhouettes of the Flayed standing on their backs, and realized that the floating masses were not animals at all, but strange assemblies of wood. Several broke in reaching the coast and a large number of the Accursed were drowned, but

155

the others disembarked safe and sound. Their multitude covered the strand. Gripped by horror, the triton fled at top speed.

All gazes fix themselves on Klevorak. Has Glauvonde reported what his eyes have seen, or, on the contrary, has his loquacious tongue taken pleasure in fabricating a tale? Only the perspicacious intelligence of the old centaur is capable of figuring it out.

Meditatively, he caresses his flanks with his thinned-out tail.

What does Gurgundo think of Glauvonde's adventure? The perplex triton blinks and shakes his head.

Noisily, Oiotoro takes the floor, punctuating his statements with loud splashes in the water. Certainly, Glauvonde is telling the truth. He has seen such monsters himself. He invokes the testimony of those of his brethren who accompanied him, two years ago, in his great voyage.

Everyone starts speaking at the same time, but Kadilda utters an exclamation and points to the beach, where three fauns are trotting along with their hopping gait. From afar, the centaurs recognize the gray beard of Pirip. Futh and Puiulex are with him. Before they have spoken, everyone has seen the distress on their faces and knows that they are bearers of bad news.

Suddenly, Kadilda remembers the distant day when Pirip, out of breath, came to the centaurs to announce the death of Sadionx and to summon their vengeance against his murderer.

In a halting voice, the faun recounts that in the morning, Futh and Puiulex had left the tribe to collect mulberries, which are more abundant in the vicinity of the Smoking Mountain. They were placidly picking the black berries from the brambles when whistling sounds had suddenly cut through the air. Futh felt a sharp pain in his arm; he had put his hand to it and pulled out a pointed stick...

Pirip handed Klevorak a small branch, short and slender, stripped of its bark, terminating in a hard point, as shiny as the nacre of seashells. Astonished, the centaurs take turns to feel it, sniff it and admire the fact that such a light object was able to transpierce Futh's arm...

Pirip resumes his story. When the surprised fauns looked up, the whites redoubled; similar pieces of wood sank into the grass to the side of them, and suddenly, through the thicket, the grape-eaters saw crouching white bodies that were spying on them. A single glance was sufficient. They have run all day to tell their brothers that, by some unknown prodigy, the Flayed have fallen from the sky or emerged from the bowels of the earth...

The triumphant Glauvonde swells with pride; he alone has told the truth: the impure ones have crossed the sea.

It does not matter. Their bare feet will not tread the forbidden ground for long. In a trice, an intoxication of wrath inflames the brains of the centaurs. What! The Accursed Ones dare to track the sovereign animals all the way to the fortunate isle! Threats of death ring out, Fists are raised. Forward! Forward! To the death! Hooves paw the ground....

Klevorak calms his people down. The sun is sinking into the waves. Before long, darkness will fall. Will the centaurs go forth to pursue the humans through the dark woods? Let them wait for tomorrow's dawn. It is in broad daylight that it is appropriate to deliver battle. Perhaps, because of their number and the pernicious weapons that their industry has forged, the Flayed will dare to stand up to the attack.

At that idea, loud laughter shakes breasts. The expectation of combat, forgotten for so many years, excites the dominators, and they employ the last moments of daylight in collecting clubs and fashioning lumps of wood into cudgels, which they whirl around, hurl into the air and catch in their hands.

Meanwhile, in spite of their impatience, Hark and Kolpitru crouch down beside the chief. Because of his great age and his injury, for the first time, Klevorak will not lead his people into battle. He informs the two giants as to the shouts of command and the rules of strategy. According to the ancient customs, the entire tribe will march behind them. The only ones who will remain with Klevorak are those whose great age retains them, as it does him: old Hekem, Miorak and the tremulous Babidam.

However, Hark proposes that Kadilda should remain too. She alone is able to dress he father's wound, and if a sudden reflection is born in his prudent brain, she will go in his name to transmit it to the combatants. As the centauress finds the odor of blood repugnant, she does not protest against the decision of the chiefs.

Darkness has descended upon the occidental beach. Only an indecisive light still indicates the horizon where the sun has set. Then the voice of Klevorak rises alone within the three tribes, and intones a solemn hymn.

He recalls how, at the cost of cruel suffering, the sovereign animals reached the fortunate island and have renewed their peaceful splendor there. Now, as far as this last refuge, the Accursed Ones have launched themselves on their track! Let a pitiless punishment repress their imprudence permanently! Peace only germinated in fields sown with blood. By nightfall tomorrow, let none of them soil the sacred isle with his presence.

The chief falls silent. A long murmur approves his words; then, going back to the thickets, the sovereign animals lie down, and the powerful rhythm of their respiration soon rises up.

Only Kadilda remains awake, for a long time, her heart quivering. At the idea that the delicate feet of humans are trading the soil of the island, she is gripped by such emotion that she presses both hand upon her throat in order not to cry out. Abruptly, old memories come to assail her mind. The prospect of the morrow's battle fills her with horror; and yet, a shameful regret troubles her of not perceiving once again the brethren of the pale child who once placed his hand on her flank. Immediately, however, she rejoices that her eyes will not see their fragile bodies smashed by the furious blows of the centaurs...

Then her thoughts become confused, and she falls asleep.

The woods wake up. The songbird-chicks chirp in the hollows of their nests. The quadrupeds shake themselves and rustle through the thickets. The nascent rays of the sun set the foliage ablaze, on which the countless pearls of the dew scintillate. The centaurs prance through the grass in the radiant freshness of the dawn. Puiulex, the faun, is trotting at their head. He will guide them as far as the brambles where Futh received his wound yesterday by his side. From there, they will easily pick up the trail of the Flayed.

The faun's pace is slow, and the progress sufficiently fastidious to make the six-limbed folk impatient. There is no evidence of the approach of the impure ones, so, in order distract themselves, they all poke fun noisily at Puiulex. Undoubtedly, Futh and he were dreaming; they had mistaken the silhouette of a birch gleaming in the sunlight for a Flayed.

"And was it a birch that pierced Futh's arm with one of its branches?"

Abruptly, the voices fall silent. Puiulex indicates a thornbush with his finger. The ground is covered with darts similar to the one that was drawn from Futh's arm. The centaurs pick them up, turn them over in their fingers and then throw them far away, clutching their clubs in their strong hands and searching the surroundings with their piercing eyes.

The recently-trodden ground, the trampled plants and the broken branches indicate the passage of a horde. A small number of humans can do as much damage as a herd of cattle. Another sign denounces them. The birds fall silent in the trees. The quadrupeds have disappeared—all of those, at least, that were able to do so, for Haidar bends down over a clump of furze and picks up the still-warm body of Lull by the ears, transpierced by a dart. All night, the hare has lain there, twitching in agony. Around him, a pool of blood has blackened the soil. At the suffering of the little brother, a surge of anger warms their hearts. Woe to the filthy race!

Bending down over the ground, without saying a word, the centaurs follow the trail. They no longer have any need of

Puiulex. The sickening odor of the impure race poisons their nostrils. Evidently, after having perceived the fauns, the Flayed have taken flight. Doubtless they anticipated punishment. One sole dread haunts their minds: what if the adventurers have already taken to the sea?

Hark, who is in the lead, utters the cry that commands a halt and silence. Everyone stops and listens, ears cocked and neck extended. A precipitate gallop is heard through the high furze. It is neither the gait of the red deer nor that of the wild boar. Besides which, the beasts do not run away at the approach of the dominators. The herd clears a path through the thicket. Tregg utters an exclamation of triumph. He has found the trail of the fleeing humans. There is no doubt about it. All of them follow it, noisily, unworried by the possibility of an enemy ambush.

The undergrowth becomes thinner and lower. The chestnut-trees are smaller and more widely spaced. Soon they will reach the heath that precedes the wood of cork-oaks and the coastal hills. Another thicket of dwarf holm-oaks, and there it is.

Hark emerges from the bushes and utters an exclamation. His brothers stop behind him, nonplussed.

Facing them, a long voice-range away on the edge of the wood of cork-oaks, is a numerous and motionless troop. Its appearance strikes the centaurs with amazement. On four feet, like their own, there are similar bodies surmounted by two heads. One resembles that of a hind, the other that of the sovereign animals themselves. Thin arms are brandishing pointed sticks or feeble clubs. Between the quadrupeds move the pale silhouettes of the Flayed. Their hands are clutching pieces of wood or stalks of an unknown shiny substance. Some are kneeling; one arm extended forwards is holding a flexible piece of wood, the other is drawn backwards.

It is Haidar whose subtle mind dissipates the astonishment of his people. "Remember what Oiotoro said. The Flayed have made Kahar their slave."

Haidar is right. The centaurs recognize the elongated head and mane of the horse. A growl of anger emerges from their throats. Their own pride is wounded by the humiliation of Kahar, whose form is that of their lower bodies. The Flayed are the torturers of everything that lives. The centaurs bear within them the soul of animality entire.

With a howl, Hark bounds forward, whirling his club. The roaring whirlwind is unleashed behind him. The heath flees under their hooves....

Facing them, the Flayed remain motionless. Those who are kneeling have their eyes fixed on their aggressors. The others, gripping their mounts with their legs, are waiting for a gesture from one of them, doubtless their chief. He is the tallest. Above his mouth, a tuft of blond hair divides his face in two, and he is mounted on a black horse bound by shiny ropes. Hark has chosen him. It is on him that his club will fall first. He rejoices in sensing him crushed beneath his feet.

The gallop of the centaurs draws closer; another few strides and the wretches will be punished...

The blond chief raises his stick and utters a cry—to ask for mercy?

The arms of the kneeling humans stiffen in an effort that makes them red in the face, and then abruptly relax. The air fills with whistling sounds and the noise of silky wings. The centaurs raise their heads...

With a frightful cough, Hark raises himself up to his full height, clutches with both hands at his throat, traversed by a dart, vacillates momentarily, falls to the ground, roars, hollows out the ground with his six limbs and vomits black blood...

Around him, a dozen of his brothers fall with cries of pain. Several tear the darts from their wounds, bite them furiously and get up. Running into a mass of bodies, however, the sovereign animals rear up, totter, trampling in place.

In all haste, the Accursed Ones charge their bows again and hurriedly launch a second volley of deadly birds. Again, four or five centaurs collapse, writhing in hideous convulsions. The rest do not wait for a third assault. Kolpitru, the giant, whose shoulder has been ripped by a dart, has bounded forward. Leaping over the cadavers, all of them charge with him, clubs raised.

The archers are gripped by terror and flee; the horses take fright, buck, and turn away, in spite of the efforts of the riders. With an enormous racket, the herd of six-limbs descends upon the confused mass of the Flayed.

Horses and horsemen give way under the impact. The clubs rise and fall, causing brains to gush out and pulverizing limbs. Frail bodies are crushed under hooves. Terrified, the horses struggle randomly, adding to the disorder. But the men dismount and, frail and naked, hurl themselves fearfully against the assailants. Sharp javelins and bronze blades sink into breasts, and stop the thrusts of formidable arms. Blood flows. Insensible to the pain, the centaurs strike and stamp, killing until the moment that a deep wound lays them down on the slippery ground. Before dying, each of them had claimed innumerable victims.

In vain, the chief with the moustache excites his brothers with his voice, encouraging them to return to the fray, exerting himself in the first rank, transpiercing Kaplam with his blade as the centaur raises his cudgel over him...

The Flayed weaken, fall back, and take shelter behind bushes or cork-oaks. With cries of victory the centaurs pursue them. Even the white chief hesitates, looks back. Sarka the Brunette falls upon him, brandishing her club. She will avenge the death of Kaplam, who made her a mother...

The centauress falls to her knees with a hoarse plaint. Armed with small trenchant blades, a dozen humans, the most agile, are attacking the dominators from behind, cutting their hamstrings with their weapons or burying them in their belies. Several of the centaurs stagger, howling, their feet catching in their entrails; others turn round, launching themselves against their new aggressors. The majority are rapidly struck down. The rest flee. It is the triumph...

No! A new danger falls from the sky. The archers have climbed the trunks of cork-oaks and, perched in the high branches, are raining down their darts. One after another, Palk, Hagdan and Kaloak collapse on to the ground, gripping it with their clenched hands.

Mad with rage, their brothers bound against the rugged trunks, surround them with their arms, rip away the bark with their teeth, and shake them with all the might of their muscles. Under the rain of darts they fall back, their eyes punctured, their shoulders bloody, and immediately raise themselves up to their full height in a somersault of fury, to struggle again, conclusively. Under the pressure of Kolpitru, an oak crashes down, with the archers who have taken refuge in it. In the blink of an eye, their trampled bodies are nothing more than a frightful fleshy pulp.

In the meantime however, the pale chief has gathered his men. From all directions, the livid bodies surge forward, precipitating themselves with a new ardor. For some time, the clubs have been broken or, wet with blood, have slipped out of hands. The decimated centaurs stifle their enemies in their powerful arms, knock them down with kicks, strangle them with their bloody jaws. To the hair, shoulders and legs of each one, eight or ten men cling, trying to deliver a mortal blow. At every moment, a huge body falls in the midst of shrill cries of victory.

Four times, in an unprecedented effort, Kolpitru gets rid of his assailants, crushing a dozen of them beneath his enormous weight...but they come back a fifth time, more numerous. The giant does not wait for their attack and charges them, with a burst of laughter...

Beside him, Haidar, Tregg and Sakarbatul, heedless of twenty wounds, stave in chests, makes skulls explode, rip out bellies. Everywhere they go, the impure buckle—but an instant later, they are swarming more furiously. What are the brothers doing? Three times, Haidar and Kolpitru raise the alarm call; no helpful arms rise in response to their appeal. But they have picked up blades escaped from human hands, and are whirling thrusts around them that cleave empty air. Tregg and Sakarbatul are striking with them.

Once again the Accursed Ones give way, and retreat in disorder.

The centaurs breathe momentarily, look around...

A great cry of amazement escapes them. In the bloody wood, covered with cadavers, from which the frightful odor of murder rises, they alone of the six-limbed folk are standing. Apart from them, there are no longer any but inert bodies, or those struggling in the final convulsions. That is why, just now, they appealed to their brothers in vain...

And their cry is so terrible that fir an instant, the clamor of the humans is extinguished, and the moans of the dying, and they can hear the sound of the source that is making the blood trickle from their wounds...

Then, immobile, they sense the approach of death.

All alone, the blond chief advances. He stops a few paces away, and his shrill voice utters unintelligible sounds. But Haidar stares at him and shudders. In the black hole of his memory two eyes light up similar to the azure eyes that are contemplating him. He remembers a lightning bolt, the fall of a tree, the miracle of the fire...

There is no time for vain thoughts. The moment has come to die. The four centaurs clutch their weapons, and brace themselves to bound forward. But the blond chief throws himself to one side. A hail of darts stops the final charge. Haidar has three arrows in his shoulder and one in his leg. Kolpitru and Tregg have fallen. Sakarbatul stumbles and does not get up again.

Beside him, Kolpitru has risen to his feet again, and one last time his voice commands. The order is that those who are alive should gather their last strength and report the news of the disaster to Klevorak. He will hold back the pursuit for a few seconds.

Haidar and Sakarbatul hesitate, wanting to die, but Kolpitru repeats his command. The order of a chief is sacred.

With a cry of adieu, the survivors launch themselves into the undergrowth and flee at top speed, leaving a red trail behind them.

Kolpitru has steadied himself on his four feet; torso rigid and head held high, he faces up to the enemy. His blood is streaming. A new volley of arrows falls upon him. He remains motionless, his body bristling with darts, like a porcupine; and so frightful is his appearance that the howling multitude dare not approach him. Only the blond chief takes a step forward, and then another...

The centaur does not move. And suddenly, the Accursed One throws way his sword and places his hand on the red torso. Beneath his frail fingers, the mass of the giant, dead on his feet, collapses.

All day long, Klevorak has remained under the willows, lying beside the river. Hekem, Miorak and Babidam are sitting by his side. Kadilda has been into the woods and has brought back large armfuls of rheki roots, and branches laden with olives to the old centaurs. Then, with great care, several times, she has dressed the wound that Klevorak bears on his left foreleg. The virgin's skill is unequaled. Into a hollow seashell filled with water she plunges a handful of vey fine moss and then places it on the wound. The damp and cool contact eases the pain. Then, very gently, she winds a liana around the pastern, so skillfully that the chief is able to walk without the beneficent moss sliding off. Everyone watches her with admiration; their stout fingers would be incapable of such delicate work.

The squatting elders exchange slow words. In spite of the weight of years they feel the cruel regret of not doing battle today alongside the young. Each of them in turn exhales rancor, and then falls silent.

Hekem thinks aloud: "The ancient law was wise that granted death to those rendered incapable by age of following their brethren to the pasture and to war."

Klevorak shakes his head. His eyes go to the white virgin, who is sitting and saying nothing.

Miorak asks: "How have your limbs not carried you away in spite of yourself, Kadilda, to follow the herd?"

The centauress shakes her shoulders. "I'm afraid of the scent and sight of blood."

Klevorak adds, gravely: "It is forbidden to shed blood for pleasure. But when the laws commands that it be shed, it is good to see, and its odor affirms hearts. Whoever smells otherwise does not have the soul of the six-limbed people."

Humbly, Kadilda lowers her head and does not reply. Klevorak's words are just.

No, the centauress does not have the soul of her people; she does not have the jovial and indomitable temperament of the centaurs; she shares neither their pleasures nor their pains. Sentiments agitate confusedly within her that she cannot specify, which her siblings could not comprehend. Her tongue is incapable of expressing them; it might be able to do so, but shame prevents it. There is a sweet and melancholy world within her, like an autumnal sky veiled with mist, which will die with her.

The hours go by. Several times the old ones think aloud. Now, doubtless, the impure ones have expiated their crime. Their feet paw the ground impatiently. Their minds grow tired of being obsessed by a single concern.

Toward evening, the waters of the river ripple, and the scales of tritons flash in the rays of the setting sun. Their flat faces appear above yellow-tinted shoulders. Have the victors returned? The centaurs shake their heads. Then the people with webbed hands sprawl in the reeds and on the grassy banks, awaiting the anticipated return.

Then, in the direction of the woods, there is a rustle of stirred leaves. Is it the victors? The oscillating silhouettes of fauns approach. They too want to know before nightfall that Futh's wound has been avenged.

Among the foremost, Klevorak recognizes Pirip, and beside him Puiulex, who left with the centaurs that morning. Mockingly, the old chief questions him: has he come on ahead of his six-limbed brethren in order to be the first to announce the victory? Puiulex coughs, spits on the ground and pretends to be laboriously shelling a hazelnut. The centaurs burst out laughing. The cowardice of Pirip's people is well-known. They are afraid of everything, including the Flayed. The odor of blood makes them feel faint.

At the sarcasms of the elders, Pirip and his brothers frown, as if taking offense; then, feigning indifference, they watch the tritons' games while scratching their thighs. But they cannot control themselves for long, and soon abandon themselves likewise to gaiety. Well, no, they know nothing of war; their great brethren have no need of their assistance, have they?

Klevorak nods his head approvingly, and silence falls again, only troubled by the capers of the tritonneaux and the faunillons. They wrestle and tumble on the strand, and the females laugh to see webbed hands clutching at cloven hooves and the pell-mell of gilded fins and bearded thighs.

The sun has extinguished its glory. The entire sky is pink. An infinite sweetness of living fills the air. The last fragments of birdsong trill madly before slumber. Then the croaking of frogs begins. Rabbits gambol, teased by the faunillons. The shadows descend and thicken. The stars light up. Faunillons and tritonneaux yawn and become drowsy. Have the centaurs been obliged to pursue the impure ones all the way to the waves? Perhaps they will not return until another sun rises.

Necks are extended and ears are cocked. Irregular sounds are approaching in the forest. That is not the entire herd. Undoubtedly messengers are preceding the others. A double gallop strikes the ground in cadence. A long murmur of joy ripples through the fauns. The tritons jostle one another on the bank. The old centaurs get to their feet and take a few steps. Kadilda is standing beside her father.

An acclamation greets two black phantoms that emerge from the wood, but they do not respond. Undoubtedly, the rapidity of their pace has left them breathless. The goat-foots run to meet them, and immediately draw aside with yelps of fear.

Haidar and Sakarbatul halt in front of Klevorak, who looks them up and down uncomprehendingly. Their appearance is horrible. Sakarbatul has an eye punctured, three wounds in his breast and a broken blade passed through his shoulder. Haidar is completely red. Here and there, the stumps of arrow protrude from his wounds.

"Where is my people?" asks the chief.

Sakarbatul says nothing.

The chief repeats his question.

Haidar points a finger at the Beardless, and then indicates himself, and in the silence, he murmurs in a feeble voice: "This is what remains of the six-limbed people."

Stupor sticks tongues to palates. Suddenly, however, a surge of fury intoxicates the chief. He growls: "You lie!" and extends his hands to strangle the impostor.

With a groan, Sakarbatul has let himself fall to the ground. His blood can be heard flowing, drop by drop.

Haidar is tottering too, and repeats: "Chief, this is what remains of the six-limbed people." Then, gathering all his strength, in a halting voice, amid universal horror, he recounts the frightful battle in which the centuries-old strength of the sovereign people has been annihilated. When he has finished his story, there is a long silence.

A centaur does not lie. The things that Haidar has said are true. In a broken voice, Sakarbatul affirms: "That is what happened."

But so many prodigies cannot enter the intelligence at a single stroke. One after another, Klevorak, Miorak, Hekem and old Babidam persist in asking questions.

It is not true, is it, that all have perished? Yahor, at last, has survived, or Hark, or Tregg the Gray?

Haidar shakes his head; they are all dead.

And Kolpitru the Giant? It is impossible that the frail hands of the Flayed have struck him down?

Yes, he too has fallen, the last.

By what sorcery were the impure ones able to triumph?

Twenty times over the centaur explains the prodigy of the arrows, the trenchant weapons made of unknown stones, and the docile horses. The old ones listen and try to penetrate the mystery of these things mentally. But they strive in vain, incapable of conceiving them. Who, then, has revealed these sorceries to the Flayed?

Haidar describes the blond chief who commanded the accursed people, his flamboyant blue gaze, and adds: "Father, do you remember, in the country of the Red Rocks, the little indomitable being who, on the night we exterminated the Flayed, struck Hark the Rude with his hand and threatened us with fire? In truth, I tell you this: it is him who has come back, and has guided the vengeance of his brothers against us."

The old centaurs do not remember, and shake their heads. So crushing is the distress that has descended upon the strand that the tritons and fauns, feeling their spirits overwhelmed, have retired without a sound to their retreats. Before envisaging the future, their souls have need of reconstitution by sleep.

Then the centaurs remain alone on the bank, now lit by the moon, which has risen above the woods. Klevorak's gaze scans those who surround him, while he counts on his fingers.

Hekem, Miorak, Babidam, Haidar, Sakerbatul, Kadilda and himself: seven. Seven remain of the multitude that was almost innumerable this morning. The moon illuminates the fleshless silhouettes in a sinister fashion: the white hair and emaciated limbs of the old ones, and the bloody and frightful phantoms of the wounded. Four ancient individuals, two dying and one timid virgin: that is all that survives of the people with six limbs. What will survive tomorrow evening?

Definitive thoughts spring up in the chief's soul, and he pronounces: "This is the end of the sovereign people. Tomorrow, the last sun of our race will rise."

No one protests. No one things of avoiding fate, of delaying the fatal moment by flight. The strength of the sovereign people has been annihilated; everything has already succumbed with it, today. The idea of surviving does not occur to them—and the roaring voice of Klevorak celebrates one last time the destiny of the centaurs.

He relates how, chased by the cold and rain, they quit the Red Rocks, and at the price of what suffering, under new skies, they established universal peace and justice. But they have succumbed in a great battle. Death is upon them.

This much is true: they are not perishing under the vile thrusts of the Flayed, by their frail limbs; it is Nature herself who has struck them down. For years, the fecundity of the centaurs has been diminishing; for years, the rain and the cold have pursued them, have tracked them as far as the fortunate island. They have reached the occidental extremity of the earth; henceforth, it will be impossible to follow the sun in its course. The divine warmth has been extracted from their loins; it has abandoned the climes in which they lived; the star is felling them without their being able to catch up with it over the moving waves.

The centaurs are ready to die.

Instead of their strength diminishing gradually and their perishing one by one under the slow bite of the cold, glorious death has carried them away all together in a single battle. It is appropriate that, in perishing, they should celebrate with a joyful heart, after the life that united them, the death that will not separate them. Their eyes will close without fear. Their destiny is complete.

With a single voice, the centaurs repeat the chief's words; then, abandoning the moonlit bank, they return to their thicket and, without anger and without apprehension, having accepted their destiny, they lie down peacefully to sleep for the last time.

Only Kadilda has not joined her voice with the others. Only she remains awake when the rest have gone to sleep. Her heart is once again separate from that of her people. Certainly, at Haidar's story, she was lacerated by pain; she wanted to be dead with her brethren—but now she revolts against the idea that it is necessary to perish tomorrow. She is young, she is beautiful, she has a thirst for life, she has not loved. Is any treaty with the victors impossible, then? Would they not allow the placid and inoffensive survivors of the sovereign people to grow old alongside them?

But such thoughts are inaccessible to the old. Even Kadilda is ashamed of conceiving them, and would not dare to speak them aloud.

Tomorrow, then, she will die—but before dying, perhaps one supreme joy is reserved for her. She will see once again the child Naram, who once stood up to the six-limbed race, and who exterminated it yesterday. He has become a tall male with a menacing voice, a murderous arm, a formidable intelligence and the heart of a king. However, since Haidar recognized him, his bright gaze has doubtless remained the same; perhaps once more it will fix itself on her; then she will die happy.

And Kadilda goes to sleep, and in the supreme night, she dreams once again the dream of old. Here is Naram, the blond child, walking in the dense woods beside her. Around them, the birds are chirping and the rabbits tumbling in the grass. He has put an arm around her waist, is holding her against him and taking her hand in his. An incomparable sweetness envelops them. His harmonious voice murmurs soothing words.

And suddenly, caressing her with his nacreous gaze, the child approaches his face to the virgin's, and places his lips upon her tremulous mouth.

As the dawn whitens, the centaurs wake up. In the cloudless sky, the stars are going out. Roseate mists catch fire in the orient. The paternal sun surges forth in his glory. The centaurs extend their arms toward him and acclaim him.

What will be the order of their death? The voice of Klevorak commands in accordance with the instinct that is in their hearts. This morning, as is customary, they will all go together to collect fruits and roots, and they will rejoice in the freshness of the dew-covered woods. Then, having chosen heavy and solid clubs, they will return to the occidental beach, beside the mouth of the river, and there, lying on the sand, filled with the beauty of the star, the profound sky and the sparkling sea, happy to be alive, they will wait for the humans.

At a slow pace, because of the old age of some and the wounds of others, the centaurs go into the pines in order to reach the nearby olive grove and the field of rheki. The perfumes of the marvelous island fill their nostrils; the glare makes the olive-trees silvery; the dark verdure of the rheki caresses their eyes. Around them, rabbits turn somersaults in the grass or sit down cheerfully and watch them pass by, smoothing their fur and twitching their ears. The roebucks and their does come to rub their muzzles against the arms of their tall brethren. The joy of that which lives is immense and peaceful. Under the empire of the Flayed, this evening or tomorrow, all will be terror and massacre; but the centaurs do not pry into the secrets of destiny and savor the charm of the final hours.

Only Kadilda finds the fruits tasteless and does not mingle her voice with the serene speech of the elders.

Sated, the sovereign animals quit the olive grove and go to a spring that emerged from between two stones close by. The taste of the water is perfect. One by one they kneel down and drink long draughts. When they get up again, a song reaches their ears. They recognize their brethren with the horned heads. They conceive a desire to salute them before going back to the river. Besides which, the young ash-trees that make the best clubs are a little beyond the goat-foots' camp.

In a meadow shaded by oaks, fauns, faunesses and faunillons are busy. Some are bringing back armfuls of branches laden with olives, oranges and ripe grapes, piling them up on a bed of moss, and drawing away in haste in search of further provisions. Others are blowing into punctured reeds. Others, very attentively, are repeating in chorus the words that the most learned of the females are teaching them; when their repetition is not quite right, the old females pretend to get annoyed; everyone laughs and cries, and meekly begins again.

Pirip himself advances to meet the visitors, his face illuminated. Klevorak questions him. The fauns are nimble and numerous; why do they not arm themselves with cudgels in order to resist the invaders? Or, if battle is repugnant to them, why not attempt to delay their destiny by flight?

Cheerfully, Pirip shakes his head. Blood horrifies his people; the only combats they know are amorous combats that terminate in the languor of satisfied desire. The fauns will not resist the Flayed, and they will not try to run away, for they cannot survive their brethren. But every year, in autumn, they celebrate the luxuriant splendor of the fruits with a solemn feast. Today, in accordance with the customary rites, they will eat, sing and dance. Perhaps the Flayed will not kill them until after the feast is over. At that hope, Pirip's eyes light up with joy, and he orders the fruit-bringers to make haste.

A grimace twists the toothless mouth of Hekem. He is scornful of the cowardly soul of the capripeds, who will allow themselves to be slaughtered without defense. But Pirip's will is sacred. The desire of his people is expressed by his mouth.

Once again hands are shaken; cries of adieu reply to one another on either side.

When the white virgin comes forward, the last to do so, Pirip smiles at her softly and says: "Do you remember, Kadilda? One day, I too knew the events of tomorrow."

And behind her siblings, Kadilda draws away, envying the puerile gaiety of the fauns.

In the ash-wood, the centaurs have chosen young trees heavy with sap and torn them from the ground. Now, as they go along, they strip away the useless branches and leaves. Having stripped them, they twirl them around. Before dying, they will strike more than one blow.

When they have reached the mouth of the river, they go into the water and refresh their weary feet. Immediately, on all sides, the tritons emerge from the reeds, surround them and interrogate them. What is the advice that the night has suggested to the old chief?

When Kadilda tells them the plan that has been agreed, the children of the waves groan loudly, and wring their webbed hands despairingly. Must the imperfections of their limbs prevent them from helping their brethren, and associating themselves with their destiny?

Klevorak scolds them. The time to die has arrived for the centaurs, but the subtle inhabitants of the water will have many happy days to come.

Gurgundo shakes his head. Between the three races there is a sacred bond. Like the fauns, the tritons will not survive the dominators. The cold and the rain, which have pursued the noble animals all the way to the fortunate island, will make the viscous people suffer cruelly. Besides which, the Flayed are invading all the lands; their ruses will not spare the children of the sea. Taking advantage of their lassitude, they will take them by surprise, asleep in the reeds, and massacre them. Why should the supreme joy of dying at the same time as their brethren be denied the tritons?

Will it be denied them? A flash races over the surface of the river. Phlanenor, who was playing at the river mouth, raises his damp face out of the water and utters a loud cry of distress, at which everyone within range of its resonance comes running.

"Harrooh! Harrooh!"

In the blink of an eye, the entire river is sparkling with shiny skin and scales. Tritons, sirens and tritonneaux precipitate themselves into the water.

The centaurs follow the bank, lengthening their tread, climbing the little rocky cape that separates the mouth of the river from the open sea. An incredible spectacle is offered to their gaze.

In the choppy waves a bizarre monster looms up, which gradually draws nearer, beating the water with a multitude of fins. Its form does not resemble anything that lives. The centaurs remember the vanished Wild Beasts. From the river bed, however, a voice rises. It is Oiotoro, noisily triumphant, exhorting his brethren no longer to doubt his words. Do they recognize now the machines fabricated by humans?

Indeed, accursed silhouettes are moving hither and yon on the back of the strange beast. Undoubtedly, the Flayed are holding council. They are pointing at the centaurs and seem to be hesitating. The mewling of their shrill voices is audible. But one of them leans over the water. Phlax the tritonneau has approached the vessel stealthily. He has been unable to contain his curiosity, wanting to see the prodigy at close range.

Just as the imprudent child extends a hand to touch one of the pendant fins, however, he utters a scream, and writhes in the water, which foams and turns red, his body traversed by a javelin...

A roar of wrath downs out the cheers of the humans. The menacing hands of tritons rise above the waves on all sides. With cries of rage, the children of the sea fall upon the vessel, take hold of it and shake it. Stupefied to begin with, the mariners hasten to grab their oars, their javelins, their axes and their bronze blades, and lash out at the green-tinted faces and viscous breasts.

Howling with agony, the tritons let go, then return to the assault more furiously. Soon the sea is stained with their blood. Many are writhing in convulsions. But continually, at the moment when they lean over the side to strike, the humans are grabbed by webbed hands, dragged into the waves and choked by irresistible grips...

In the struggle, the skiff has drifted. The rising tide had brought it close to the shore. The centaurs encourage their brethren will their clamor. Suddenly, Sakarbatul bends down, pulls a fragment of rock out of the ground and, with an effort that makes his bones crack, hurls it.

It falls over the side of the vessel, which groans, sinks, and bobs up again, coming apart. Water rushes through the gaps. With gurgles of joy, the tritons come back more ardently, all grabbing the fractured poop at the same time...

The sea penetrates the vessel, seething. The frightened mariners jostle one another, hurling themselves toward the prow—but the skiff suddenly capsizes like a wounded beast, and slowly sinks beneath the waves, creaking dully.

The Flayed utter fearful plaints, wringing their hands; then, throwing away their useless weapons, they dive and try to swim to the shore. Before they have taken a few strokes, the children of the sea have seized them, crushing them in their muscular arms...

One by one, the white bodies disappear in the troubled waters. The centaurs cheer their brethren, who raise their victorious hands to salute them.

But old Babidam's finger points out to sea. Beyond the wooded point that is the northern limit of the river-mouth, another monster appears; behind it comes another, and then a third. Their innumerable fins strike the water rhythmically. Attracted by the noise of the battle, they are making haste. Already, the anxious faces of the Accursed Ones are distinguishable, examining the surface of the sea.

Suddenly, there are gestures of despair; their eyes have perceived the pieces of broken wood that the river is carrying away. They have divined the catastrophe, and are preparing their weapons.

If Gurgundo and his people wished, they could easily escape. That is not their intention. They turn somersaults and launch themselves forward with cries of defiance.

The Flayed are on their guard. Volleys of arrows great the swimmers and cover the sea with agony. All those who survive accost the first skiff and take hold of it—but the mariners strike them with ax-blows; further darts rain down on them from the other vessels.

With cries of pain, the tritons turn round, pulling fragments of wood from their wounds, return to the attack, grabbing hold with their hands and teeth, cracking the sides of the vessel, while other dive and shake the undersides of the skiffs.

The sea foams under the efforts of powerful limbs. A second skiff sinks beneath the surface with all those manning it. Not one escapes the children of the sea. But the battle is too unequal. Four more wooden monsters have arrived to help the others. Axes, swords and javelins slice and pierce naked limbs and defenseless torsos. The sea is strewn with cadavers.

The war cries fall silent. There is no longer anything but death-rattles. The humans, leaning over the bloodied waters, lie in wait for survivors. From afar, the centaurs see the faces of their brethren rise up again. The vanquished make them a gesture of adieu—and then, in a single band, intoning the song of death, they launch themselves into the attack once again.

Gradually, their voices die away, and there is nothing any longer to be heard but the strident cries of the humans, drowning out the innumerable murmurs of the waves.

Such was the end of the tritons, the children of the sea.

The centaurs have not quit the steep shore. For them too, the final hour is approaching. They descend the cliff and move on to the sandy occidental beach. One anxiety grips them: must they fall, impotently, under the arrows? Will they not have the joy of striking out as they die? Another hope inflames them: it is that of dying before sunset; that before the great shadow closes upon them, their eyes will be filled for one last time by the divine light.

But this is how the fauns met their end.

All morning, in accordance with custom, the busy goat-foots have run through the forest paths. In heaps, they have deposited the harvest of swollen grapes, yellowing oranges, blackened olives and all the fruits with which the fecund autumn has laden the branches of the trees on the grass in front of the oaks. Then, awaiting the consecrated hour, they have crowned their horned heads with vine-branches, and girdled their limbs, necks and waists with foliage. And just at the moment when the sun has attained the middle of its course, when the heat of its rays are lighting up the underwood, Pirip, clapping his hands, has given the signal for the fête.

While the faunillons bound over the lawns in frenetic gambols, the males and females divide into four groups. Taking turns, the members of each one will feeds on succulent fruits, blow into punctured reeds, sing the consecrated songs and dance recklessly under the oaks, making the dry leaves fly. That is what the fauns have done, at the festival of autumn, since time immemorial.

Usually, the rejoicing lasts until sunset. Today, it will last until death.

Now, several times already, each of the fauns in turn has sung the beauty of autumn, blown into the melodious reeds, bounded over the moss and the undergrowth, and become intoxicated ion the sugary savor of grapes and dates, and everyone is excited by the increasing delirium of all. It is the hour when a madness of joy is unleashed among the goat-foots. Their light souls are entirely given over to the vibration of the fête. Nothing exists for them outside of the clearing strewn with fruits and foliage, where hairy legs spin hectically at the whim of the pipes and the songs and the laughter, in the acrid odor of billy-goat that fills the atmosphere.

There are whistling sounds in the air and the sound of wings...

What are these birds? Why is Turlu no longer dancing? Why has Sprink dropped his pipes? Why, ceasing to suck the yellow fruits, have Stryx and Futh clasped their hands to their sides? Why, instead of a song or a burst of laughter, is a jet of blood springing from the throat of Puiulex? And why is little Pilp, instead of rolling in the dry leaves, lying very tranquil now, face down in the moss?

Why? It is because of the whistling birds, which alight bearing death on their wings. Let death be welcome! The fauns do not fear it, nor do they flee it. Drunk with joy and ripe fruit, the wounded feel no pain. Until the exhaustion of their strength, they sing and dance, leaving red traces in the grass, and then, when they fall, their faces remain serene; no anguish contracts their features; momentarily, their limbs tremble, and very quickly, very softly, they exhale their last breath, intoxicated by the beauty of the dream. And their vitreous eyes and their wide dead mouths are still laughing with the joy of having lived.

One after another they fall, insouciantly, under the rain of arrows. The fête will end today before sunset.

In accordance with custom, Pirip utters a summoning cry. All that remain of the pacific people take one another by the hand and enlace themselves in a single round, singing at the top of their voices. With astonishing acrobatic leaps, the dancers bound as high as the forks in the trees and fall back on to the grass. Then a few of the better jumpers remain motionless. Their siblings let go of their inert hands, join up again, and tighten the round.

And gradually, the circle shrinks. They were twenty; now they are fifteen, twelve, ten...

The others are asleep in the red grass; they leap over their bodies with an entrechat.

Now they are nine, seven, six...

Now they are four. They stop.

Pirip's leg is transpierced by an arrow; the other three are out of breath. Ahead of them, the laurier-bushes part.

It is them! It is the Accursed Ones, half-hidden beneath pelts that they have stolen from the beasts! They advance with caution, hatred in their meager faces, clutching their weapons in their clenched fists...

The tallest one is in the lead. He is holding a sword in his hand. The skin of a lynx covers his shoulders. A large tawny moustache bars his face. His sparkling eyes are fixed on Pirip, and Pirip remembers Haidar's words. And more distantly, far away in the gulf of the past, he perceives the white body of a woman, and hears the plaints of a tiny human, choking...he sees, bounding over Sadionx, an adolescent Flayed whose eyes are like those that are contemplating him. He sees him again, brandishing the fire before the frightened herd of centaurs.

Destiny is sovereign. Once, the Accursed Ones succumbed under the blows of the sovereign animals. Today, it is the turn of the fauns to fall before them. The past does not return. Yesterday, the fauns were masters of the forests; today, it is the newcomers. All that Nature wills is in the order of things. The law of all that lives is to accept destiny.

A few clusters of grapes are lying on the moss. The fauns pick them up and hold them out to the humans, their faces cheerful. Their turn to exist has passed. Without hatred and without fear, they render homage to those who will be the masters of the woods in their stead.

Astonished, the Flayed stir and draw their bows. With threatening gestures, they signal to the fauns to stop...

Insouciantly, the goat-foots take another step forward. Under a volley of arrows and javelins, all four fall to the ground, each pierced by several mortal blows.

The blond chief turns round and seems to abuse his companions. Then they all approach the recumbent bodies, consider them and touch their limbs curiously. They laugh as they stir the still-warm breasts of the faunesses with their feet.

The blond chief has advanced toward Pirip, who is lying on his back, and he looks into his face for a long time. Twice he passes his hand over his forehead. Then, as he moves through the cadavers scattered in the undergrowth, a smile of triumph lights up his pale face. One of his brothers brings him a horse. He launches himself on to the animal's back and grips it between his knees. But his hand rises, swinging a javelin.

Pirip, whom he believed to be dead, has quivered. The faun's eyes are open again, and his mouth is laughing at the blue eyes he has recognized.

The chief's javelin whistles through the air and nails Pirip to the ground, quite dead.

Such was the end of the fauns, the children of the earth.

On the occidental beach, the seven centaurs are crouching down, their clubs positioned beside them, their forelegs extended on the ground, their arms folded over their breasts, and their faces turned toward the sun. They fill their calm eyes with its splendor. The day is declining in its glory. The mauve sea catches fire under the blazing rays. Light clouds, purple, gold and azure, are preparing the star's radiant bed on the horizon.

The centaurs exchange serene remarks while awaiting death.

Will it come from the sea? The skiffs have not yet appeared in front of the occidental beach.

Will it come from the forest? A little while ago, a herd of frightened deer was seen fleeing along its edge.

It does not matter. The centaurs are ready.

The minutes go by. The star descends. A prodigious flamboyance extends in the sky.

Suddenly, Kadilda whimpers, and Haidar announces, in a calm voice: "Here they are."

The edge of the wood is animated. Everywhere, between the rugged trunks of the pines, the Accursed forms are gliding. The setting sun illuminates their livid skin and draws glints from their bronze blades. Several are mounted on horses. They are swarming, as numerous as ants.

The centaurs pick up their clubs, slow rise to their feet and face up to the enemy. Klevorak fills his nostrils with air and announces: "The hour has come."

Then, arms extended, with his great voice, which vibrates in the peace of the evening, he blesses the sun that has given life to the centaurs, the water that has slaked their thirst, and the earth that has nourished them. And after him, each voice repeats the same words.

Kadilda is due to speak last, but the words expire in her throat. She hides her face in her hands and presses her trembling flank against the chief's flank.

Klevorak places a heavy hand on her head and says: "Accept destiny."

At the same time, however, her ear hears the halting voice of Haidar, who is to her left. "You can live. Flee southwards at a gallop. Life is good."

Kadilda raises her head and gazes softly at the wounded centaur, who, because he loves her, has been raised to a sentiment unknown to his race and who accepts that she might not die with the others. But she shakes her head. Now she is strong. She will fall beside her brethren.

Klevorak gives the order. The sovereign animals do not wait in a cowardly fashion for death. Once again, their strong hands clasp one another. Then, having taken a firm grip on their clubs, all seven advance at a slow pace, in a single line. When they are within half a voice-range, the old ones forget their age, and the injured their profound wounds; in a supreme effort, they will all charge together, and will all perish together, striking out.

On seeing the centaurs approaching, the humans stop and hesitate. They seem to be considering, with astonishment, the withered limbs, the wrinkled faces and the hirsute beards of the old males, and also the astonishing energy that is keeping Haidar and Sakarbatul, wounded the day before, upright and rigid, their heads raised, squeezing their cudgels in their fists. Undoubtedly, the assailants feared that they might meet adversaries more redoubtable and more numerous, and perhaps their implacable hearts are softening.

Haidar murmurs in Kadilda's ear: "Do you see him?"

The centauress makes a sign. At the first glance, she has recognized him in the crowd of his brethren—and she contemplates him, all other emotion abolished.

It is him. His stature has increased. His limbs have acquired more strength. A tawny moustache cuts his masculine face in to. But the incomparable grace of his body remains the same. The gleam in his eyes has not changed. The hand that holds the sword is the same hand that was one placed on the virgin's flank. It is him. It is the child Naram. He has escaped the ambushes of hunger and cold, as he escaped the fury of the centaurs. He has rejoined his brothers. Today he is their chief. He surpasses them by virtue of his strength and intelligence, as he does by his stature and his beauty. Everyone is listening meekly to the orders he is shouting, in a voice less high-pitched than before—the voice that caresses the ears of the white virgin delightfully.

Kadilda is suffering. And Kadilda is happy. Naram will never know how dear he was to her. He will never know how often the virgin's thoughts returned to him; the azure gaze will never again fix itself upon the centauress; and never again will a human hand be placed on her body; that is her suffering. But an infinite joy inundates Kadilda because, once more, she has seen the one whose memory has embalmed her soul since the distant day when, on awakening, she perceived him for the first time, over there, in the abandoned land, near the River of Swans. Soon, the centaurs will die, gazing at the sun. She will die with her eyes full of the beauty of Naram, the pale child, who has become the chief with the imperious gaze and the sovereign gesture.

Intoxicated by her dream, Kadilda advances. Naram is there; what else is there? But Haidar, who is marching beside her, is astonished not to hear the whistle of arrows. What are the Flayed up to?

Now, on the orders of the blond chief, the archers are lowering their bows. They are gripping long think lianas, which they are stretching out, and getting ready to run toward the centaurs. The riders strike the bellies of their horses with their heels. On his black charger, Naram's tall stature looms over his companions.

The moment has come. Klevorak looks around. Then, whirling his club, he utters a war cry and bounds forward, His brethren repeat the cry, gather their strength, and bound forward simultaneously.

Undoubtedly, the humans did not believe the sovereign animals, old and wounded, to be capable of the supreme effort. They hesitate, stop. Their horses sniff the odor of the six-limbed people, and take fright.

With shrill cries, Naram encourages his warriors, suppresses Kahar's somersaults, drives him forward, and is the first to hurl a long liana, which unrolls, whistling. Other, similar lianas escape from the arms of his brothers, like flying serpents. They fall among the centaurs, enlacing their torsos and their arms, tangling around their legs, causing them to stumble in the final charge.

The Flayed utter shouts of triumph.

But with a single tension of their muscles, the sovereign animals have broken the feeble lianas, scattering them in inoffensive fragments. And, clubs, raised, they launch themselves into the midst of the impure people. Under the impact of breasts, bodies fall to the ground; they are crushed beneath hard hooves; the centaurs' raised arms come down heavily.

In a dream, Kadilda glimpses grimacing faces, hears choking cries of agony. She feels her feet digging into soft flesh...

The audacity of the Accursed Ones is punished. The dominators will not fall into their infamous hands alive. Humans collapse pell-mell under their blows.

Then, renouncing their reckless plan, the Accursed Ones seize their blades and their javelins, and strike.

One after another, the centaurs fall. First, old Miorak feels a dagger sink into his belly. His feet catch in his intestines and skid. He crumbles with a raucous cry. Then Sakarbatul, who has got up twice, remains motionless in his turn. Babidam, Hekem and Klevorak are struggling against clusters of assailants hanging on to their flanks.

Kadilda has remained isolated beside Haidar, who is shielding her with his body. A forest of arms is around them, brandishing swords, clubs, axes and javelins. Several times, the centaur scythes them down with furious sweeps of his club. Then a blade cuts through his breast from side to side. Haidar utters a moan of distress and falls to his knees.

A dozen Flayed rush him, plunging daggers into his shoulders, into his neck, into is bloody torso. He sighs, and lies down on the sand.

Terrified, the centauress takes a step forward, closes her eyes and awaits the mortal blow.

A commanding voice makes her shiver. She opens her eyes again, astonished to be alive. Facing her, the humans have lowered their weapons, and are standing still. Out of their ranks, mounted on his black horse, Naram, the blond chief, advances on his own.

Naram! The centaur's legs tremble beneath her. A turbulent joy carries thought away. Everything is forgotten. Nothing exists except Naram, coming toward her, who want to save her! She recalls his hand, the hand she can see, and which once rested on her flank. She recalls her strange dream. Joy drives her crazy. He is there; he is coming toward her. She makes an inarticulate whimper, smiles at the chief and extends her arms toward him....

The black horse takes fright, rears up and lets itself fall on the breast of the centauress, She flinches under the weight, and straightens up. The horse has fallen because of the impact. Where is its rider?

An unexpected burden grips the virgin's back. She moans and turns her head. It is not a dream! Naram's face is close to her own. With one bound, the chief has launched himself on to her back. The human's muscular thighs grip her flanks. One of Naram's arms winds around her torso. His breath wanders over the virgin's neck.

Faint with sensuality, tenderness and love, she lowers her eyelids, blushes, abandons herself, and extends her lips to the human, as in her dream.

Violently, Naram seizes her hair, twists it in one hand, and with the other, with a howl of triumph, passes a bronze bit into the mouth of the new beast of burden that he has just conquered.

The clamor of the impure ones celebrates his triumph...

Too soon! Klevorak has rid himself of his assailants. He perceives his daughter, roars horribly, and cleaves through the human ranks, crushing them underfoot.

Naram sees him coming and tries to flee, but he is tangled in his own bonds. The impotent Accursed Ones utter cries of terror. The old chief brandishes his club over the head of the man...

But before the blow falls, the white centauress has reared up. Naram! Who dares to strike Naram?

The murderous weapon falls upon the virgin's head. Her skull fractured, Kadilda collapses on the sand. The man she loves is alive. Her lips, still bloodied by the bronze bit, are still smiling, and she stammers: "Naram…Naram…"

His eyes crazed, Klevorak looks at the virgin, dead by his own hand.

Naram is already upright, picking up his blade. His brothers are running…but the old centaur is on to the blond man with a single bound. He picks him up in his mighty hand, lifting him off the ground, whirls the howling body around his head, striking to the right and the left, opening a path, and, at an irresistible gallop, launches himself toward the sea, dragging with him the formless rag whose bones are dislocated and whose flesh is bloodying the sand…

When the waves lick his red hooves, the chief turns round. With a powerful gesture, he hurls the cadaver away; it crashes into the pale mob, and he launches himself into the waves, which splash around him.

On the quaternary horizon, the blazing disk of the sun is declining. What does the shrill yapping of the Accursed ones matter? What does the vain whistling of their arrows matter?

With a rhythmic effort of his muscles, Klevorak, the ancestor, his eyes staring, swims toward the Occident. To the one who gave him birth, the last of the centaurs will render the life he has received.

To meet the old chief, the paternal star descends upon the waters, and, in an immense flamboyance, extends his arms of light. The entire sky is ablaze; a fiery atmosphere bathes the centaur; indescribable voices buzz in his ears; divine effluvia envelop him.

Ahead of him, to the right and the left, from the horizon to the zenith, everything is golden, everything is red, everything is light. The star fills the sky, fills the sea, takes possession of the old centaur, collects him, seizes him, and drags him down with him. The terminus of the voyage is attained.

In the universal blaze, Klevorak the Chief feels his soul dissolve. He raises his arms with a great cry, and is swallowed up in the Sun.

GULLIVER IN THE LAND OF THE VICHEBOLKS

The following pages have been presented to us as a re-production of a manuscript catalogued under the heading "Miscellaneous" in the British Museum. Are they really due to the pen of Jonathan Swift? Are we dealing with one of those hoaxes of which the history of literature contains numerous examples? The extreme prudence that is our rule compels us to reserve our judgment. The only point that seems beyond doubt is that if they are not the work of the celebrated Dean they are surely the work of one of his contemporaries. One cannot conceive, in fact, in an ulterior epoch, and in view of the progress of our civilization, that any critic, no matter how bilious he might be, would have hazarded such a bitter satire, so devoid of plausibility, at a portion of humankind.

One might have thought that the insatiable curiosity that obtained me so many singular and terrifying adventures in Lilliput, Brobdingnag, Laputa, the land of the Houyhnhnms and elsewhere would have eased with age, and that I would no longer have dreamed, after sixteen years and seven months of travels, and having gray hair, of anything but enjoying a well-earned rest in my little house in Rotherhithe.

That would underestimate the force of one of the most deeply-rooted human instincts: the atavistic attraction of nomadism, which cannot be destroyed by long centuries of sedentary life.

It is necessary to add that losses of money and the worries regarding the establishment of my children combined with that instinct to cause me to lend a favorable ear to the assurances that we given to me by a long-haul captain from Cork, with regard to the precious materials—gold, amber, furs, ivory, fossils, gemstones, etc.—which, he said, could be encountered in large quantities beyond the polar circle, among the indigenes of the icy regions of northern Europe and Asia, and which could be acquired, thanks to their ignorance, on extremely advantageous terms of trade.

This information seemed to me so precious and tempting that I did not hesitate to propose an association to Captain Sanders, and, when he had accepted the terms, to offer him command of a large schooner, which I fitted out accordingly with a few friends, and on which I embarked with him on the twelfth of March in the year 1721, in order to seek my fortune one last time.

Such were the origins of that ill-fated voyage. It has left me memories so repugnant that, added to my previous experiences, it has completed giving me such a frightful idea of human beings that I have deferred writing the narrative of it for some time. If I have resolved to do so, it is only in the hope that it might constitute a useful warning to my fellows. My sacrifice would be less painful if I thought that I might, at that price, convince my compatriots to shield themselves more effectively against the imprudences into which the love of money is capable of drawing us, and put them more carefully on their guard against chimeras as contagious as they are absurd, and liable to ensure before long, if they are rigorously pursued, the total and irremediable destruction of our civilization.

May the horrible example of the Vichebolks weaken the empire of those anxious minds who, under the pretext of obtaining an illusory improvement, limit themselves to destroying the mediocre realities with which our reason enjoins us to be content, and thus crushing us beneath an excess of afflictions, leading us so far astray as to attribute to the divinity the responsibility for miseries, three-quarters of which are due to our own folly.

The first weeks of our navigation were rendered rather perilous by encounters with giant icebergs with which the belated melting of the ice populates the ocean. It was necessary for us to seek shelter in a haven in the Lofoten islands, and it was not until the end of April that we crossed the polar circle and entered into contact with the indigenous elements.

We quickly perceived that, either because Captain Sanders had been poorly informed, or because the customs and habits of those savages had changed in twenty years, we were not gaining very much from their commerce. Not only were they rather poor, but they were very well acquainted with the value of precious metals and refused our trade gods disdainfully. When I strove to obtain a few pounds of amber from a Laplander or Eskimo chief in exchange for a little gunpowder and eau-de-vie, he said to me, ironically: "Go offer it to the Vichebolks."

The same response having been made to me several times, as our affairs were going from bad to worse, I asked Captain Sanders who these Vichebolks were, and whether there was any means of getting in touch with them. He replied to me in a anxious tone that they were barbarian tribes whose territory commenced two or three hundred miles beyond North Cape. Prey to the grossest superstition, they claimed to regulate all their actions according to the injunctions of an idol named Vietso, of which a handful of bloodthirsty priests arrogated the right to dictate the decrees. Their customs were so revolting that until now, navigators have avoided entering into relations with them.

What he told me did indeed attest to a corruption so disgusting that perhaps, if I had been the master, I would have imitated that reserve for the sake of the peace of my eternal soul. Unfortunately, between the twenty-fifth and twenty-sixth degree of east longitude, we were assailed by a frightful northwesterly tempest. In order not to be swallowed up, it was necessary for us to flee before the wind, which whipped up monstrous waves. On the third morning the sea having become calmer, we found ourselves a short distance from a low-lying coast, where the entrance to a natural harbor was discernible.

Setting a course for it, Mr. Sanders admitted to me that he suspected that we had been draw a long way eastwards, and that the harbor might be that of Koumos, which is the Vichebolk capital. In spite of the repugnance that the name inspired in me, the crew's fatigue, the damage to our ship and the dearth of water—several barrels had been smashed by the tempest—rendered it virtually indispensable to take refuge there. We therefore resolved, for better or worse, to put a brave face on it and, setting suspicions and excessive scruples aside, to make the best of the opportunity that had been presented to us. Who could tell whether Providence, gripped by pity, might not be offering us an occasion to make up our losses?

Before midday we dropped anchor in a bay well-protected by two cliffs against the bad weather of the open sea, and I scanned the mass of buildings, crumbling ramparts and half-ruined palaces that constituted the city with my telescope. After a few moments, a canoe manned by four rowers set off from the bank and came toward our ship. I noticed with compassion the wretched aspect of the aborigines, emaciated and half-naked beneath rags held together by a few threads. One of them, who seemed to be their leader, was sitting in the stern. By means of a megaphone, I invited him in several languages to come aboard.

I was uncertain at first whether he had heard me, but after having studied us for some time, he gave an order to his slaves, who came alongside; he jumped toward a rope-ladder that we threw down to him, clung on to it, climbed it and emerged on to the deck a few minutes later.

The fellow's clothing was a bizarre mixture of precious furs, rags and embroideries, but his attitude immediately revealed as much baseness as arrogance.

We soon succeeded in understanding one another. Although the Vichebolk nation as a whole only speaks an Asiatic jargon completely unintelligible to Europeans, the priests of Vietso, doubtless with the objective of better concealing their deliberations, willingly make use of Occidental idioms. It was, therefore, in reasonably correct English, in an arrogant tone that was belied by the anxiety of his shifty gaze, that their delegate questioned me about the purpose of our voyage.

I told him, in a civil tone, that, constrained by the tempest to land in the glorious country of the Vichebolks in order to make a few repairs, I would be glad to take advantage of the opportunity to engage in commerce with them—and I listed the goods that my ship contained, with which I was in a position to furnish them in exchange for local products.

Sinnekar—such was, I subsequently learned, the name of my interlocutor—replied to me, sniffing, that according to their laws, everything that my ship contained had belonged to Vietso from the moment that it had penetrated into their waters, but that, for humanity's sake—he looked sideways at my carronades, whose covers I had deliberately removed—the priests of the god might perhaps deign to reach some accommodation with us. In any case, it was indispensable that I should go with him, immediately, to the Linkrem in order to obtain their orders.

I told him that I would gladly go, under his safeguard, accompanied by twenty well-armed sailors and Mr. Sanders. At the same time, loudly enough for him to hear me, I instructed the first mate to open fire on the city if I had not returned by eight o'clock.

With a few strokes of the paddles, we reached land. Apart from the villages of certain cannibal populations of Africa, I have never seen anything as wretched as that miserable city, which, however, so travelers say and as can still be judged by its remains, had enjoyed, prior to the introduction of the cult of Vietso, a measure of prosperity, and even of splendor.

We traversed a series of dirty and tumbledown streets bordered by hovels filthier than Irish pig-sties among which the debris of sumptuous buildings rose up in places. A ragged crowd contemplated us with even more bewilderment than curiosity, and fled in terror as we passed, driven back by the whiplashes of a dozen militiamen with yellow faces and slanting eyes who served us as bodyguards.

When I expressed to my guide my pity at the feverish aspect and emaciation of these poor people and asked him whether the population had not been ravaged by some epidemic, he replied with an air of satisfaction that what I saw was the result of the magnificent constitution of the country, and challenged me to find a single person in all of Koumos—except for the priests of Vietso and their servants, who carefully maintained their vigor in order that no surprise attack might overturn the regime—who had an ounce of fat on his bones.

After having waded through mire and loose stones for three-quarters of an hour, we finally reach the seat of Vietso—which is to say, a kind of castle, fortified and barricaded, guarded by soldiers who were armed to the teeth, whose uniforms were in tatters and whose faces, like those of our escort, attested an Asiatic origin.

After having made us wander for ten minutes through corridors whose floor-tiles gleamed and empty, dilapidated rooms full of filth, into which the glacial wing penetrated through broken window-panes, we arrived in a flagstoned antechamber where my guide invited me to wait with my men, from whom I had refused to be separated.

After an hour, as I was reflecting that I might have been imprudent enough to let myself be drawn into a trap, and was mediating mentally as to how dearly I would sell my life, he reappeared and informed me that the priests of Vietso would do me the honor of receiving me.

Not without commending my soul to God and recommending Mr. Sanders to be ready for any eventuality, I followed my guide and soon penetrated into a room that had the appearance of a courtroom.

A dozen individuals clad in sumptuous robes were sprawled there in heavy armchairs with faded gilding. One of them, whose bright-eyed face was ornamented by a long beard that came down to his navel, was somewhat reminiscent of the prophets of Israel as depicted in my old Dutch Bible. He was the high priest, and I subsequently discovered that his name was Stoitol. He looked at me intently, with an imposing expression, and invited me in good English to acquaint him with the purpose of my visit.

Briefly, I repeated the explanations I had given Sinnekar, to which he listened attentively, not without exchanging a few smiles and winks of intelligence and commiseration with his colleagues.

When I fell silent he proffered, in a condescending tone: "Friend! Appreciate your good fortune. You set out with the aim of acquiring a few mediocre and perishable baubles, but you have reached the bosom of virtue and felicity. Know that henceforth, you are liberated from the bonds of egotism and property under which the rest of the world groans. All that Vietso possesses is yours."

I was charmed to find that amiability in the old madman, and replied that I did not ask for so much, but would be content with authorization to sell my trade goods at a low price to the population—which, to judge by what I had seen, would welcome them.

A general burst of laughter greeted me. When it died down, a kind of bulldog with bloodshot eyes, named Skytrot, informed me brutally that, from now on, as Sinnekar had informed me, everything that my ship contained belonged to Vietso, whose priests would take responsibility for dividing it up in the best interests of everyone, and that I had to give orders accordingly when I went back aboard.

I manifested my amazement at this procedure forcefully, and asked what would happen if I refused to allow myself to be robbed.

The entire tribunal began growling in the manner of hungry dogs seen fighting over a bone. Like a baying mastiff, Skytrot howled: "You will be tortured and put to death, as all the corrupt individuals have been who have attempted to resist the orders of Vietso and shield the aberrations of vice against the reign of his wisdom."

And, yapping in chorus for a good quarter of a hour, all the members of the tribunal, trying to outdo one another—thus I discovered immediately what my experience confirmed, that loquacity is the essential virtue of the Vichebolks— explained to me that, a few years before, their glorious country had been almost as badly governed as the nations of the Occident, by a tyrant assisted by a criminal aristocracy. The fortunate revelation of Vietso had put an end to that intolerable system and established equality for all: no one any longer possessing anything, had anything to envy anyone else. Thus, all the evils that had previously never ceased to divide people had been extirpated at a stroke.

When I was able to get a word in, I declared firmly that, in my quality as an Englishman, I had no wish to judge the constitutions of other peoples, and that, although this one appeared utterly wretched to me, it might be that the regime of Vietso was excellent for them, but that, being English, it was of no relevance to me; that, my cargo being mine, I only intend to be dispossessed of it at a good price; that, if anyone wanted to rob me it would cost the aggressors dear; and that, if we were massacred, England would be able to avenge us.

And, leaving my interlocutors astonished by the violence of my language—I had already remarked in the presence of certain kaffir kings that threat is the only kind of reasoning that is accessible to the barbarian mentality—I walked out, with so resolute a step that no one dared to stop me, rejoined my men in the antechamber, left the palace and returned to me ship without experiencing any other inconvenience than being escorted by a ragged and verminous mob, whose howling sometimes seemed to indicated mendacity and sometimes the temptation to fall upon us and rip us to pieces.

The very next day I gave the order to put to take on water and to begin the repairs, determined not to prolong that uncomfortable and certainly perilous sojourn.

Under the guard of ten well-armed men, we established a workshop on the shore, where the carpenters set to work. After a short time, all the wood of which we had need was brought to us, in exchange for a few handfuls of flour, by unfortunate starvelings who then spent the rest of the day watching us in amazement while twiddling their thumbs.

Forty-eight hours after my reception by the Vietso, I saw Sinnekar returning, accompanied by one of his colleagues, whose ferrety face I had noticed during my visit, and whose name was Innelen.

They explained to me that, thanks to their representations, Stoitol, who was the high priest, had refused Skytrot authorization to massacre us, but they begged me not to prolong a deplorable resistance.

I replied that, being English, I would defend my property to the end, and would not surrender it unless I were paid.

And as they spouted more effusively their sermons on the horror of property and the vanity of money, I became angry and demanded whether they took me for a fool. Did they think that I had not noticed that they were as fat and glittering as the rest of the population was fleshless and feverish, and that I had not understood that the great miracle of Vietso really consisted of having reduced a host of unfortunates to such indigence of strength and intelligence that they were so degraded as to allow themselves meekly to be exploited by a gang living on their misery like mushrooms on the decomposition of other plants.

They replied hotly that I did not understand anything; that the people were happy; that, if I failed to recognize the merits of Vietso, the fault was in the veils that prejudice had thrown over my intelligence; that, furthermore, no one had any desire to use violence on my person; that, if they had any money to offer in exchange for my trade goods, they would do so with pleasure, but that it was a long time since those vile metals had disappeared from Koumos, and that, as all industry had been obliterated in the country since it was no longer in anyone's personal interest to work, there was nothing to offer me to satisfy my rapacity.

I replied that I had obtained information, and that I was ready to deliver the whole of my cargo to the Vietso if they would simply give me in exchange the treasure of the former tyrants, preserved in the principal tower of the old fortress.

Innelen and Sinnekar protested forcefully that that was impossible; those gemstones belonged to the Vietso and were, in consequence, inalienable.

To which I replied that I did not give a hoot, but would not release so much as a nail unless I were paid.

And we went our separate ways, very annoyed.

So opposed were our pretentions, my conversations with those cunning individuals could only be repeated while we carried out our work. I must say that I pressed forward with the utmost energy, less because of the apprehension I had of an attack as because of the extreme malaise caused by the spectacle of which I was witness.

Let the reader understand me! I was, perhaps, somewhat less revolted by the rascality of the clique that had usurped power than sickened by the condition of stupidity into which the mass of the citizens had fallen. It is, in fact, true, monstrous as the thing had appeared to me at first, that the unfortunate people, as much because of the laxity of their temperament as the weakness to which famine and disease had reduced them, had arrived at the stage of allowing themselves passively to be guided by whiplashes, shorn and slaughtered like a flock of sheep. Only a few savage acts of violence, at intervals, marked a surge of despair. Wilted by the declamations of Stoitol, they were ferociously repressed by Skytrot and his Asiatics, acclaimed in cowardly fashion by the host of their slaves.

The disgust induced in me by such a humiliating abasement of human nature even surpassed the indignation that I felt in my quality as a merchant, in seeing the enormous natural resources of the country unutilized.

Fortunately, I had a secret hope that I was not entirely wasting my efforts.

One evening, when I was comforting myself with a good bottle and limiting myself to responding to their reiterated threats that I would be raising anchor in three days' time, Innelen and Sinnekar—they were, as I have said, the two most cunning members of the gang—ended up confessing to me, in lowered voices, that, although it was impossible to dispossess the Vietso of its treasure officially, Innelen, who was in charge of it, might perhaps find the means to remove a part of it in order to buy my cargo, which consisted of foodstuffs of which even the priests of the Vietso themselves were beginning to feel a most pressing need.

You might perhaps be surprised that I did not refuse point blank to become the accomplice of what was obviously nothing but a crime—to which I will reply that it would be very difficult to do business if one were overly delicate. On the other hand, as the regime of the Vietso itself did not appear to me to be anything other than the most scandalous of crimes inflicted on a wretched people deprived of its rights, I persuaded myself that there was a kind of morality in robbing it.

We therefore moved closer together and, with our elbows on the table, I ended up coming to an agreement with Sinnekar that I would surrender my cargo in exchange for his brining me gems to the approximate value of a hundred thousand pounds sterling. You might perhaps think that sum excessive for merchandise that had only cost me eight thousand, but it is necessary to point out that we do the same with negroes, who are worth less than Vichebolks; that the risks of the enterprise were considerable; and that, in any case, as long as they remained in the hands of those imbeciles, all the jewels of Golconda would not be worth a farthing.

Having thus agreed terms, Sinnekar and Innelen invited me to begin disembarking my crates and barrels right away. I replied that I would not do that until I had been paid. They protested. I pointed out the difference that there was between their word and mine, and repeated that everything would stay on board until I had the gems in my hands. Moreover, my repairs being almost finished, I would doubtless be raising anchor in forty-eight hours, resolved to clear a passage with cannon fire if anyone tried to stop me.

The two fellows went away grumbling, but they came back the next day, after nightfall and presented themselves on deck each carrying a package under his arm. There emerged therefrom a profusion of jewels and precious objects: rings, bracelets, necklaces, watches and snuff-boxes, in barbaric taste but rich in gold. I estimated their value to be at least a hundred thousand pounds—and, indeed, on returning to London, got even more for them.

Having locked those trinkets in a safe place, I immediately gave orders for the cargo to be unloaded on to the dock. The worked was carried out without interruption for twenty-four hours. The entire population uttered cries of enthusiasm on seeing barrels of wine and spirits disembarked, along with the sacks of rice and sugar, hams and vegetables that formed the greater part of it, but they were held back by the Chinese guards with whips and clubs. Naturally, the rumor had spread that I had ended up giving in to the Vietso's threats, and although I felt some humiliation in thus confirming the unfortunate horde in its superstition, I judged it imprudent to offer any contradiction.

So sickened was I, however, and so distrustful of those brigands and victims of delusion, that scarcely had my last hogshead been unloaded, instead of filling my ship with the precious timber that was abundant and waiting until the next day to set sail, as I had promised Sinnekar, I took advantage of the brightness of the night—in those latitudes once can see daylight in the middle of the night—and raised anchor; by sunrise I was out of sight of the coast.

Although I have brought back from that expedition a certain opulence, it has left me with an inexpressible malaise. I had not previously thought that our species could descend to such a degree. I feel that having seen it in that state of degradation will cause me sadness until my dying day. The notion that I have of humankind has been diminished and dishonored by it. The idea that the people in question were once like others upsets me. For the first time, the fragility of our civilization and its pretended conquests has become apparent to me. I can no longer defend myself from the idea against which I previously rebelled: knowing that the filthy Yahoos so justly scorned by the noble Houyhnhnms had once been human. The regime of the Vietso is doubtless the transition that brought them from our species to bestiality.

My horror was further increased by the fact that I perceived, during our return journey, that several of my sailors had been subject to the contagion of the condition of insanity in which the unfortunates lived among whom we had just spent a few weeks. I was warned by the boatswain that a dozen of them had formed a conspiracy to proclaim the worship of the Vietso, throw me into the sea with the captain and take possession of the ship and all its contents.

I assembled the sailors on deck the next day and informed them that I had learned that a mutiny was in preparation. I had no doubt that my amicable warning would be sufficient to remind reasonable man of their duty, but that it was only just that the ringleaders should be punished. Drawing my pistols, I blew out the brains of Watson and Murray, who were the two worst offenders.

That firm action did not raise any protest, and I have no doubt that it was with great relief that the rest of the crew returned to obedience. It is very probable that if, in a few years time, the sovereign of those hyperborean regions had shown an analogous decisiveness, the ignoble worship of the Vietso would not have developed, and that a significant portion of humankind would not have fallen back into barbarity.

In any case, this example ought to prove to us that there is no doctrine, no matter how absurd or baleful it might be, that is not capable of winning minds by contagion. It ought to constitute a salutary warning for us.

As my life reaches its end, having definitely terminated my adventures, I shall dare, by way of conclusion, to put my compatriots on guard against the perilous temptations in which an immoderate love of lucre risks steeping them. It is better to renounce some profits than to become, under the pretext of gaining a few pounds, the propagators of follies that are capable of ruining our civilization completely—and if, by virtue of imprudence, they happen to open the door to the contagion, let John Bull remember that the cat-o'nine-tails is the best quinine against that malign fever, the most dangerous from which humankind has suffered since the days of the year one thousand and the Black Death.

MR. CUFFYCOAT'S CURIOUS ADVENTURE

On Sunday the twenty-eighth of June 1914, as was his habit, Mr. Cuffycoat, having informed his housekeeper that he would be dining at his club, slipped into his smoking-jacket and, before going out, studied himself one last time in his wardrobe mirror.

The sight of his round face, his colorful cheeks, his blue, slightly protruding eyes and his entire solid and upright person had not been a surprise to him for quite a long time. It never failed to procure him a comfortable sensation—comfortable rather than esthetic, strictly speaking. The age of fifty had softened his features and marked his flesh with red blotches. Two warts, one of which bore a spiky tuft of hair, were tending toward a ridiculous enlargement. One of his incisors, recently chipped, caused an asymmetrical gap in his jaw, which irritated him. He noticed, moreover, that his shirt, poorly ironed, had a crease, and would have to be changed, even at the inconvenience of undressing. As for the smoking-jacket, although he was not a slave to any excessive snobbery, it would surely be opportune to replace it in the autumn. He similarly postponed a visit to the dentist until the same epoch.

All things considered, he was no more displeasing than the average gentleman of his age in possession of an annual income between a thousand and fifteen hundred pounds and living in South Kensington. One might even say that he resembled the majority of them in an incontestable fashion. As everyone knows, fauna adapt to the conditions of the environment in which they live. The chameleon takes on the color of the foliage that shelters it, and the neck of the giraffe is elongated exactly as much as is required to browse the fresh shoots of tall trees. Mr. Cuffycoat presented a completely satisfactory specimen of the human variety that, in the bosom of family hotels, taxis and tube trains, has ended up distinguishing itself in several notable characteristics from cave-dwellers.

To tell the truth, though, it was not exactly his physical personality that Mr. Cuffycoat was weighing up, as a disciple of Phidias or George Brummell might have done. Even though Jemima Barnet, and several other young women having today attained a rich maturity, would once gladly have placed their delicate hand in his for life, he obtained no vanity from that. That was merely the cupboard, the correctly-fashioned chest of drawers, no more, in which a soul dwelt.

Or, rather than a soul—there are too many thorny misapprehensions attached to the meaning of that term—I propose to say to you: a spiritual essence. And there again, at the risk of prolonging this introduction, I am obliged to persist. It would be inexact to think that Mr. Cuffycoat disposed on intellectual gifts or moral quantities of an extreme refinement. You might have consulted the list of his social and philosophical works at the British Museum, and even opened some of them. They do not surpass in any way the average of those sold at Tooth & Sons. As for the delicacy of his conscience, I am convinced that if he refused the preference shares that he was offered by that rogue Percy Lyon for the launch of Vaseline Mines, it was less because it was fraudulent than because the fraud in question seemed to him to be too gross not to end in criminal proceedings.

All that, I am aware, does not sufficiently distinguish Mr. Cuffycoat from many other gentlemen who frequent the second-rate restaurants of Piccadilly, and I would not have thought of making him the hero of this tale if he had not imposed himself on public attention by a more characteristic shibboleth.

It is appropriate—I have no doubt that you will agree with me—to credit everyone with the gifts that belong to him. It is a absurd pettiness to contest them. I would never deny that Lady Nashburn has asthma, the third-ranked pearl necklace in the realm and very solid religious principles. Mr. Doomberry—James Doomberry, the one who lives in

Montpensier Street—is an exceptional conchyliologist. Among all the regulars at Turtle's Bar, Jack Hitcphin is the foremost in deciphering the puzzles in the weekly papers and David Robertson in the game of draughts.

Mr. Cuffycoat's specialty is of a much higher order. You are not unaware of the degree to which many people—distinguished minds such as Marcus Aurelius, Pascal, William James, John Stuart Mill and many others—have been haunted by all the philosophical, sociological and political problems that never cease to occupy the most prominent place, after the advertisements, in the columns of the newspapers. Hence, endless discussions, enormous volumes. headaches, troubled digestions. Mr. Cuffycoat has had the rare merit of cutting short all those divagations on that dangerous terrain.

Of that ensemble of questions he has made two categories. There are those that can only preoccupy neurasthenics. Those, as they emerge from Cambridge. he has locked in a drawer, throwing the key into the Thames from the middle of London Bridge. That way, he is sure of no longer hearing any mention of them. Then there are those that it is appropriate for a gentleman in Mr. Cuffycoat's position to talk about at a dinner party or in the pages of the *Athenaeum*. With regard to those, Mr. Cuffycoat has the good fortune to possess the truth. In the same epoch, armed with a hook, he has carefully made his choice from all the stock that his masters had accumulated in him during his schooldays, and having eliminated everything that was not of the finest quality, he has verified, weighed, labeled and catalogued all the rest, and has arranged them admirably within the cupboard or chest of drawers that his mirror presents to him when he looks into it. He can give his word, as a gentleman, that he has undertaken that operation with minute care; thus, all the scoria, all the false semblances and all the dubious items having been set aside, he has at the disposal of his contemporaries the complete arsenal of Truths desirable in a well-made intelligence.

Although the list is not as long as you might think, I shall not try to enumerate its items for you, but I shall give you the

Ariadne's thread that will permit you to navigate through the furniture, if you are curious to do so.

In substance, this is the nub: Providence—a pseudonym whose secret is in the drawer whose key has been lost at London Bridge—has arranged everything in this world for the happiness of humankind. Undoubtedly, there have been a few misunderstandings between them, the importance of which universal history has grossly magnified. They have been diminishing incessantly, and, for two centuries, it has been possible to affirm that everything is settled to a remarkable degree. In the last fifty years, particularly, the pace of progress has been so vertiginous that it has been able to surprise minds less alert than Mr. Cuffycoat's. Having the good fortune to possess the Truth, however, he had recorded all of that as a perfectly normal receipt.

Science, by means of its new discoveries, incessantly augments the means of human enjoyment, and brings about a parallel amelioration. A host of statistics offers peremptory proof of the daily increase in its conquests; look at those concerning potatoes, pigs and longevity. Those that have the appearance of contradicting the others—the increases in alcoholism, criminality, etc.—are of absolutely no significance, as I could easily demonstrate to you if we had the time. The Truth—with a capital T—that Mr. Cuffycoat has solidly installed in his cupboard is that within every State, increasingly fortunate citizens are entering into increasingly satisfactory relations, and in the same way, States are in the process of substituting for the anarchic rivalries of old the pacific settlement of their disputes, while waiting for humankind as a whole to form a single reconciled family in which the entire world will eat breakfast, play football, do a little work, constitute stocks and embrace one another at the same times of day.

It is a great fortune for a nation to possess citizens like Mr. Cuffycoat. It is necessary to recognize that the deposits of wisdom that he contains are not yet as extensively exploited as the coal-mines of Yorkshire or American oil-wells, but already, its rich alluvia are flowing through the liberal and conservative press and between the lips of Statesmen. It will not take long for the entire country to satisfy its spiritual needs therewith as generally as it butters its toast and takes a bath.

If it were reasonable to attach himself to such futile impressions, Mr. Cuffycoat, in the radiant peace of the summer evening, would experience a surfeit of satisfaction in possessing such vast reserves of Truth to provision all the clientele that comes knocking at the door of the cupboard. A master trader, he only draws for his security a more kindly indulgence for the enervation that is manifest, on his arrival in the smoking-room, by Phil Norwood and Jack Clinton, who are mixing their whisky with a dose of the evening newspapers. It appears that some sort of Archduke has been assassinated somewhere in the Balkans. They anticipate on the basis of this repugnant news item the darkest of European tragedies.

It is sufficient for Mr. Cuffycoat to open the cupboard discreetly and extract a few pinches of Truth therefrom to do justice to that nonsense. The error of Norwood and Clinton is to view the twentieth century through the lens of the age of cave-dwellers or the Hundred Years War. Even assuming that Austria and Serbia conserve a few tiresome atavistic survivals, the great powers are there, on the alert. Peaceful Germany— see Lord Haldane—is there to retain its ally by the sleeve. If France exhibits a residue of nervousness, we have the *Daily News*.

A broad smile cleaves Mr. Cuffycoat's mouth. "Don't worry about it!"

And that evening, at bridge, docile fortune, multiplying honors in his strong hands, ratifies his anticipations and counter-arguments with particular docility.

The World War was not only for Mr. Cuffycoat, as for you and me, the occasion for much private anguish and preoccupations of a general nature. It caused him an appreciable intellectual contrariety.

Naturally, you cannot imagine for an instant, whatever its repercussions might have been, that it had disturbed Mr.

Cuffycoat to the point of attempting a vain search to find the key thrown in the Thames from London Bridge, or revising the contents of his cupboard. The Truth has the property that, unlike fish and hollyhocks, it can be preserved indefinitely without there being any need to touch it. A fire-damp explosion costs the lives of two hundred miners; it is a regrettable accident for their families and for the Company, because of matters of pensions and compensation, but it does not devalue the gift that Nature has made to human beings in putting coal at their disposal. The World War is a disagreeable news item. It is as ineffective against the Truth as against universal gravitation. The shock that it has caused so many superficial minds is an opportunity to affirm more energetically in the face of their neurasthenia the principles of the eternal order.

Nevertheless, the best-informed moralists recommend the avoidance not only of sin but of the temptations that clear its path. You might well have enclosed the Truth in a solidly-built cupboard, but beware of woodworm and burglars who might force the lock. Mr. Cuffycoat could not be in doubt that, however imperceptible that European scuffle was from a cosmic viewpoint, and however secondary it appeared from a genuinely philosophical viewpoint, it nevertheless projected into the atmosphere of everyday life all sorts of microbes, complications and annoyances. It filled the newspapers with its news, the streets with its posters, and conversations with its din. It intervened in private life in the form of difficulties with food-supplies and vexatious regulations. It lay in wait for Mr. Cuffycoat at his club. It assailed him in his domestic hearth with neither truce nor repose, from the day when the son of Mrs. Bartle, his housekeeper, was sent to the Flanders front. The first zeppelin raids on London rendered its splatterings even noisier.

The government made every effort to protect the principal public establishments, the banks and the armaments factories, but the Truth is a product far more precious than administrative papers, leases and shells. Mr. Cuffycoat did not hide from himself for an instant, therefore, that the moment was particularly opportune to undertake a long-planned voyage to Australia. Thus, he would shelter the treasure of which he was the depositary from any unhealthy contact. At the same time, he could complete his research on the customs of primitive peoples, and, associating himself with the patriotic efforts of his countrymen, reassure the populations of Melbourne and Sydney by means of a few lectures with regard to the phases of a worldly accident that was doubtless regrettable, but the importance of which it was necessary not to exaggerate.

Therefore, having instructed Mrs. Bartle to air his apartment for two hours every morning, and informing Norwood and Clinton that he would be absent for a couple of months, he went to Liverpool to embark on the Cunard Company steamer *Merry Mary*, departing for Adelaide.

The first days of the journey were favored by exceedingly fine weather, and the Mediterranean crossing, accomplished in the best possible conditions, permitted Mr. Cuffycoat to ascertain the extent to which the disasters of submarine piracy had been exaggerated by Lord Northcliffe's newspapers. In the Red Sea, he saw several dugongs and a large number of troop-ships. The Indian Ocean did not give rise to any observation on his part worthy of being recorded. At that distance, events in little Europe appeared in their veritable perspective, and he made it his duty to deliver a commentary on it to his neighbors at table, a Scottish lady with and angular profile, who was going to distribute Bibles and trousers to the natives of the islands, and an obese Dutch lady covered in jewels, who was rejoining her husband in various plantations of species, rice and sugar cane, whose value had been multiplied tenfold by the war.

It was probably a hundred miles or so from the northwestern coast of New Guinea that one of those contingencies intervened that are completely imperceptible from Sirius but the multiplication of which, since August 1914, has significantly increased charter fees and the cost of maritime insurance. In spite of the administrative investigation of which it was the object, the loss of the *Merry Mary* with all hands and cargo has never been fully explained, but it appears incontestable, in view of the fine weather, the absence of any reefs in that region and the on-board prohibition of spirits, that it must be attributed to Boche malfeasance. Either a submarine had succeeded, thanks to criminal complicity, in prolonging its depredations even in those distant seas, until the day when it was definitively sunk, or, more probably, the steamer had encountered a badly-secured mine of a kind forbidden by international treaties but mass-produced in large quantities in the factories of Wilhelmshaven.

The fact is that, forty-five second later, everything went to the bottom...and like the crew and the rest of the passengers, Mr. Cuffycoat would have concluded his earthly career in that deplorable, but ultimately minor, incident, if he had not chanced, on emerging from the turbulent waters, to perceive an empty chicken cage floating alongside him. He clung on to it with his last reserves of strength and had just recovered his breath when, similarly rising up from the abyss in her turn, the adipose Dutchwoman, stuck a completely bald and repugnant head out of the water, and nearly spoiled everything by trying to climb on to the apparatus as well. It was obviously too frail for two people, and there was no comparison whatsoever between the value of that old lady and the cupboard confided to Mr. Cuffycoat. He therefore delivered a vigorous swing of his fist to the lunar face, which disappeared, and remained bobbing on the waves for hours—long enough for him to lose consciousness completely.

When he recovered his senses he was lying on a beach strewn with fragments of coral, seashells and wreckage, on the edge of which were verdant clumps of mangroves.

A few moments were sufficient for him to take account of the fact that half his body was grievously scratched, that there was blood on his forehead, and that his worldly possessions were limited to his waistcoat, his shirt, torn trousers, two socks and one badly-damaged shoe. In his pocket he had a purse containing twenty shillings, and, thanks to a rubber envelope, his wallet, containing his check book, documents and a few banknotes, was intact. No inn seeming to be close by, Mr. Cuffycoat had to admit that this fiduciary equipment would not procure the same commodities as in the Strand or Oxford Street; and, as he was dying of hunger, disdaining the advice of Dr. Turveymoon, who had advised him formally to avoid crustaceans, he set off in pursuit of crabs, and cracked a good dozen of them between his teeth.

Thus restored, the situation appeared to him in its true light. Without his being exempt from trivial inconveniences, he had an exceptional opportunity to abstract himself from the annoying contingencies that were momentarily obscuring the European firmament, and supplementing the Truth with a host of precious and original observations. No doubt the commerce of the innocent peoples inhabiting this region would reconstitute a link in the invisible but certain chain linking the Golden Age of antiquity, anterior to history but discovered by Rousseau and Aphra Behn,[8] to that of the future, as yet obscured by a few wisps of mist.

Evidently, the vicinity of a grocery and a confectioner's shop would have assisted Mr. Cuffycoat more rapidly to refurbish the cupboard of which he had custody, but heat rendered a simplification of wardrobe tolerable, without any great inconvenience. With some bark and a few lianas, Mr. Cuffycoat improvised a second shoe, and an excellent had capable of warding off sunstroke. After a few days, with his temporal and spiritual reserves duly reestablished and polished, he set forth.

By the racket of roars that rose up in the nearby forest as soon as darkness fell, he judged it preferable not to plunge into it and to content himself with following the coast, sustaining

---

[8] Mrs. Aphra Behn's *Oroonoko; or, The Royal Slave* (1688) is the first text discussed in Lichtenberger's study of utopian socialism. The novel's narrator opens the story with a description of the alleged Golden Age in which the simple indigenes of Surinam are allegedly dwelling—or were, before slavers and colonists arrived.

his strength with oysters, crabs, coconuts—which he found much inferior to their reputation—and seabirds brought down by thrown stones, which reeked frightfully of lamp-oil. Although it would have been more agreeable to see the silhouette of a small hotel or the humblest vending machine, he was pleasantly distracted by the spectacle of several flying squirrels, and noticed with pleasure, unfortunately out of range, a herd of kangaroos.

On the third day, Mr. Cuffycoat went to sleep, as usual, exhausted by fatigue. In the early hours, he dreamed that, at table at the club with Norwood, he served him a few slices of Truth, appropriately seasoned, for which Norwood thanked him by seizing him, as was his habit, by the button of his jacket. Instead of letting him go, however, the sympathetic gentleman's finger dug into his side in an increasingly irritating fashion—to the extent that Mr. Cuffycoat ended up struggling desperately until the moment when he woke up and perceived the flint point of some sort of harpoon on his breast, from whose tip his gaze rose beyond the black fist that held it to envisage the grimacing face of the most abominable Guy Fawkes that the most convinced anti-papist had ever been capable of imagining.

Mr. Cuffycoat hastened to address his best smile to this visitor and a few cordial words of welcome, while a number of his fellows gathered around him, prancing around with horrible capers and sinister howls.

For want of knowing the local language, Mr. Cuffycoat could not follow very exactly the discussion that began, but it was evident that he played an important role therein. A venerable elder who would have delighted maids and babies in the central cage in the Zoo came to examine him with particular attention. When, eventually, he acquired a better understanding of the local folklore, he understood that it had been very much a question of eating him, and that only his thinness and the unusual color of his skin, which gave rise to the fear that he would be difficult to digest, had spared him that form of burial.

They contented themselves with tying his hands behind his back and imprisoning his neck in a fork whose two points were drawn together by a bit beneath his chin. A frightful negro child took hold of the shaft and rained blows upon him every time he attempted to pause in order to get his breath back. It was thus that he was led to the nearby indigenous village, where the women greeted him with a chorus of howls that reminded him unmistakably of a suffragette meeting in Whitechapel.

The life that Mr. Cuffycoat was forced to lead furnished him with a fine opportunity to testify to the degree to which a free thought is capable of raising itself above the perishable rag to which it is attached. If the Truth of which he had taken delivery a quarter of a century earlier had been less thoroughly verified and endorsed, there is no doubt that it would have run a grave risk of stumbling in the course of the adventure.

In fact, the role of the ladies of the country being to serve their husbands as beasts of burden, his own was effectively that of a beast of burden at the disposal of other beasts of burden. With blows from fingernails, teeth and clubs, he was instructed in the arts of pounding grain, skinning game and watching the roasting-spit.

In that capacity, one of the most painful tasks that had been confided to him was that of supervising the cooking of two old men, who formed the main course of a kind of Christmas dinner, the character of which was both religious and exquisitely gastronomic.

Certainly, the fine works of Sir John Lubbock and a few other sociologists had prepared him not to take exception in a puerile fashion to certain customs whose singularity only disconcerts us for want of adequate reflection. Anthropophagy has, as its first principle, a praiseworthy spirit of economy; nothing is as culpable as wasting food. In the second place, it proceeds from a spirit of veneration for our ancestors; what more honorable tomb could be offered to them than the bellies

213

of their posterity? Thirdly, it is beyond doubt that it tends to satisfy an instinct analogous to that of our academic appetite. Having no books to devour in the equatorial region, because of the rudimentary state of printing in that latitude, one assimilates what ought to be therein by preferentially eating the brains of those presumed to be capable of writing them.

Plausible as the philosophical substratum of that doctrine might be, however, it shocked prejudices in Mr. Cuffycoat so deeply anchored that he found a veritable relief in the fact that his humble status prevented him from taking part in the feast. That relief was not such, however, that he did not feel that he had the right to take the first available opportunity to break a contract that, in truth, he had not signed.

By virtue of all the blows, his back was nothing but a single wound, like the spines of donkeys in Arab lands. He was fed in an ignoble manner, with the offal of prey and rotten fish. Glances of which he was the object on the part of two frightful Megaeras gave him glimpses of new perils, of which the example of Joseph shunning the flirtation of Potiphar's wife demonstrated the imperious duty. He did not, therefore, believe himself to be failing in any delicacy one evening when the entire tribe was drunk on palm-wine in freeing himself by filing through his shackles with a trenchant sea-shell, and, having got rid of his fork, making off as rapidly as his legs would carry him.

Having run all night and a part of the morning, without any sign indicating to him that he was being pursued, he conjectured that his hosts had reconciled themselves to his taking "French leave." Spotting a pretty little inlet between the coral reefs where a little stream flowed, he allowed himself to collapse on the edge of a coconut grove and, after having swallowed two or three rancid mouthfuls, went to sleep, exhausted by fatigue.

When Mr. Cuffycoat woke up the sun was already low on the horizon. Suddenly, he had the idea of ending the day by bathing, which would relax his bloody feet and soothe his bruised back. It was, in any case, the time of year when he had the custom of devoting himself to that sport at Brighton, or on one of the beaches of northern France.

He therefore went down to the edge of the sea and was getting ready to take off his rags when an unexpected apparition caused him genuine amazement and caused a supplementary redness to rise to his sunburned cheeks.

In the very edge of the waves, nonchalantly lying on the sand, was a lady whose face, quite pleasant, suggested an age of about forty. Although clad in a rather outmoded manner—it was twenty years since those bell-skirts had been the height of fashion—she was not without some pretention to elegance. Leaning on her elbow, she seemed to be fishing in a box of chocolates with ivory tweezers, although Mr. Cuffycoat determined subsequently that she was merely tickling a holothurian with a shark-bone.

Mr. Cuffycoat had received an excellent education. He was cruelly conscious of the fact that his appearance was insufficiently decent for an introduction. Innocent of any contact with a comb, a brush or soap for more than three months, burned by the sun, covered in wounds and dirt, he must offer a frightful sight. Besides, the far-from-abundant garments that the shipwreck had left him had suffered the cruelest simplifications since. The truth is that they were reduced to such a minimum that there was hardly anything worth mentioning. How gladly he would have given all the bills in his wallet for a forty-five shilling suit!

In spite of these painful circumstances, he told himself insistently that, in these regions, the first duty of a gentleman was to put himself at the disposal of that lady. So, coughing lightly and bowing decorously, he took two steps forward and expressed the pleasure that he would experience if he might in some way be useful to a lady of standing. At the same time, he excused himself immediately for the incorrectness of his attire. It was very difficult in that latitude to procure the slightest thing...but if, by chance, it were possible to give him an address...

The lady must have been accustomed to traveling, and possessed of considerable self-control. She did not manifest any disapproval of her interlocutor's wardrobe and even gave evidence of more curiosity than amazement at his appearance. She replied to him immediately in very correct English—she had hardly a trace of a foreign accent—that she was very touched. Certainly there were few resources here. It was a significant stroke of luck to encounter a man of the world. Furthermore, had she not already had the pleasure...?

That was precisely what Mr. Cuffycoat was in the process of asking himself. That accent, that face, even that costume, obsolete but not devoid of pretentions, reawakened distant memories in him...

A movement on the lady's part enlightened him. While adjusting her skirt she had just uncovered, instead of feet, a tail: a tail of a very pretty model, with a hint of the mackerel about it, in sparkling colors...but, all in all, a tail...

Mr. Cuffycoat uttered an exclamation. Abruptly, he remembered a season near Folkestone when he had encountered, in the house of his friends the Buntings, that singular individual unexpectedly sprung from the sea, around which there was a mystery that was so piquant, and which had turned poor Charteris' head so terribly.

He bowed again. "Miss Waters," he said, "please excuse me if, at first, I didn't recognize you. The unexpectedness of the encounter...Cuffycoat, the friend of the worthy Buntings...at Sandgate Castle...[9]

Miss Waters smiled graciously and blushed slightly. Mr. Cuffycoat was really too kind. Alas, in twenty years, a woman changes a great deal...

"Besides which, I must look a perfect fright. One tries to keep up to date. Your fashion magazines, when, by chance, a shipwreck procures some of them for us, arrive so badly damaged by damp, fish, lobsters, and all the rest...and our couturiers, you know...always demands, strikes, broken promises..."

---

[9] Author's note: "See H. G. Wells, *The Sea Lady*."

She shook her head dolorously. Mr. Cuffycoat agreed, but with a hint of distraction—for he had experienced an abrupt flash of enlightenment. In sum, it had been a risible error of judgment that had led him to believe that he would find the innocence of primitive humankind in the indigenous populations. All the discoveries of modern science teach us that it is from the sea that universal life emerged. It is there, no doubt, that a special humankind subsists, continuing to practice the virtues from which terrestrial humankind has temporarily departed, but toward which it is returning by means of great strides...

In consequence, a delightful plan took sketchy form in his mind while he replied a trifle distractedly to Miss Waters' questions. The Buntings were in very good health. Melville had died some ten years before. Adeline Glendower had not married. At present, skirts were very short..."

In response to the reiterated pleas of his interlocutrice, he even tried to describe the costumes recently glimpsed at a charity auction at a ministry. Unfortunately, he did not know the technical terms. He hazarded: "If you would authorize me to accompany you to your couturier, perhaps I'd be able to explain it by means of a model."

As the siren seemed to be looking at him with some surprise, he judged that he might as well come straight out with it. "Miss Waters," he said, "you'll excuse me, in the circumstances I which I find myself, for speaking frankly..."

And, pouring out his heart, he explained all the inconveniences to which the war in the old world had given birth for him, and those that he had just experienced on the part of the Papuans. Painful as the hypothesis was, the precious cupboard—he pointed to himself—in which the essential Truths were contained seemed at risk of deteriorating before long, and—who could tell?—being cleft from top to bottom by some irreparable fissure. By contrast, might not a judicious immersion in the brine render that item of furniture all of its shine and all of its watertightness?

In other terms, he, Cuffycoat, was asking Miss Waters for permission to go home with her, with the hope of savoring in her company the peace of the great depths, of rediscovering the calm, the innocent tranquility that permits the mind...

A strident burst of laughter interrupted him.

The peace of the great depths! Tranquility of mind! Alas, Mr. Cuffycoat was surely joking? Yes, undoubtedly, at Sandgate Castle she had put on a show. When one is unfamiliar with the customs of society, one does not bore one's hosts with a account of one's own troubles... But submarine existence is a nightmare, something atrocious. Unrelentingly, everywhere, there are battles, massacres, creatures devouring one another...

"To go home in a little while, it will be necessary for me to clear a path through the most ignoble gang of octopodes—veritable apaches—you can imagine. And on a daily basis one has to defend oneself against the attacks of sharks. We've been obliged to have our house armored with coral in order to breathe easily there. Even then, the narwhals and the swordfish come to pass their trenchant blades through the interstices. There is not a moment when they are not fighting and killing one another. And hideous and voracious monster incessantly rise up from the great abysses that are far worse than those ridiculous Boche about which you make so much fuss. It requires all the energy of a woman of the world to conceal the horror of that way of life from you. I cannot depict it any better for you than by confessing that, when I long for a moment of tranquility, it's on land, in the company of humans, that I come in search of it."

On the land...in the company of humans...tranquility...

Mr. Cuffycoat stood there open-mouthed, bewildered. He persisted, timidly: "You truly believe...a simple change of air for a few days..."

Miss Waters cut him off with a hint of dryness. What would they think at home if she brought a gentleman back to the house? A gentleman dressed like that? Bathers certainly allow themselves all kind of license in their dress, but there is

218

a limit. A young woman—even one no longer young—has to observe certain proprieties. Old Mr. Waters is something of a stickler for etiquette. In any case, one primordial reason dispensed with any other. Miss Waters scanned the gentleman with a sharp gaze.

"Where are your gills?"

"My...my gills?"

"Yes, your gills, your breathing apparatus...in sum, what you need to respire under water. You don't have any? It's impossible, then—even more impossible than driving an automobile without the chauffeur's permission. I'm sorry...but I have to take my leave. If you would be so kind as to lend me a hand..."

Striving to put on a brave face, Mr. Cuffycoat did his best to support the beauty. She staggered rather gauchely until she was knee-deep in water. Then she stretched herself out, and drew away with a flick of her tail; then, raising her upper body out of the water one last time, she flashed Mr. Cuffycoat a smile and, with one last wave of the hand, disappeared.

Mr. Cuffycoat remained motionless, disconcerted. Suddenly, he pricked up his ears and shivered. In the peace of the falling dusk, an atrocious howling was beginning to be discernible: the war-cries of the Papuans launched in his pursuit.

In a few bounds he had reached the edge of the great forest...

He paused momentarily, for the growls of all the ferocious beasts were already rising from its shadows, where their shiny eyes were gleaming. But for a second time, at closer range, the clamor of the cannibals resounded in his ears. He did not hesitate any longer, and deliberately plunged in among the wild beasts.

It is at this point that we must confess that, greatly to our regret, we lose track of Mr. Cuffycoat.

One would dearly like to know in what manner the inestimable Truth of which he was the depositary was preserved in the jungle, but the rarity of strollers and mailmen in that locality, and the contingencies of submarine warfare leave us in the most painful uncertainty.

The sole evidence that is perhaps worth the trouble of reporting is that of an Irish sailor picked up two months later in the region by a schooner from Hull. If he is to be believed— and his words must evidently be treated with caution—he had been wandering the island for several weeks after a shipwreck. The most curious thing he saw was a tribe of orangutans whose entire way of life testified to a state of civilization at least equal to that of the aborigines. It had also reduced to slavery several individuals whose facial features bore an unmistakable resemblance to those of Papuans. The strangest one even offered a vague resemblance to less primitive races. In the barking and mewling that constituted his manner of self-expression, it was possible to recognize, at times, the inflections of a European language. Thus, every time that, having been found remiss, he was punished by one of the anthropoids, he was heard to groan at length, and his plaints could be translated exactly by the words "All right; very well," as pronounced by an American who might have had seals in his family.

Is it necessary to establish a connection between that rather suspect deposition and the ultimate destiny of Mr. Cuffycoat? That is a point on which I forbid myself to make a decision. We only suspect that, whatever his fate might have been, he kept inviolate until the end the precious stock of Truth confided to his care, of which rather rich specimens are fortunately conserved in the majority of Academies and scientific bodies of the two worlds.

NOTE

The editor of this periodical[10] has been kind enough to authorize me to communicate to his readers the story that they have just read, and which was presented to me as coming from the eminent pen of Mr. Wells.

It differs singularly from the most recent stories of the celebrated writer, but it is not without some analogy to his previous publications. It would not, therefore, be impossible that it is a matter of a particularly prophetic "anticipation" of his youth, or even an imperfect draft of a work that he will give us in the next phase of his evolution.

Some exacting mind might perhaps remark that I could easily have settled the question of its origin by addressing myself to Mr. Wells, whose kindness would have informed me. That is a procedure which I flatly refuse.

The work of a genius such as Mr. Wells ceases to belong to the individual and becomes the property of humankind. It would therefore be intolerable that the imperialism of a single individual should decide its tenor. It would not be worth the trouble of having created war and democracy if it were necessary for us to tolerate henceforth such a despotism of the individual. At a time when all the nations of the world are submitting themselves to the universal suffrage of determining their political destinies, it would be pitiful if literary problems of an infinitely narrower range were removed from the judgment of the nation.

I would therefore be glad if the readers of this periodical were to hold a referendum—ladies are naturally admitted—in order to decide whether or not this fantasy belongs to Mr. Wels. If the answer is yes, it will figure, in spite of all his protests, at a modest rank, in his complete works. If the answer is no, it is in vain that it will have been written, from the first

---

[10] Author's note: "This fragment first appeared in the *Revue Mondiale*."

line to the last. It will be withdrawn and will remain attached throughout the centuries to the name of the presumed forger whose name is probably: André Lichtenberger.

MOWGLI RETURNS FROM THE FRONT

[The fragment that follows was originally communicated to us under the signature of a certain Rudyard Kipling, of whom no other work is known. The English press, when it was published in a Franco-British periodical, took the liberty of linking it insistently to the immortal *Jungle Book*. Edgar Poe and other writers have already remarked that bizarre verbal analogies sometimes seem to correspond to obscure psychological affinities. Our readers might perhaps deem that what links a paper-scratcher who remains virtually anonymous to one of the most dazzling geniuses of British literature is worthy of printing as a curiosity.]

The Song of Bagheera the Captive

In the night I have scented the odor,
Of the jungle where fear reigns,
Of the jungle where the struggle is honest—
Blood on the thicket, blood on the branch—
Where, beneath the fangs
Of living victors
The bones of the dead,
Crunch nicely...
Long live the jungle!
Scratch, my claws!
Me for me;
You for you;
Life against life;
Murder and madness;
Strike out straight,
Such is the Law.

How Mowgli, the man-cub, who was the brother of the wolves and hunted for fifteen years in the jungle before enrolling in the *rukh* of the great Gisborne, quit the service of the waters and forests of India to put on the khaki uniform and go to Europe to fight in the Great War, first in the Dardanelles and then on the Front in France, is a story that would take a long time to disentangle.

In truth, what decided him was not, I think, the incorrect aggression of the Boche against Belgium, nor the interest of civilization and the threatened rights. For of Europe and Belgium he knew almost as little as Bagheera the panther knew about thermodynamics or the planet Mars, and the rights of man stopped, for him, at the defense of the *rukh* against fire and deforestation.

I believe, however, that he was beginning to find life in the compound tiresome. He argued ferociously with his father-in-law Abdul Gafur, whom he had never entirely forgiven for his sorceries of old. I suspect that his wife Ayescha, who had become terribly coquettish, gossipy and devout, was annoying him. Then the enrolment of the great Gisborne in the khaki army delivered the decisive blow.

The fact that the white sahibs were fighting among themselves over there was their business and the fact that Inspector-General Muller was abruptly thanked for his employment and, it was said, put in a prison in Bombay, caused his some pleasure because of an untoward blow with a riding crop with which the German had struck him one evening, partly in play and partly in anger. (Old Muller had never suspected that on the day in question, scarcely a tenth of a second had separated his heart from Mowgli's pointed dagger.) But when, one morning, the great Gisborne took his pipe out of his mouth to announce to his subordinate, between two puffs, that he was leaving in three days to join the *terain* and follow the trail of the war, Mowgli was astounded.

At a cry for help from Balooo or Bagheera he would have bounded into the depths of the jungle. From the day he knew that Gisborne was leaving, the invasion of the Boche evoked for him that of the red dogs of Dekkan. There had been no need for them to call for help for Mowgli to know that in the hour of peril, his place was beside old Akela, Wontolla the solitary and the lahinis with the bristling fur. In the jungle, throats are cut, but one does not learn to betray one another. All for one and one for all, that is the motto.

That is why, knowing these things, Gisborne was only three-quarters surprised when, one morning, while strolling back and forth on the deck of the old *Irawaddy*, bound for Bab-el-Mandeb, he heard himself hailed by a seductive voice and recognized his former forest warden in his khaki uniform. Mowgli looked a trifle miserable, suffering cruelly from sea-sickness. Gisborne scolded him. Was he not crazy to leave the service, the bungalow, his wife and children? He shook his head, yawned and excused himself nonchalantly. When Bagheera took it into his head to hunt elsewhere, he went.

I shall not tell you about Mowgli's campaigns. The details would be almost as difficult to reconstitute as the exact sentiments that were inspired in him by the war of right.

In Egypt, he savored the infinite joy of finding himself on firm ground again. I fear that his best memories might relate to certain dives in Alexandria.

It was necessary to re-embark for the Dardenelles. The Mediterranean was no more merciful than the Indian Ocean. Mowgli conducted himself brilliantly at Koum-Kalch, where he spitted several Turks. The Military Medal rewarded his exploits. In the following weeks, however, things become obscure. It is evident that he suffered from the thirst and the heat, and had to be evacuated to Moudros with dysentery.

Where the nightmare thickens further is when we find him again on the Front in France. Attached to a liaison service, the great Gisborne, one nasty winter evening, was making his way through a muddy trench on the Somme, lowering his head among squalls of snow, when he stumbled over a bundle of cloth from which emerged a cough. He uttered and oath, and then an exclamation, for he had just recognized two large blazing eyes and a mouth that was still trying to smile, but no longer could.

The two men exchanged brief and banal words, and separated. Gisborne retained a dolorous memory of that encounter. It seemed to him that one of the vilest acts of the Boche—in which he was somewhat complicit himself—was to have dragged into that misery the freshest and chubbiest little atom that had ever come to babble in a wolf's lair. So, a week later, it was almost with relief that he learned that the Hindu fusilier about whom he asked for news in passing had been evacuated because of a bad bronchitis to a sanitary formation at the rear, where he had doubtless croaked. "For they all croak," the sergeant concluded, philosophically.

Just the day before, Gisborne had noticed, in the process of dying in the French trenches, a pretty little Algerian donkey, enrolled in the war almost as unconsciously as Mowgli himself—and its utterly inoffensive and astonished gaze had pursued him. For five minutes he associated the two cases, and the similarity saddened him. Then, as nothing is eternal, and the bombardment of the 105s was getting closer, he thought about something else. That evening, he limited himself to writing to Chadwell, who had succeeded him in the *rukh*: "You can tell the wolves that they will not see their big brother again. He has been evacuated, dying, to the rear and must have croaked. The war is over for him."

The assertion was only partly correct. The war was indeed over for Mowgli, but he was not dead.

Sometimes, the hearth-fire is believed to be extinct, but in a corner, an invisible ember is asleep beneath the ash. Touch it with a few twigs or dry leaves, and a tiny flame springs forth.

Something similar happened aboard the liner *Indus,* in the Indian Sea, off the coast of Bombay. There was, in fourth class, among other human wreckage, a bundle of dirty rags. It did not budge or speak. The men described it "the sick monkey." It was also the Reformed Indian Soldier no. 9433, formerly known as Mowgli—and the beasts of the jungle had once named him "the little frog."

How can what was weighing upon him be described? It had been made with years of nightmare, with heat that burns and cold that bites, with snow, with snow, frost, wind, hunger and thirst; with the calcinating sand of the desert and the glutinous mud of Flanders; with the mist in which everything gets bogged down and swallowed up; with the stink of chloroform, and that of wagons crammed with humanity, of noxious holds, of a hundred sewers, with that of Boche trenches. There was also an uninterrupted rumble of bombardment, the whistle of bullets, the moans of the damned, the exhaustion that imports sickness into the marrowbones. All of that was crushing that rag, reducing him to something that was no longer a man, but merely a passive, diffuse, repugnant scrap...

But that evening, on the calm ocean, a new breeze blew. The sea was scarcely rippled. The oblique sun was blinking its last muted ray. Two yellow butterflies whirled around...and suddenly, the rag moved. It uncurled into a long emaciated phantom and came to lean on the side of the boat. It coughed throatily, avidly breathed in the air charged with the first aromas of the soil.

When a cat has been ill and recovers its health, it licks itself from top to toe. The next morning, instead of the sick monkey, there was a tall, thin fellow, vacillating but correct in his clean clothing. As he passed, a sailor sniggered: "Look! There's a new one in the menagerie!" A gaze fell upon him so heavy that he turned his head away involuntarily, muttering. Once, in the jungle, Shere Khan the tiger had been unable to meet that gaze.

Two months later, crouching opposite one another, Abdul Gafur and his daughter Ayescha were conscientiously eating hot rice stuffed with curried vegetables, and while plunging their fingers into the bowl, the old man started a discussion with his daughter, with increased vigor, of a subject that had often been raised before. Now that the sahib Chadwell had received the news in a letter from the sahib Gisborne himself, there was no longer any doubt that that good-for-nothing Mowgli had been killed. Having mourned appropriately, was Ayescha going to consume herself in an indefinite widowhood? She had enough property, to which the pension would be added. In those conditions, there would be no lack of advantageous opportunities.

Facing these prospects, the breast of Ayescha, a taste for which was a little too strong for all the foresters who had felt it—which is to say, if gossips can be believed, every male for ten leagues around—rose up with compunction. How large would the pension be?

Suddenly, however, she uttered a muffled cry and her complexion turned gray. As for Abdul Gafur, he was gripped by a tremor similar to the one that had shaken him on the occasion when his future son-in-law had set a pack of wolves on him. At the entrance to the cabin a long silhouette was standing, in which two fiery eyes were sparkling, only too recognizably.

Mowgli made a brief hand gesture in the direction of his father-in-law. "Get out!" And, crouching down in his stead, he plunged his fingers into the dish and started eating.

Mowgli's return to his penates was accompanied by less triumphant delight than that of the prodigal son. Undoubtedly Ayesha, once she had recovered from the initial shock, lavished generous testimonies of her affection upon him. Impressed by his son-in-law's medal, Abdul Gafur showed him a half-sly, half-superstitious deference. And throughout the region, the reappearance of the victorious warrior excited a flattering curiosity. To listen to him recount his voyages and exploits, idlers and old wives gladly sat for long hours nibbling pancakes on mats, as at the stories or prayers of some wandering holy man, fakir or Yogi.

But in finding himself back among his own kind, Mowgli experienced no joy. It was not that the little flame that had lit up in the depths of the sick monkey aboard the *Indus* was completely extinct, but it remained unsteady and fugitive, as if the frightful things that had accumulated during year after year of Gehenna continued to weigh upon Mowgli, enveloping him in a filthy, damp mist of anguish, in which people and things assumed strange, distant and disconcerting aspects.

In truth, you see, even though thousands and thousands of leagues now separated them, the Boche still had Mowgli in their sights. Hideous tentacles gripped him, were attached to him. His sleep was interrupted by atrocious visions from which he woke up feverish and panting. His eyes were hollow, his appetite uneven. He went for days without unclenching his teeth, or babbling interminable and incomprehensible litanies in a precipitate and monotonous voice.

With regard to his fellow humans, he was manifestly suspicious. Even Ayescha suffered from his hypochondriac moodiness. He spent hours counting his children on his fingers, disconcerted by their number, which seemed to him to have benefited from excessive blessings of Providence during his absence. That mania was inevitably noticed and suggested that Mowgli's mind had not entirely come back from the land of the devils. But he brought back incontestable merits from his struggles, and his madness acquired him a universal surplus of consideration.

He did not seem to care about that, fled from his neighbors and spent the best part of his time in solitude. To tell the truth, he soon began to leave the bungalow at first light and not return until after sunset. Sometimes, he even remained absent for two or three nights in succession—to which Ayescha, having complained the first time, reconciled herself like a reasonable woman.

Where did Mowgli spend those days and nights? It was quite simple. At a furtive pace, slipping, so to speak, along the palisades, he went out of the compound as dawn broke. And from there, in a matter of seconds, he reached the forest. Abruptly, the dew-soaked foliage closed over him, swallowing him up. And then, for hours on end, he coiled up, stretched out or crouched down, his eyes half-closed.

That is what all jungle-dwellers do when, wounded in the battles of war or love, they flee their own kind and hide their distress or their shame in inextricable thickets amid the sweet and warm putrescence of the odorous soil. Often, they stay there for days on end. No one knows on what they subsist—perhaps the fecund sap of the fermenting earth, laden with germs.

Sometimes, they die there. Stripped in a few hours by ants, their carcasses do not take long to dissolve into the mud. At other times they survive and, having grown thin and weak, resume looking after themselves. Then, they will kill again, and the jungle will soon resound with their challenges of love and combat.

Thus, in the shelter of luxuriant foliage, Mowgli, folded up in himself, fled the pursuit of Things, trying to disgorge his pollution. Doubtless obscure and powerful forces responded to his appeal, issued from the womb of the earth in which the whim of the gods, thousand of centuries ago, created life...

Sometimes, the thunder of cannon, oceans, and the howls of rage and pain of all the hells ceased to rumble in his ears. He was no longer choked by ulcerous fluids, corruption and filthy stinks. Sparks zigzagged through the mist. Beyond the nightmare, indefinable, almost ungraspable memories were born. Suddenly, sounds sang in his throat, and his lips stammered words. Sometimes, they were no longer human words.

One morning, at the awakening, the trepidant life was more forceful. In all the thickets the birds unleashed their trills with a sort of fury. Wholl, the squirrel, chased his brothers through the branches. Two gazelles traversed the clearing, teasing one another with their young horns. Busily, Sahi the porcupine trotted by with his nose to the ground, rattling his coat of mail. And suddenly, from a clump of lentisks, a gray wolf emerged, with a bald head and a bloody mouth.

From Mowgli's breast resounded the age-old welcome of beasts that hunt: "Good prey to you, Comrade!"—unintelligible, of course, to the inept ears of humans, but in the jungle, how amicable and how traditional.

Astonished by the words he had pronounced, Mowgli shut up. Already, however, according to the courtesy that is the rule, the wolf had replied: "To you, Comrade, good prey!" Then, after a momentary hesitation, it advanced at a prudent toward the thicket where Mowgli was lodged, muzzle curious and eyes wary.

His heart beating, Mowgli stood up. "Peace be with you; I am of your blood!"

Fangs bared and tail hanging down, however, the wolf recoiled, snorting. Suddenly, with a howl of terror, as if *dewanee*—the madness—had gripped it, its bounded backwards, spun around and made off...

Why would Mowgli have pursued it? Is it because he would have given anything to flee as the wolf was fleeing, to vomit up himself, pestilential with all the diabolical pestilence of humans?

He curled up for the rest of the day, holding his breath. A short distance away, burrowing rats were going back and forth, but they avoided passing close to the thicket that hid him, and the birds did not perch in it, not even the intrepid Darzee.

When dusk fell, Mowgli quit his refuge, and through the jungle, whose thousand mysterious noises fell silent as he approached, he set about making his way back to the dwellings of men. He felt an immense distress. A glimmer, however, was vacillating in the depths of his soul. A need for affection hastened his pace.

He reached the compound. The mass of the bungalow stood out in the shadows, pierced by a light. As lightly as a cat, he approached the window. There was a sound of voice. He shivered, crept the last few meters, peeped in. With an arm round Ayescha's waist, Mahbub the buffalo-hunter was eating from the same plate as her.

Mowgli drew himself up to his full height and took a step forward. Then, with a long cry of distress, to which all the voices of the jungle responded, he bounded backwards like the wolf, turned on is heel, and started fleeing recklessly through the undergrowth.

When his instinct warns him that an inundation is imminent or, on the contrary, when implacable drought is advertised, Hathi and his brothers quit their pasture and set off on a journey. And for days on end, imperturbably, fanning their ears, trunks on the alert, they tramp for miles in the direction of new terrains to which their choice guides them. It was thus that Mowgli, fleeing humans, plunged into the jungle, the great maternal jungle, palpitating with life, palpitating with murder, which has been the same for centuries, full of odors, howls, claws and teeth, and caresses.

To begin with, in order that he could not be pursued, in accordance with the art taught to him by Baloo the bear, he carefully covered his tracks. For a week he zigzagged, changing direction continually. Then, for an entire day, he paddled along the bed of a stream, frightening young crocodiles. When he emerged from it on to a rocky banks where his wet feet made no imprint, he breathed more freely. Now the humans could no longer catch him. And who could tell whether, by running so fast and fleeing so far, he might not end up shaking off Things?

At first, they clung on to him. It was not only his soul that they had infected but his nose, his beast and his muscles. In the jungle, in order to live, it is necessary to kill. Mowgli had forgotten the discreet pursuits, the subtle feints, the decisive assaults. Scatterbrained rabbits and stupid fawns made mock of him. He often had to content himself with slugs, caterpillars, crickets and other small creatures. There were days when even vermin were lacking. One evening, obscurely, he felt death within him and curled himself up. At dawn, a rustle of branches woke him up. Ten paces away, trailing a broken leg, a sambar was panting. He collected his remaining strength, pounced, buried his knife in the throat, and drank the warm blood that spurted out. It was a superb prey. Mowgli lived on it for several days. A new vigor was born in his flesh. The little glimmer of the *Indus* ignited flared up, radiating heat...

The scavengers in the surrounding bushes insulted him, their entrails tormented by hunger. He replied to them angrily and they fell silent, not so much frightened by his threats as disconcerted by the contrast between his form and his language.

Among scavengers, Tabaqui the jackal is the most voracious and the most cowardly. He dare not kill, and lives on pillage and duplicity. The reek of gamy venison drew him to Mowgli like a fish-hook. For hours he remained there, contemplating him and whining.

For three days, Mowgli watched him prowling around from the corner of his eye, but he gave no indication of it, still having his pride. None of the beasts of the jungle had responded to his calls; to be refused by Tabaqui would be intolerable.

It was not until the fourth morning that, spotting the wretch lurking in the shadows, he hailed him: "Tabaqui with the hollow belly, there is what you need to fill it here."

He saw Tabaqui shudder and jump to his feet, ready to flee, but Mowgli did not budge. The acrid aroma teased the nostrils of the starveling; he started trembling in all his limbs.

Mowgli continued, his voice bantering: "Tabaqui has become very proud. Doubtless he kills himself now. Once, he was less difficult. When I hunted with Akela, he trotted behind us and licked up the drops of blood in the dust."

His ears flattened and his tail between his legs, Tabaqui was drooling. Finally, he murmured in a halting voice: "Lord, powerful Lord, that flesh is perfumed."

"This flesh is just ready," replied Mowgli nonchalantly. "Such that I would be capable of swallowing the last shreds—unless I had a whim to spare a few crumbs for a brazen mendicant I would treat as a friend."

Tabaqui crept forward on his belly, tortured by fear and hunger.

"Have pity, Lord. Your words are soft. Your language is that of the jungle, but"—he uttered a yap of distress—"it is not only your form that is human, powerful lord, it is your odor."

Mowgli frowned, shrugged his shoulders, seized a femur to which a little rotten flesh was adhering, and threw it hard at Tabaqui, who yelped with joy and pain. The bones cracked under his famished jaws. With his mouth full, he hiccupped: "Lord, Lord, incomparable protector of the poor, may your name be blessed—but what name?"

"I am Mowgli, the man-cub that the wolves raised, and that Bagheera and Baloo the bear educated. I was the friend of Hathi. I killed Shere Khan the tiger and decimated the red dogs of the Dekkan. And now I have come back from among humans to find my brothers again."

In the jungle, lives are precarious, but stories are transmitted indefinitely. Except that they become confused and overlap, and one does not know whether they relate to before the Deluge or last year. Licking the bones, his eyes half-closed, Tabaqui gazed at the images rising within him.

"Mowgli the man-cub...that was the name. On the council table, the skin of Shere Khan... The frog unleashed the little people against the dholes. These stories are in the Book. Are you Mowgli, then?"

"I was Mowgli. Then there have been stories. But now I am Mowgli again. Where are Bagheera and Balooo?"

Tabanqui blinked. "Their bones whitened many moons ago. I know something of it!" He passed his tongue over his chops, hideously.

"And the gray brothers?"

"Perhaps once, or twice, or more, the rains have fallen since they quit their lairs, No one knows where they hunt today."

Indeed, it sometimes happens that wolves change residence in search of prey, and their lairs remain abandoned forever.

"And Hathi? Hathi and his sons?"

"Lord, Hathi and his sons have decamped. Certain rumors warned them that powerful white men armed with the red flower and aided by turncoat elephants were advancing from here and there to capture them and put them in chains.

They made off at a gallop, breaking everything—but the grasses and foliage have long grown back; their tracks are lost."

At Tabaqui's responses, a heavy sadness descended. The flame vacillated, Mowgli uttered a lament: "Then all those of my blood are dead or vanished?"

Almost sated—he is never completely so—Tabaqui's stomach was grateful. He took stock once again in his memory of the chronicle of murders and emigrations. Finally, as if talking to himself, he yelped: "Of course, there is still Kaa..."

Kaa! Kaa the python, who had once received him on his back in the Waingunga and saved him from the fury of the dholes and that of the little people of the bees. How had Mowgli not thought of Kaa"

"Kaa is still hunting in the same thickets?"

Why would Kaa move; his strength surpasses all others. His gaze alone is sufficient to paralyze his prey.

"Lord, Kaa dwells where Kaa dwelt. But dare you approach Kaa?"

Disdaining to reply, Mowgli has already resumed his course. He walks again, for days on end...and as he plunges further into the virgin heart of the immense forest, gradually, the Things fade away, become pale, relax their grip...

Nose to the wind, ears pricked, legs braced, Mowgli sees once again the quivering life of the jungle. There is no longer anything real but the prey to be killed in order to eat, the water to be lapped to slake his thirst, the path lost to be found again by sniffing the ground, while prowling through the undergrowth, breathing in a thousand scattered, fugitive and indescribable atoms through every pore.

Amid the soft or violent odors, amid the cries, the challenges, the appeals, the death-rattles, amid the crackle of branches and rustled grass, among the obscure swarms, Mowgli makes every effort. Flanks throbbing, he seeks and finds, follows slowly, retracing his steps with a thousand circuits, the invisible track that he followed many years before in order to join the humans, and it is the track of his old soul that he is picking up. And behind him, harpooned by the thorns, stuck in the marshes, torn to shreds by all the stones and all the brushwood, desiccated by all the suns, effaced by all the dusts, by the healthy sweats, by the sharp perils, by the honest battles, the Things collapse.

Where is the sick monkey? Where is the moving ocean? Where is the bizarre khaki livery? Where is the cold, the fog, the indescribable mud? Where is the servile forester? Where is the husband of Ayescha, the son-in-law of Abdul Gafir, the son of Messua? Here is Mowgli, the brother of wolves, the little frog. He has grown up, his features are hollow, perhaps his flesh is less polished, but his tendons and his muscles are as hard, his legs indefatigable, his gaze sure. With the nurturing jungle he stuffs himself and imbues himself. He steps himself in it, eats and drinks it. He is it; it is him. A curse upon the rest! Here is the harmonious and healthy play that nothing can falsify, adulterate or corrupt. The sap streams from the branches he breaks as he runs. So dense and so violent are the perfumes that it is a struggle for him to force a path through them. Life is so vibrant that one could believe that one can see the corollas blossoming and the mosses becoming green. All the voices of creation are rumbling like the lowest note of a harp. His human muscles lift him up like a gazelle, like a great bird. Here is Mowgli.

And here is Kaa.

For two days, Mowgli has no longer been hesitant, has no longer been searching, has no longer been sniffing. As straight as an arrow released by a bow, he heads for his goal. Down with everything! Behind with everything! There is no longer anything but the jungle that grips him. Here were his hunting-grounds. With him, Bagheera killed the nilgai in that clearing. Here is the trail where the dholes were barking at his heels...

And here is Kaa, the same Kaa.

On an outcrop of rock warmed by the midday sun, the giant python has coiled and knotted the thirty feet of his spotted body. His large flat head is dangling down to ground level. His eyes are like dead opals. He is dreaming.

Before this apparition, the human stops. But Kaa straightens up. His body unrolls and dilates with the sound of a sword being drawn from a steel sheath. Slowly, at the end of six feet of formidable neck, the enormous head swings back and forth like a shuttle. His eyes are red, searching, staring.

A hiss escapes his throat, and he asks, amicably: "Hsssh! Have you slept well, little frog? Has your hunting been good?"

Among the coils of the yellow and black living cable, Mowgli has resumed his place, and installs himself. Kaa surrounds him with a rampart that is also a soft pillow. The head of the serpent rests on the human's shoulder.

In a whisper, playing with his knife, Mowgli tells his tale. He has traveled miles and miles, traversed nameless waters and lands. The things he has seen cannot be described. His adventures are prodigious. Gradually, his speech becomes excited.

Kaa interrupts, laughing: "Not so loud. I'm not changing my skin."[11] And then, as if talking to himself, he adds: "This little frog is comical. Humans are like that. They are born, grow up and die before one has had time to get to know them. And each of their sneezes, according to them, is a memorable event. Little one, it's only yesterday that I saved you, as a child, from the thieving monkeys. Today you're an adult. Tomorrow your hair will be white. The day after, your bones will be scattered in the brushwood. Don't make such a fuss about these little things. You remind me of that old fool the white cobra, who took seriously the pieces of stone and teeth confided to his guard by kings. Just tell me this: have you had good hunting?"

"Terrible hunting, Kaa, compared with which, what are all killings! The red flower destroys men by the thousand.

---

[11] Author's note: "Pythons are partly deaf when they slough their skin."

Four times the rainy season returned, and they did not cease killing one another. Kaa, it was an unimaginable horror."

With a soothing gesture, Kaa puts his head next to Mowgli's and says, indulgently: "Little One, you're not yet very wise. It requires many deaths to make the living. And the jungle of spring is the daughter of the rotten jungle of autumn. These are old stories, Little One. Do you think that Kaa is unaware of these battles of which you speak? Ten times twenty times, the rains will fall without people ceasing to massacre one another. Every night the maledictions of their destroyed cities rise of toward the stars. However..."

Kaa reflected for a few minutes. Slowly, the years and the centuries filed through his memory.

"However," he concluded, "I don't believe that was humans. It was, if I remember correctly...yes, in truth...there were brown ones and black ones...they were ants. Anyway, it's not important!"

He yawned. And, uncoiling the rings of his body with a sound of tearing silk, he added cheerfully: "I'm hungry, little frog. Shall we go hunting, the two of us, as we did yesterday?"

So they did.

And Mowgli never, ever returned to the world of men.

The Song of the Sun, the Land and the Water

There is the Sun, the Land and the Water,
The rest is smoke, soon flown away.
Scratching his lice and nibbling his nuts,
The Bandar-Log cries: "The jungle is mine!"
But if he feels the dart of the horse-fly that stings him
Or his she-ape has a stomach-ache.
He fills the woods with his howls.

Tomorrow, however, the sun will rise.

When Tabaqui has his share of carrion,
Destiny is just and life is good.

But if Tabaqui feels his belly hollow
His endless barking curses the gods.
Whether your back is bare or not, Tabaqui.
Tomorrow your nameless bones
Will be swallowed up regardless
In the old earth to which all the living
Return indefinitely to melt.

At the end of summer, in the panting jungle
Gnawed bones strew the dead leaves,
And frightful reeks that the breezes bring
Charge the air with pestilential vapors.
But now, bursting from the caverns of the sky
Springs the great assault of the torrential rains
Beneath their streaming
Everything piles up
Old rotting things
Drain away in impure floods
And when, tomorrow the trunks give birth to young
leaves
Nature will forget her murders and mourning.
And like a baby, fresh from its first slumber
She will offer, seductively, to the candor of Men,
Her innocent forehead, and her new kisses.

There is the Sun
      There is the Land,
           There is the Water.

SF & FANTASY

Henri Allorge. *The Great Cataclysm*
Guy d'Armen. *Doc Ardan: The City of Gold and Lepers*
G.-J. Arnaud. *The Ice Company*
Charles Asselineau. *The Double Life*
Cyprien Bérard. *The Vampire Lord Ruthwen*
Aloysius Bertrand. *Gaspard de la Nuit*
Richard Bessière. *The Gardens of the Apocalypse*
Albert Bleunard. *Ever Smaller*
Félix Bodin. *The Novel of the Future*
Louis Boussenard. *Monsieur Synthesis*
Alphonse Brown. *City of Glass; The Conquest of the Air*
André Caroff. *The Terror of Madame Atomos; Miss Atomos; The Return of Madame Atomos; The Mistake of Madame Atomos; The Monsters of Madame Atomos; The Revenge of Madame Atomos; The Resurrection of Madame Atomos*
Félicien Champsaur. *The Human Arrow; Ouha, King of the Apes; Pharaoh's Wife*
Didier de Chousy. *Ignis*
Captain Danrit. *Undersea Odyssey*
C. I. Defontenay. *Star (Psi Cassiopeia)*
Charles Derennes. *The People of the Pole*
Georges Dodds (anthologist). *The Missing Link*
Harry Dickson. *The Heir of Dracula*
Jules Dornay. *Lord Ruthven Begins*
Alfred Driou. *The Adventures of a Parisian Aeronaut*
Sâr Dubnotal *vs. Jack the Ripper*
Alexandre Dumas. *The Return of Lord Ruthven*
Renée Dunan. *Baal*
J.-C. Dunyach. *The Night Orchid; The Thieves of Silence*
Henri Duvernois. *The Man Who Found Himself*
Achille Eyraud. *Voyage to Venus*
Henri Falk. *The Age of Lead*
Paul Féval. *Anne of the Isles; Knightshade; Revenants; Vampire City; The Vampire Countess; The Wandering Jew's Daughter*
Paul Féval, *fils. Felifax, the Tiger-Man*
Charles de Fieux. *Lamékis*
Arnould Galopin. *Doctor Omega; Doctor Omega and the Shadowmen* (anthology)
Judith Gautier. *Isoline and the Serpent-Flower*

Léon Gozlan. *The Vampire of the Val-de-Grâce*
G.L. Gick. *Harry Dickson and the Werewolf of Rutherford Grange*
Edmond Haraucourt. *Illusions of Immortality*
Nathalie Henneberg. *The Green Gods*
V. Hugo, P. Foucher & P. Meurice. *The Hunchback of Notre-Dame*
Romain d'Huissier. *Hexagon: Dark Matter*
Michel Jeury. *Chronolysis*
Gustave Kahn. *The Tale of Gold and Silence*
Gérard Klein. *The Mote in Time's Eye*
Fernand Kolney. *Love in 5000 Years*
Louis-Guillaume de La Follie. *The Unpretentious Philosopher*
Jean de La Hire. *Enter the Nyctalope; The Nyctalope on Mars; The Nyctalope vs. Lucifer; The Nyctalope Steps In; Night of the Nyctalope*
Etienne-Léon de Lamothe-Langon. *The Virgin Vampire*
André Laurie. *Spiridon*
Gabriel de Lautrec. *The Vengeance of the Oval Portrait*
Alain le Drimeur. *The Future City*
Georges Le Faure & Henri de Graffigny. *The Extraordinary Adventures of a Russian Scientist Across the Solar System* (2 vols.)
Gustave Le Rouge. *The Vampires of Mars; The Dominion of the World* (w/Gustave Guitton) (4 vols.)
Jules Lermina. *Mysteryville; Panic in Paris; To-Ho and the Gold Destroyers; The Secret of Zippelius*
André Lichtenberger. *The Centaurs*
Jean-Marc & Randy Lofficier. *Edgar Allan Poe on Mars; The Katrina Protocol; Pacifica; Robonocchio; Tales of the Shadowmen 1-9*
Xavier Mauméjean. *The League of Heroes*
Joseph Méry. *The Tower of Destiny*
Hippolyte Mettais. *The Year 5865*
Louise Michel. *The Human Microbes; The New World*
Tony Moilin. *Paris in the Year 2000*
José Moselli. *Illa's End*
John-Antoine Nau. *Enemy Force*
Marie Nizet. *Captain Vampire*
C. Nodier, A. Beraud & Toussaint-Merle. *Frankenstein*
Henri de Parville. *An Inhabitant of the Planet Mars*
Gaston de Pawlowski. *Journey to the Land of the 4th Dimension*
Georges Pellerin. *The World in 2000 Years*
Ernest Pérochon. *The Frenetic People*
Pierre Pelot. *The Child Who Walked on the Sky*
J. Polidori, C. Nodier, E. Scribe. *Lord Ruthven the Vampire*

P.-A. Ponson du Terrail. *The Vampire and the Devil's Son; The Immortal Woman*

Henri de Régnier. *A Surfeit of Mirrors*

Maurice Renard. *The Blue Peril; Doctor Lerne; The Doctored Man; A Man Among the Microbes; The Master of Light*

Jean Richepin. *The Wing; The Crazy Corner*

Albert Robida. *The Adventures of Saturnin Farandoul; The Clock of the Centuries; Chalet in the Sky; The Electric Life*

J.-H. Rosny Aîné. *Helgvor of the Blue River; The Givreuse Enigma; The Mysterious Force; The Navigators of Space; Vamireh; The World of the Variants; The Young Vampire*

Marcel Rouff. *Journey to the Inverted World*

Han Ryner. *The Superhumans*

Brian Stableford. *The New Faust at the Tragicomique; The Empire of the Necromancers (The Shadow of Frankenstein; Frankenstein and the Vampire Countess; Frankenstein in London); Sherlock Holmes & The Vampires of Eternity; The Stones of Camelot; The Wayward Muse.* (anthologist) *The Germans on Venus; News from the Moon; The Supreme Progress; The World Above the World; Nemoville; Investigations of the Future*

Jacques Spitz. *The Eye of Purgatory*

Kurt Steiner. *Ortog*

Eugène Thébault. *Radio-Terror*

C.-F. Tiphaigne de La Roche. *Amilec*

Théo Varlet. *The Golden Rock. The Xenobiotic Invasion; The Castaways of Eros; Timeslip Troopers* (w/André Blandin); *The Martian Epic* (w/Octave Joncquel)

Paul Vibert. *The Mysterious Fluid*

Villiers de l'Isle-Adam. *The Scaffold; The Vampire Soul*

Philippe Ward. *Artahe*

Philippe Ward & Sylvie Miller. *The Song of Montségur*

MYSTERIES & THRILLERS

M. Allain & P. Souvestre. *The Daughter of Fantômas*

A. Anicet-Bourgeois, Lucien Dabril. *Rocambole*

A. Bernède. *Belphegor*; *Judex* (w/Louis Feuillade); *The Return of Judex* (w/Louis Feuillade)

A. Bisson & G. Livet. *Nick Carter vs. Fantômas*

V. Darlay & H. de Gorsse. *Arsène Lupin vs. Sherlock Holmes: The Stage Play*

Séamas Duffy. *Sherlock Holmes in Paris*

Paul Féval. *Gentlemen of the Night; John Devil; The Black Coats ('Salem Street; The Invisible Weapon; The Parisian Jungle; The Companions of the Treasure; Heart of Steel; The Cadet Gang; The Sword-Swallower)*

Emile Gaboriau. *Monsieur Lecoq*

Goron & Emile Gautier. *Spawn of the Penitentiary*

Steve Leadley. *Sherlock Holmes: The Circle of Blood*

Maurice Leblanc. *Arsène Lupin vs. Countess Cagliostro; Arsène Lupin vs. Sherlock Holmes (The Blonde Phantom; The Hollow Needle); The Many Faces of Arsène Lupin*

Gaston Leroux. *Chéri-Bibi; The Phantom of the Opera; Rouletabille & the Mystery of the Yellow Room; Rouletabille at Krupp's*

Richard Marsh. *The Complete Adventures of Judith Lee*

William Patrick Maynard. *The Terror of Fu Manchu; The Destiny of Fu Manchu*

Frank J. Morlock. *Sherlock Holmes: The Grand Horizontals; Sherlock Holmes vs Jack the Ripper*

Antonin Reschal. *The Adventures of Miss Boston*

P. de Wattyne & Y. Walter. *Sherlock Holmes vs. Fantômas*

David White. *Fantômas in America*

Pierre Yrondy. *The Adventures of Thérèse Arnaud*

SCREENPLAYS

Mike Baron. *The Iron Triangle*

Emma Bull & Will Shetterly. *Nightspeeder; War for the Oaks*

Gerry Conway & Roy Thomas. *Doc Dynamo*

Steve Englehart. *Majorca*

James Hudnall. *The Devastator*

Jean-Marc & Randy Lofficier. *Royal Flush*

J.-M. & R. Lofficier & Marc Agapit. *Despair*

J.-M. & R. Lofficier & Joël Houssin. *City*

Andrew Paquette. *Peripheral Vision*

Robert L. Robinson, Jr. *Judex*

R. Thomas, J. Hendler & L. Sprague de Camp. *Rivers of Time*

NON-FICTION

Stephen R. Bissette. *Blur 1-5. Green Mountain Cinema 1; Teen Angels*

Win Scott Eckert. *Crossovers* (2 vols.)
Jean-Marc & Randy Lofficier. *Shadowmen* (2 vols.)
Randy Lofficier. *Over Here*

ART BOOKS

Jean-Pierre Normand. *Science Fiction Illustrations*
Raven Okeefe. *Raven's L'il Critters; Rave's Faves*
Randy Lofficier & Raven Okeefe. *If Your Possum Go Daylight...*
Daniele Serra. *Illusions*

HEXAGON COMICS

Franco Frescura & Luciano Bernasconi. *Wampus*
Franco Frescura & Giorgio Trevisan. *CLASH*
L. Bernasconi, J.-M. Lofficier & Juan Roncagliolo Berger. *Phenix*
Claude Legrand, J.-M. Lofficier & L. Bernasconi. *Kabur*
Franco Oneta. *Zembla*
L. Buffolente, Lofficier & J.-J. Dzialowski. *Strangers: Homicron*
Danilo Grossi. *Strangers: Jaydee*
Claude Legrand & Luciano Bernasconi. *Strangers: Starlock*